Aspiring author Anthony Walker may be a newbie on the path of becoming a novelist, but that does not stop him from working arduously towards bringing forth a novel creation that is intended to keep each reader engrossed in the enthralling story which revolves around its main character, Gloria, who is spiraled from her state of innocence into the assassin she is destined to become. A must read!

I would like to take this time to express my deepest form of gratitude to my family, friends, and supporters who have provided me with the exact amount of encouragement that I needed to proceed forward with completing the novels I have created which are meant for the world to consume as a wave of enlightenment.

Anthony Walker

THE VICISSITUDE OF A FEMME FATALE

AUSTIN MACAULEY PUBLISHERS™

LONDON * CAMBRIDGE * NEW YORK * SHARJAH

Ordering Information
Quantity sales: Special discounts are available on quantity purchases by corporations, associations, and others. For details, contact the publisher at the address below.

Publisher's Cataloging-in-Publication data
Walker, Anthony
The Vicissitude of a Femme Fatale

ISBN 9781647500672 (Paperback)
ISBN 9781647500665 (Hardback)
ISBN 9781647500689 (ePub e-book)

Library of Congress Control Number: 2021909469

www.austinmacauley.com/us

First Published (2021)
Austin Macauley Publishers LLC
40 Wall Street, 33rd Floor, Suite 3302
New York, NY 10005
USA

mail-usa@austinmacauley.com
+1 (646) 5125767

In acknowledgment, I would like to extend a special thanks to senior editor, Nikki Main, as well as the other faculty members involved who form the compartments of the Austin Macauley Publishers for affording me the opportunity to gain credibility as a published author under their brand.

Chapter 1

The clouds hung in the sky as a dreary sight, and though no rain had yet begun to fall, one wouldn't have been able to know the difference from the amount of wetness that suddenly formed on face. Even if she wanted to, there wasn't anything that could be done to slow the stream of tears that flowed out from her eyelids. Gloria found herself to be ashamed, embarrassed, and, quite frankly, fed-up. *How could I have been so stupid?!* is the question she constantly berated herself with.

At 15 years old, Gloria should've been enjoying the fruition of her youth, but instead, she was weighed down by an all-too-heavy burden for her conscience to bear. The problem, which only worked to add more strife to her already-tumultuous life, began over the weekend on a Saturday night of partying for the last time before the school semester was set to commence once more after a much-needed spring break.

Gloria was fairly new to the school she attended, since she was currently experiencing her fourth foster family in as many as three years. The only two people she had to consider anything of a friendship with were a Muslim girl of her age by the name of Malala who accentuated her daily wardrobe and heavily applied makeup in accordance with those who acquainted themselves in the favor of the new age culture of Gothic rock music.

Gloria's other companion was a husky black kid named Jeremy who was someone that everyone assumed had grasped the identity of being a gay person, since his clothing often bordered on the more sensitive side of the type of apparel that an average boy his age should be wearing. With Gloria in her non-descript attire of jeans and baggy tee-shirts, the three made for the perfect oddities but were entwined nonetheless by their similar realities of being viewed as the outcasts amongst their peers.

Gloria suffered the fate of being the outcast of her new home as well. Landing into adoption with a penurious family who was only interested in using her presence and warm body as a means to exceed a bit further over their monthly income of food stamps and cash subsidies. Although the household remained to be that of a predominantly Caucasian persuasion amongst husband, wife, and their two underage sons, race was never a matter of concern for Gloria as long as she was provided with a roof over her head, and she was provided with a roof over her head and she remained safe.

When Gloria first arrived at the home along with a case worker by the name of Jessica Santiago, introductions were formally made with her new adoptive parents portraying themselves in the roles of gracious hosts while doing everything in their power to make a good impression on the case worker. Even by inviting Ms. Santiago to join in on their small 'Welcome to our Home' feast they prepared to celebrate Gloria's arrival. However, as soon as the red brake lights of Ms. Santiago's vehicle became invisible to their range of vision, the whole demeanor of the household switched.

Gone were the warm smiles that first greeted her upon her arrival, which were rapidly replaced by the solemn looks of disdain and contempt for her presence in the home. Gloria acknowledged the temperament she found with a simple shrug of her shoulders and began walking in the direction of the room that she was shown to be staying in with her head down. The emotion was nothing new for Gloria to experience, since she appeared to be a form of disease to the number of families she'd been placed with who only sought to care for her as a means to broaden their financial gain devoid of any caring emotions for her wellbeing.

Gloria instantly became worried from the sight of the father who was named Buck, reaching behind his couch to hoist a Confederate flag onto hooks that she now noticed were screwed in tightly on the wall. She'd been in enough history classes to fully understand the gist of what it meant for someone to show pride in such a flag, so Gloria quickened her pace to the room, as the family eyed her with mischievous smirks attaching to their faces.

Gloria entered the small room and immediately noticed that there was no lock on the doorknob. The fear that set in when she heard footsteps approaching caused her to spring on the bed and retrieve her cellphone from her pocket. She quickly scrolled through the few numbers that she stored and made certain that Ms. Santiago's number was at the ready on speed dial. Suddenly, the bedroom door swung open, and Buck stood at the entryway with an expressionless look on his face. He saw Gloria practically shivering on the bed as she sat with her phone squeezed tightly in her palm, eyeing him suspiciously.

As Buck examined her for a long moment, Gloria placed her finger on the send button while secretively hoping to be able to hold him off long enough for her to alert Ms. Santiago to any altercation that might occur. To her surprise, however, Buck never bothered to take a step further than the doorway as he merely nodded his head at her transgression before he started to speak.

The interaction between them didn't last too long, with Gloria being forced to listen to the rules of the house as the young boys who were named Dale and Jacob, at the ages of six and seven respectively, stood behind their father, making ugly faces and hand gestures. The boys' mother, Patty, soon came after them, wafting cigarette smoke through the air, to drag them away almost kicking and screaming to finish their homework as Gloria learned more about her living arrangements.

As long as the money they received for her care kept flowing in on schedule, there wouldn't be any problems for Gloria. There was even a change for the better when Buck informed her that she would receive a weekly stipend of ten dollars. A smile that Gloria couldn't hide beamed wide on her face from concept until she absentmindedly began to wonder if she was being fattened up for the kill, especially since any form of currency given by members of the foster families she'd come to encounter was something that was never heard of.

The money and rules that Gloria was given doubled so that she wouldn't be too inclined to give away any information as to the goings on in the household. She had the power to come and go as she pleased; just as long as she didn't do anything to wake up the kids, it didn't matter what Gloria did. The only exemption to the rule was if Gloria somehow managed to lose the spare key that she'd been given, it wouldn't be automatically replaced and she would then have to abide by a ten o'clock curfew.

If it wasn't for the racial tension of the Confederate flag hanging proudly in their living room, Gloria could've grown to endear old Buck and his chain-smoking wife, Patty. The kids, not so much, but at least it wasn't like the last circumstance of her placement where she was constantly living in fear of the intemperate husband who drank so much, he held no qualms about relieving his stress by way of physically abusing her or his devoted wife who received the bulk of his rage.

The case worker, Ms. Santiago, almost suffered a major heart attack when she saw all of the bruises on Gloria's body during her scheduled monthly visits. Gloria tried her best to give off the explanation that she'd been jumped on by a bunch of girls at school, since the drunk husband, Dan, threatened to kill his wife before he came looking for Gloria to do the same thing to her, should any law enforcement become involved in the matter. However, Ms. Santiago knew that something was amiss when she came to see the similar bruises to the ones that Gloria had on his wife, Miranda's, battered features.

Needless to say, Gloria was immediately removed from the home under the close supervision of Ms. Santiago and the police. It took nearly two months for her wounds to fully heal, but a glimmer of hope surfaced for the wife, Miranda, after Ms. Santiago informed Gloria that she was justifiably released from police custody for almost fatally stabbing her husband to death after she finally had herself enough of enduring one of his many drunken assaults on her. Ms. Santiago was still wary to let Gloria out of the sight of her supervision, but after a year, Gloria came to be placed in the home of Buck and Patty Benning.

Schooling wasn't much of a vital factor in the Benning homestead. Patty only rose in the morning to bring her sons to school on the premise that they would be cared for during a majority of the day which gave her the opportunity to do anything she wanted without having them around to drive her crazy. Buck, on the other hand, had excellent skills in his trade of carpentry, but since little work was left to be had due to economic downturn, he found himself spending a lot more of his time drinking in the local bars with a bunch of his out-of-work buddies.

The scenario was the same way many times over where the decision to attend school was left entirely up to Gloria. Her parental supervisors never truly cared; as long as the funds kept rolling on in for their patronage, any further need for emotions in Gloria's regard seemed to be unnecessary. Wisely, Gloria chose to participate in as many school activities she could handle in order to escape the humdrum of the day, although things never changed much for the better whenever she happened to attend.

In school, Gloria was forced to congregate with her fellow outcasts, Malala and Jeremy, during break periods, such as lunch and recreation in their own private seclusion, apart from the mass of kids who chose to ignore them anyway. When the semester came to a close to begin the spring-break vacation,

Gloria became conflicted with her emotions by the need of wanting to have something to do for the few weeks of school closure.

Gloria's only interaction with the Benning clan occurred when she sat down for a place they had reserved for her at the end of the table to eat. Luckily, Patty was an excellent cook of southern cuisine, so whether any meal throughout the courses of breakfast or dinner, Gloria was able to eat herself a hearty meal which only became interrupted whenever food was thrown in her direction from the two boys of the family.

Gloria never uttered a scornful word to the boys for their acts of mischief. Instead, she simply pushed aside any food that landed on her, then excused herself from the table to wash her dishes before returning to her room. At least Buck had the gumption to place a small television set in her bedroom to give Gloria some form of company to quell the ills of the loneliness that she faced. She was all the more surprised to find that the set actually operated in color.

Other than the three-month shopping trip to buy Gloria clothing from a local thrift shop, there wasn't much of a further regard for her wellbeing. Gloria's cellphone became the contraption which was vital in enabling her to escape the boredom that Gloria endured. She never received any calls outside of maybe Malala, Jeremy, and Ms. Santiago's random checkups, but Gloria still couldn't fathom what she would do without it.

The phone was supported to function by way of a basic monthly plan which included the gratuities of unlimited calling and text messaging. Gloria only had limited access to the internet, but she had enough video games programmed to keep her occupied for hours on end, paid for by the Department of Foster Care Systems for the simple reason of being able to constantly ensure the safety of the many young they allowed into the homes of strangers.

In the early afternoon hours of the past Saturday, Gloria found herself to be startled by an instant message alert she came to receive while watching her favorite television show. As she thought about it, Gloria surmised that the message may have been some kind of advertisement, so she wasn't going to show much concern toward the text. When the alert came again, she decided to check it in the hopes to stop the text from reoccurring, but after Gloria read the intended message, she could only manage to evoke a look of utter disbelief as she stared at the phone in her hand with her mouth hanging agape in absolute befuddlement.

Gloria was rendered speechless. The text message was actually an invitation to attend a back-to-school party at a fellow student's house. The text seemed to have been sent at random for all those who attended her institution at Lincoln High who may have been interested in going. Gloria found herself faced with two questions now:

(1) How did they get her phone number? And, (2) should she make the effort to attend? Since any forthcoming answer to the two questions raised were as conflicting as they were intriguing, Gloria decided to place a call to her two friends for their much-needed opinions on her finding.

Gloria came to discover that Malala and Jeremy had both received the very same invite that she did. She also found out that it was Jeremy who took the measure of submitting all of their names and numbers to the school registry in order to receive updates on school events as an attempt for them to blend in with their peers. Gloria didn't have any inclinations about taking the invite seriously, but as she took a look around her spare bedroom within the Benning home, a smile rapidly made its way across her face with the possibility of actually being able to have some fun with a night out looming strongly in her mind.

After travel directions were obtained, Gloria made the arrangements to meet her two friends at the house where the party was located. Choosing to ride the public bus as her means of transportation, Gloria sank herself into a seat and stared out of the window while lost in thought. She began to contemplate upon the many possibilities of her future by wondering if she could ever find herself in the midst of a loving family who would actually care for her wellbeing or what just might become of her upon her eventual release at what is to be considered the adult age of 18. As Gloria reveled in the thought, a 40-minute bus ride to her destination ended in a flash as she took a deep breath and stepped off of the bus.

Chapter 2

Gloria was immediately impressed by what she came to see. After a short walk, she found herself on a paved roadway which led to a mansion type of estate, covered in its surroundings by manicured lawns and decorations that she could feel the vibration of, with every step she took. A vehicle suddenly blared its horn behind Gloria rudely, and she was forced into menacing teenaged girls who were snickering in Gloria's direction. She began to second guess her decision to attend the party but figured that she had come too far to turn back now, so she continued along on the lengthy path toward the home.

The atmosphere of the house was jam packed and vibrant, with teens milling about having a good time talking amongst themselves. Gloria wondered if she was dressed appropriately enough for the occasion, in her bulky sweat suit with her hair pulled back into a tight ponytail, as she watched the other girls strut around in stylish high heels while wearing dresses with makeup on their faces. Gloria never had a thought enter her mind about being able to pull off a provocative look of any kind. She never had any reason to, since she was always passed around between foster family after foster family.

Of course, Gloria could've shown some kind of regard for the boys of her age group, but they always seemed to want to taunt her with jokes instead, rather than reveal any sentimental interest in her emotionally, so she never experienced the type of infliction which would allow for Gloria to embrace more of the feminine characteristics that she possessed. She was snapped out of her reverie when Jeremy came running over to greet her. After they embraced in a wholesome hug, Gloria held him at arm's length and noticed that Jeremy had now been outfitted in a more conservative look for the evening with dark blue slacks and a dress shirt.

"You're looking mighty handsome this evening, Mr. Barnes. Are you trying to make an impression on somebody in particular? Because I might be willing to let you sweep me off of my feet with the right pickup line," Gloria stated playfully in a mocking gesture while batting her eyelashes. To her surprise, however, Jeremy responded with a whisper in her ear that he just might take her up on the offer. It was then that Gloria came to realize that Jeremy had the strong stench of liquor on his breath to go along with his blurred speech from being intoxicated.

As she regarded him more intently, Gloria started to experience a funny feeling of self-consciousness as Jeremy's gaze upon her seemed to confirm the seriousness of his statement. They locked eyes for a few tense moments before Gloria put an end to the uncomfortability by simply stating, "You're drunk," as she continued walking toward the house. "Here… You can get drunk too," Jeremy slurred in response as he tried to push a Styrofoam cup into Gloria's hand.

After taking a sniff of the contents in the cup, Gloria pushed it away in disgust, feeling as though the smell had the sensation of a raging inferno in her nostrils. "That stuff stinks!" she implored while hurriedly handing back the cup to Jeremy as fast as she could. "Don't knock it, till you try it," he lamented in return as he drained the remainder of the fluid in one long gulp and continued the rest of the walk with Gloria in silence to the house.

The party was hosted by a fellow student named Tommy 'The Tank' Sanderson. A popular senior who played the position of an All-Pro running back for the school's football team. Tommy's parents were both prominent healthcare professionals who were not scheduled to return from the vacation they took to the Bahamas for another week, so his goal was to host the biggest blowout party of the year without the interruption of his parents' constant supervision, and the festivities never failed to disappoint.

Set on two vast acres of land, it seemed like the estate was able to occupy the entire student body of the school with no problem. Emotions were all stabilized by the spirits of liquor and beer which were consumed in the choice of cans or disposable cups. A keg of beer was already present, but a majority of the kids brought along their own liquor bottles of different fashions which were pilfered from their parents' very own cabinets or were purchased with the help of an older acquaintance of theirs who were allowed access to the party in return.

The pulsating music that blared through the massive speakers that were brought in came about by way of a live D.J. who mixed the latest cuts on digitized turntables. A rather large and heated infinity-edge pool was accompanied by a cruse sign that read 'Only bottoms allowed.' A rule which was strictly heeded to by a bunch of brazen girls who were splashing around joyfully in the water naked from the waist up.

Also available for their comfort were the two separate spa areas being expertly used by those feeling flirtatiously affectionate toward one another. Coupled with the picnic tables scattered about, which never seemed to be empty of the assorted refreshments provided, the element of the 'Back to School' party was every bit the teenager's dream where the only true rule being enforced was to have as much fun as possible.

The rules of the home involved were fairly simple. You could do whatever you wanted to on the outside, but the indoors was strictly reserved for the ladies who cared to spend some time with their gracious host, Tommy the Tank, and his football teammates. A poolside cabana was available for those who needed to make use of the bathroom or a quick shower to wash away the chlorine after taking the provocative swim in the swimming pool, so there was not much need to enter the main portion of the home unless there was a life-threatening situation to be reported outdoors.

Gloria was a bit overwhelmed by the ambiance of the party but found a way to ask about Malala's whereabouts from Jeremy. He took her through a doorway which led to a spacious kitchen area that was outfitted with stainless steel appliances, marble countertops, and custom cabinetry. Gloria knew that Tommy drove a nice car for a 17-year-old, but it was apparent to her now that his parents were well off. She found herself coming to envy him for a mere moment, until she saw Malala waving in her direction.

It was comforting to see that Malala never bothered to waiver from her normal appearance the way that Jeremy had. Although she did happen to put considerably less makeup than she usually applied, Malala was the same gothic girl that Gloria endeared her to be. She found Malala nursing a Styrofoam cup similar to the way that Jeremy had been, as Malala stared at a bunch of the school's cheerleaders who must've all taken the same 'Home Economics' class as they prepared baked cookies and muffins while the boys in attendance stood themselves in wait to sample the finished products.

"Prime examples of our youth gone awry," Malala commented in a way that only she could as she took to examining those in her immediate surroundings with disgust.

"What are you drinking? Something strong too?" Gloria asked eagerly to change the subject before Malala strayed too far into one of her theories about the many vicissitudes involved in life. Gloria was here to let her hair down for the evening and have fun, and that is exactly what she did, as Gloria removed the hairband she wore to let her frizzy locks cascade down to her shoulders.

Malala said that she was just drinking a simple iced tea at that moment and suggested that if Gloria wanted something a bit stronger, she should try the fruit punch. Gloria was hesitant about stronger; she should try the fruit punch. Gloria was hesitant about it at first, but as she looked at the huge punch bowl with ice floating amidst the red fluid within, she came to figure that the concoction looked innocent enough; what harm could there be in having one cup?

Gloria held the cup in her hand after it was filled and gave to it the same sniff test she performed on Jeremy's drink. What appeared to be an innocent drink at first went down smoothly enough but soon brought on a harsh burn to Gloria's chest after she shrugged her shoulders and swallowed the fluid in haste of her thirst.

Before she become repulsed by the juicy drink however, the fruity aftertaste caused Gloria to question what just occurred. Gloria realized that she may have drank the contents of the cup a bit too rapidly, since aside from the initial reaction to the burn, she actually felt fine. She returned to the punch bowl to refill her cup once more and try again. This time around, Gloria did much better by way of simply sipping the drink which only allowed the burning in her chest to last a second to each sip before subsiding. An oncoming grumble in her stomach led Gloria to question the last time she'd eaten, and without being able to properly recall, her roaming gaze came to land upon the food being prepared by the cheerleaders.

*****

Tiffany has been a head cheerleader since her freshman year in junior high school, so the distinction naturally carried over in her later years as she led the all-girl cheer squad against Lincoln High's basketball and football rivalries. Since it was her mission to be in the running for the top honor of becoming 'Prom Queen,' Tiffany made certain to know the names of all her fellow peers who attended the school which happened to be the only reason that she even bothered to acknowledge Gloria and her dreary friend Malala.

A look of utter disgust swept across Tiffany's face from the sight of Gloria in her oversized sweat suit and Malala never departing from her drab Goth appearance. She wondered how some girls could allow themselves to be so bland and malignant to their sense of self-worth. Tiffany examined the texture of her manicured nails and knew that she would never be able to subject herself to that type of torment. She was destined for greatness, and nothing was going to stand in the way of her goals, even if it meant stepping over girls like Gloria and Malala to do so.

A variety of the girls present doubled as caterers for the affair by preparing pastries or meals such as fried chicken with macaroni and cheese to replenish the picnic tables and the stomachs of the partying masses. A mischievous smirk developed on Tiffany's face as she suddenly came to think of how fun it would be to lighten up the night's festivities with a prank. When she caught sight of the hunger building in Gloria's gaze, Tiffany couldn't help but to giggle uncontrollably to herself.

Tiffany removed the small tablets she'd stolen from her older brother's mixture of drug paraphernalia, which is always poorly stashed in the top drawer of his dresser, and began to veraciously crush the pills into a fine powder. Tiffany used the same pills herself to know of their effects and was gleefully hurrying to execute her plan. When the tablets were crushed enough to her satisfaction, Tiffany separated the powder evenly in half and retrieved two freshly prepared cupcakes to further her scheme. Tiffany applied frosting to the cupcakes with perfection, then used the crushed powder as though it were a decorative confectioner's sugar.

After admiring the result of her effort, Tiffany administered the sweetest smile she could muster before ambling herself over to where Gloria and Malala were watching her movements intently.

"Hey, Ladies! Can I offer you two some tasty treats!?" Tiffany cooed with the fleeting hope of maintaining her mischievous smile. Her fellow cheerleader and friend, Alexandria, held only pure hatred for Malala ever since the gothic girl had the audacity to throw paint on her last winter for wearing the new fur jacket that Alexandria's parents gave to her as a Christmas present, so the success of Tiffany's plan was all that Alexandria was wishing for as she watched the progress of her friend's movements.

Gloria was famished. She eagerly nodded her head in full anticipation of the sweet pastry to placate her needy palate. So much so that her mouth began to salivate from the mere sight of the delectable cupcakes being in Tiffany's hands. Malala, on the other hand, immediately declined the offer. Surmising wisely that anybody bearing a smirk as wide and fake as Tiffany's, Malala knew that the bubbly cheerleader was up to something sinister.

Malala clearly saw the wayward cheerleaders for what they really were. Slutty debutantes who long developed fake personas to conceal their evil intentions. A smirk did come to form on Malala's lips, however, when she remembered the amount of embarrassment she caused Alexandria last year with the fur coat debacle. The ensuring suspension she received for the course of her action at the school was well worth the effort, Malala thought, as Alexandria eyed her from afar with malicious disdain.

When Malala left for a split second to refill her cup with iced tea, Gloria eagerly allowed herself to feast on the cupcakes that Tiffany gave her. With a bit of mesmerized awe, Tiffany watched as Gloria rapidly devoured the baked goods as though she hadn't eaten in centuries. Satisfied that her method of deceit went along accordingly, Tiffany smiled meekly before spinning on her heels and saying, "I hope I get your vote for 'Prom Queen' this year," while she waved dismissively to return where Alexandria awaited, smiling brightly.

Alexandria was sorry to see that Malala didn't fall for the ruse as well, but as long as her friend Gloria stood in line to receive the planned humiliation in retaliation for the one that she was forced to endure at the hands of Malala's maliciousness, Alexandria would find herself pleased nonetheless with the end result. She and Tiffany shared a private joke amongst themselves then failed miserably to conceal their laughter as they mocked the image of synchronizing their watches while waiting patiently with the sight of Gloria licking her fingers clean of cake residue.

*****

The cupcakes weren't exactly fulfilling, but they were a very good start. Gloria finished the remnants of her drink and instantly began to feel the warming effect of its distillation on her insides. No doubt the punch bowl was spiked, although the two parts tequila and beer did nothing to distinguish themselves from the assorted fruits added to flavor the drink. Gloria was led to believe that the liquor she ingested had everything to do with the mesmerizing effect it had on her psyche. Little did she know, however, that there was something much more dubious afoot.

A cantankerous succession of emotions began to rapidly invade her inexperienced mind all at once. From feeling extremely happy in one instance, to Gloria suddenly becoming overwhelmed by a wave of depression that was quickly replaced by the act of her seductively licking beneath her top lip with her tongue, though Gloria couldn't begin to fathom why. Sweat began to form on Gloria's forehead with a profuse amount of wetness that she couldn't ignore. Gloria took off her sweater and discarded it immediately as though it were in flames, then glared at it while panting heavily in the midst of her contempt.

Gloria saw Malala watching her and became giddy all over again while beaming a smile so wide that it threatened to hurt her face. Malala took witness of Gloria's strange behavior and instantly became concerned for her friend's welfare. She'd already had two of the spiked punch herself to know that the drink was in no way strong enough to showcase the type of side effects that Gloria was exhibiting. As she came to see Tiffany and Alexandria off to the side, beaming hysterically in mischief, Malala knew then that whatever was happening to her innocent friend was a direct result of their cunning. As Malala made her way over to comfort Gloria in her disposition, her inebriated friend began hopping up and down as though she were a young child eager for a romp in the park.

Gloria felt no cooler standing with just her sports bra on, but the condition was ebbed and forgotten about when she waved her hand in front of her face, only to have it blur back in her vision with psychedelic transparency. Though Gloria heard it as though it were coming to her from the other side of the earth, she was broken out of her transfixed stupor when Malala called out her name.

When Gloria zeroed in on Malala's position more precisely, she found herself to be ecstatic upon recognition but couldn't understand for the life of her why her friend wasn't standing still. It wasn't until Gloria looked down at her own feet to realize that she was the one jumping up and down on her toes did she come to determine who was truly at fault for the display of foolishness.

"I want to have some fun! Let's have some fun, Mally, pleaseeeeee!!!" Gloria lamented emphatically. Sometimes fun entails suspiciously eyeing

Tiffany and Alexandria who were both off to the side, laughing giddily in merriment of their scheme.

"I think you've been drugged," Malala stated candidly while looking deep into Gloria's eyes.

"What do you mean drugged?! You're crazy! You know that I don't do drugs! Come on and dance with me!!!" Gloria reported as she took to pirouetting clumsily in step.

Malala didn't know what to do. She couldn't bear to see her friend in this kind of predicament of being taken advantage of. Finally, Malala suggested that they go outside with the hopes that senses. She grabbed on Gloria's arm and was surprised to see that Gloria actually allowed herself to be led into the warmth of the evening breeze that awaited them.

A song the D.J. played reverberated loudly within the confines of Gloria's mind that forced her to sway seductively to its rhythm. She used Malala's hand to guide herself into a trance of mimicking the most exquisite moves she could conjure up of the Salsa dance in her head. When Gloria finally opened her eyes, Malala stared at her, smiling. She was happy to see that the night air was helping to relieve some of the symptoms that Gloria was experiencing.

Malala began thinking of the ways that she could get even with the two conniving cheerleaders for what they did to her friend, when she came upon the sight of something that made her and Gloria take on a look of bemused shock amongst themselves.

The sounds of erotic moans caused the two young women to glance in the direction of the source, and when they happened upon their findings, Malala and Gloria's jaws dropped open in disbelief at the sight of seeing Jeremy with his tongue deep in the mouth of a girl who seemed to be enjoying every moment of his affection toward her. No matter how much she tried, Malala couldn't remove the look of shock from her facial features.

Now that she thought about it, Malala truly couldn't remember Jeremy for actually assuming the role of a gay person on his own volition. It was a mistake that everyone took him for, especially since Jeremy never expressed any desire for having any intimate relations with the same sex around her and Gloria before.

As her recollections became more clearer, Malala remembered that Jeremy was the only son of his mother's six children, with all five of his older siblings being girls. With her household surviving primarily off of the assistance of welfare subsidies, Jeremy was naturally the recipient of the clothing his sisters handed down to him which was something that was just not up for further discussion afterward since Jeremy was nowhere near the age to make his own decisions.

Aside from his two eldest sisters, every other sibling had the privilege of experiencing a different father figure who all possessed the dismal characteristic of being non-existent in their lives.

Jeremy was forced to endure the many taunts and ridicule that his sisters sent his way. Calling him a number of things that ranged in vulgarity such as 'sissy boy' and 'punk' was a way for them to cope with the breakups and other problems they would come to encounter at the hands of the many men who traveled in and out of the sisters' lives.

With the way Jeremy was acting now, Malala surmised that he was simply waiting for the perfect opportunity to find the freedom that he so desperately craved to have in order for Jeremy to express the insatiable desire he had building within himself. A task he seemed to be doing quite dutifully at the moment by way of entwining his tongue with a girl that he probably didn't even know all that well.

Malala actually began to feel a tinge of pride at the showing of Jeremy's liberation. Gloria, on the other hand, couldn't be so sure about what she was feeling. With one glance at Jeremy's display of voyeurism, she started to feel embarrassed, guilty, betrayed all at once. Only, for the life of her, she couldn't understand why was it because she valued Jeremy to be more than just a friend?

Certainly Gloria thought about what it would be like to maybe kiss Jeremy on more than one occasion, but that was merely from the result of her own inability to experience such a sensation. So, were the emotions that Gloria was exuding an inclination that she wanted to have something more in the terms of a relationship with Jeremy than just him simply being her friend? Gloria couldn't be sure that she could answer her own question truthfully at the moment.

When Jeremy saw that his erotic display was being watched, he creased a sly smile on his face in the direction of his mesmerized audience before continuing on with the act of his lustful conquest. Suddenly, Gloria felt herself becoming extremely nauseated, but she refused to lose her integrity in the face of Jeremy's self-rejuvenation. Gloria wanted to desperately go somewhere in that moment to be alone with her contentions and to hopefully stop the strange occurrences that her body was demonstrating. The surprise feeling of a tear in her eye was the exact signal that Gloria needed to make her departure.

When Malala became tired of viewing Jeremy and his female companion being gathered within their tethers of lust, she began heading toward the picnic tables that held the refreshments. After glancing back, Malala noticed that Gloria was sprinting in the opposite direction toward the house, screaming something incoherently. Since the weather did drop a bit, Malala simply assumed that Gloria was going back to retrieve her sweater as she shrugged her shoulders noncommittally before continuing on to the tables with food on her mind.

Although the night air became a bit cooler, Gloria wouldn't have noticed. With music thumping loudly in the background to go amongst the moans and groans of those engaging themselves in sexual trysts under the wilds of a darkened sky, Gloria was determined to find some of the solace that was needed for her to attend to the bubble of emotions that she was experiencing. She wasn't even sure where to find such a comfort zone at the loud bash, but as her steps neared the house once more, Gloria thought that maybe her best chance was to sneak off into one of the bathrooms or possibly even a closet area to find herself the privacy that she so desperately needed.

Chapter 3

Upon reentering the house through the very door she exited, Gloria began to feel the delirious effects she was experiencing all over again. It felt as though being confined to a limited amount of space was a trigger mechanism that allowed Gloria's condition to go haywire again, with a wave of dizziness consuming her that almost caused her to topple over. Gloria steadied herself on a wall in the kitchen and clenched her eyes tightly in a silent prayer in the hopes that the current circumstances of her state of mind would subside rapidly.

When the sound of muffled laughter caused Gloria to open her eyes once more, see saw Tiffany and Alexandria trying their hardest to conceal the jeering of their snickers in a failing attempt. Gloria didn't know what was happening to her. Surely, she had come to witness the demeanors of those who were drunk to know that the symptoms she was experiencing was the result of something entirely different. She just didn't know what.

"I think I might've been drugged," Gloria commented to herself, but the sentiment was loud enough for her pranksters to hear as Tiffany retorted with, "You certainly have been, Ms. Ramirez, you naughty girl," in the midst of her chuckles. Gloria somehow felt the beat of the D.J.'s music permeate the traces of her soul as she began to sway once more to its seductive rhythm. Her eyes widened in shock, however, from the sound of her audience bursting into a fit of laughter which instantly worked to leave Gloria embarrassed.

Desperate for a place of comfort, Gloria blindly took off at a sprint to run deeper into the recesses of the home, to find herself a place where she could be alone with her shame. As she exited the kitchen and rounded the corner, Gloria came to find herself in a large family room area that was currently occupied by a raucous commotion that caused her to stop dead in her tracks.

Gloria didn't know what was going on at first as she ventured upon the group of boys who were huddled together in deep conversation while others looked at the spectacle with crazed anticipation. When the group broke themselves up into a sudden lined formation, Gloria realized that they were attempting to practice some type of football drill with furniture pushed out of the way to create the amount of space needed to carry out their demonstration.

Troy Beasley was the team's Quarterback. A position he was currently reenacting as Tommy the Tank crouched behind him in wait. Troy began his play calling by chanting the words, "Blue 22… Blue 22… Hut! Hut! Hut!!!" just before shoving the makeshift football that was made up of a throw pillow into Tommy's arms as the Tank began his sprint. Gloria thought for a moment that she was imagining things with the sight of Tommy barreling toward her.

The display was to show how the team implemented the very same play to win the divisional championship for their school in a tough game against their rivals at Taft High by a score of 32 to 30 as the final seconds ticked away. Just one of the many accomplishments Tommy 'The Tank' Sanderson was able to accumulate during the course of the football season.

All of which earned Tommy a coveted spot on the city's All-Pro football team as well as allowing him to be amongst the intense talks of top talent scouts who desperately sought out prospects such as Tommy for their prestigious colleges.

The scene was reconstructed perfectly where, on a final third and long play, the team's offensive line demonstrated how they moved the team of the rival defense in one direction to allow Tommy the amount of space and protection he needed to make his 40-yard dash into the end zone to give his team the win.

As soon as the throw pillow was pressed into the Tank's arms, Tommy could almost smell the freshly cut grass that was packed under the spikes of his cleats during the game as he simulated how he faked a sidestep to his left before rapidly bolting in the opposite direction on his past toward greatness.

Tommy remembered that as soon as his path became cleared, all he had to was run. After he moved himself past the few defenders set to tackle him successfully, there was nothing left to challenge Tommy's sprint besides the open air to the goal line. This time around, however, Tommy wasn't running on his cherished field of dreams, and the limited amount of space that the room afforded had him rapidly approaching an object in his path that couldn't avoided easily.

When Tommy stopped himself within inches of her and erected a sly smile, Gloria became all warm on her insides as she dropped her head down bashfully in the attempt to hide the sudden wave of elation she was feeling. Gloria was well aware of Tommy's prowess by way of admiring him from after on many occasions, so she was certain that she could never have someone like him take her on as a girlfriend. That privilege was mainly designated to girls like Tiffany and Alexandria who diligently prepared themselves from the ages of toddlers to snag a modern day prince like Tommy the Tank as someone who could sweep them off of their pedicured feet and whisk them away into the beauties of their fantasy life which included rainbows and picked fences.

Tommy was a teenage heartthrob, so, naturally, Gloria became one of the girls who admired his stocky six-foot frame which was developed in muscle from a consistent workout regiment. His green tinted eyes worked to accentuate the texture of his dark complexion that could be attributed to his family whose ancestry traces back to the islands of the Mediterranean coast. Another distinct trait that set him apart from most others and practically had recruiters salivating out of their mouths to intercept him was the fact that Tommy also happened to be academically gifted. He may not have been a straight 'A' student by any means, but he never received anything below a 'C-plus' average on his grades.

Brains plus brawn had the girls like Gloria daydreaming about the endless possibilities of them being Tommy's girlfriend. Now, here she was, inches away from inhaling Tommy's sweet-smelling cologne. It felt as though they were the only two people left on the planet for a more moment until Tiffany materialized herself from what seemed like thin air to whisper something in Tommy's ear.

Whatever was being said in secret caused the smile on Tommy's face to widen all the more. When the furtive message was finally concluded, Tommy tilted his head back and yelled over his shoulder, "We got a live one here, boys!!!" as he smiled salaciously in Gloria's direction. She didn't know what Tommy meant exactly by his lament, but realizing that she was at the center of Tommy's concern in that instance left Gloria with a compulsive urge to discover what might happen next.

Gloria didn't even notice when Tiffany made her departure, but when she returned, Tiffany mischievously shoved another cup into her hand, and Gloria immediately smelled the strong scent of the liquor held within. She instantly felt a shiver come to her spine as Tommy grabbed her hand and urged her along with, "What's wrong, baby? Go ahead and drink it so we can have some fun," in the hope of loosening Gloria up a bit more.

Gloria took one more look at the innocent-seeming white liquid and was determined to maintain her reservations about not touching another drink until her thoughts somehow managed to land upon the previous image she had of Jeremy that caused a tinge of jealousy to emerge. At that moment, Gloria made the determination that if Jeremy could have his fun…then why couldn't she?

Gloria absentmindedly swallowed the liquid she held down her throat in one quick gulp and was forced to grasp at her chest in an attempt to soothe over the fire that began to rage within her. "Whoooo! It's going to be a good night tonight!!!" Tommy lamented excitedly as he took ahold of Gloria's hand and led her further into the guise of deceit. The last thing that she remembered afterward was being led through a maze of rooms while members of the football team rooted loudly in celebration. Besides that, everything to Gloria became a blur as her memory became totally blank.

*****

Gloria had awakened the day after the party she attended with an excruciating headache. Her head was spinning madly as she scanned the area of her body with her hands and discovered that she was still wearing the same clothing from the night before. It was then while lying in the position on her back and looking toward the ceiling when Gloria came to realize that she was back in her room at the Benning home.

Gloria groggily rose herself into a sitting position with her eyes glazed over in half-open slits before she slammed herself back down into her bed with where her head continued the ruminations of its throbbing. With the passing thought of seeing something in vision that shouldn't have been there, Gloria shot her eyes open with a sudden fear.

When she came to sitting position once more, Gloria happened to land her gaze on the surprising sight of old Buck staring back at her from the doorway with a look of utter disgust plastered across his face.

"Had a fun night out?" he asked after a moment, and Gloria could easily discern from the sound of his tone that the question Buck raised was a rhetorical one as she waited for him to continue.

"Are you a whore, young lady?" Buck asked to Gloria's complete astonishment as though the inquiry were a simple one for the mind of a teenage girl to answer. This time around, however, the question proved to be a bit too much for Gloria to bear with her becoming enraged with anger to raise the response, "Who are you calling a whore?!?!" while she seethed at Buck through clenched teeth.

"Well… Seeing as how you were half naked…" Buck began in retort. The words 'half naked' caused Gloria to fervently scan the areas of her body once more to notice that she was only wearing the sports bra that Gloria had on after discarding her sweater back at Tommy's house. She instantly became embarrassed as Buck continued on with, "…and lying on the front steps as a bunch of boys your age hopped into a car and sped off!!!" he lamented dramatically with his own anger rising.

Gloria took the time to consider Buck's accusation rationally and realized that she could hardly recall anything in her memory to account for any plausible explanations of how she came to arrive at the home, so she had no choice but to accept Buck's version of the events to be true. Gloria was forced to suffer in the old adage where if someone was too drunk to get themselves home on their own accord, that person would come to be callously dropped off at their doorstep while the bell was rung with enough awaiting vehicle in order to escape the awkward questioning that was sure to come from the occupants of the residence.

Buck was still standing in the doorway expectantly in wait for an answer to his question. Gloria tried in vain to shake the throbbing she had in her head to focus correctly, which only worked in the opposite of making it pound harder, as she replied, "No, Buck, I am not a whore. I just drank a little too much at the party I went to last night." Her revelation seemed to bring about a small measure of relief to Buck, since, coincidentally, he'd actually had another foster girl staying with his family before who not only sold her body for money but did so at the behest of a crazed pimp with whom old Buck had to lock horns with in order to secure the dignity of his family.

Buck certainly didn't want to go through any type of experience like that again, so he made a vow to himself to keep a closer eye on Gloria's behavior pattern as he grumbled, "We may have to rethink the terms of our agreement, starting with a reasonable curfew," before he left scratching his head while trying to figure out what he should do with the troubled girl in his care.

The remaining hours of her Sunday was pretty much tame, with Gloria playing a few videogames before she tuned in to watch some of her favorite shows on television. The only thing to raise some serious concern about her actions during the party was when Gloria found dried splatters of blood around her sore private area after she removed her clothing to take a shower. At that moment, all Gloria could do was pray that she didn't do anything stupid as she climbed into the shower, hoping that the steamy water would be enough help to wash away the regrets of her raucous night.

*****

Gloria woke up groggily for her first day back to school but felt invigorated to start the remainder of the school year anew. Though she couldn't remember much, Gloria was hoping to have made some new friends at the party and was eager to find Malala to see if her friend could fill her in on any gaps for the lapses in her memory. Gloria thought about calling her on the phone, but seeing that she was already running late, she dressed in the best outfit that she could muster before bolting out of the door.

Gloria maintained the broadest smile she could ever remember herself exuding when she stepped into Lincoln High. A smile that rapidly deteriorated with the sight of everyone starting in her direction suddenly, before furtively mocking her with whispers and giggles. The jeering only seemed to intensify when Gloria saw Jeremy posted up at his locker, surprisingly, in the same company of girl he happened to be unapologetically interlocking his tongue with at the party.

The makeshift couple was smiling coyly amongst themselves until their emotions dramatically changed from being modest one moment, to becoming utterly sinister upon the sighting of Gloria's presence. Before Gloria could have a chance at saying something, Jeremy looked her up and down in disgust while shaking his head dismissively and throwing his arm around the shoulder of his new female companion before walking off together, laughing at Gloria's expense.

Gloria remembered her now. The girl's name was Mandy, a loner at the school as well. Gloria came to hear passing rumors that Mandy was the promiscuous type, but at that moment, she awkwardly wished that it was her under Jeremy's arm and not some random girl he just met. When she caught

30

sight of Malala existing the bathroom, Gloria's spirits immediately perked up a bit, and she shouted out her name to get Malala's attention.

Malala felt a bit contemptuous by her sighting of Gloria, but this was her friend. Malala remembered the time when Gloria was there for during her period of suffering when Malala took to cutting herself to relieve the stress of her daily depression. Malala made a personal vow to be there for Gloria no matter how egregious the resolve may be. Although the matter amounted to be a real doozey, Malala just couldn't believe that Gloria would be the type to do anything this brash. Malala took a deep breath to clear away the disdain from her conscience nonetheless when Gloria made her way over.

Gloria was relieved to see that Malala didn't exhibit the same type of scorn that Jeremy had in store for her. She even seemed to be genuinely concerned for the state of Gloria's wellbeing, which was an aspect further confirmed when Malala asked, "Are you all right?! Why did you go all crazy like that at the party? That's not like you!" Gloria just knew that she did something stupid in that instant. It was just too good to be true for her to have some fun without incurring some type of consequence. Malala was right. 'Fun, entails the outlook of disappointment,' at least in her case, Gloria thought, as she remembered her friend's dismal epithet that was used at the party.

Gloria made an exasperated sigh and wondered what she could have done to be so reviled now by everyone at the school? Before she had the chance to answer her own question, the morning bell rang loudly to signal the beginning of class. Malala grabbed Gloria by the shoulders and looked her deeply in the eyes before saying, "Meet me at lunch so we can talk. And, don't worry… No matter what you did, I'll still be here to help you through it." Gloria could only nod her head slowly in response as she considered the seriousness of Malala's words. She was left with the parting sight of her friend's back as Malala hurried off to get to class. Gloria inhaled a deep breath and began to make her way to the start of her own class while wondering how much stranger the day could get.

Chapter 4

Mrs. Cramer's English class was always noisy before it officially began, since the teacher often took the time to allow her students to settle down from the morning chaos of arriving at school to actually start learning something. Mrs. Cramer was determined to make sure that her students became educated with something more than just how to be cool on reality television or how many friends they might be able to make on the internet. She didn't want to bore them with the drab teachings of Bard and Shakespearean analogies, so she focused instead on the topics that would enable them to apply what they would come to learn as an everyday skill, such as the composition of novel writing and practicing journalism. Mrs. Cramer took the time to finish off her morning coffee as she always did in the staff room before she entered the classroom to command the full attention of her students.

The classroom was especially rowdy today, as it always was during the first day back from spring vacation, with everyone taking the time to reacquaint themselves with one another and catch up on the stories and gossip they might have missed out on. When Gloria entered the classroom, however, the element became bizarrely serene with her suddenly realizing that she was once again the object of deceitful giggles and whispers. The path to her seat was a long one for Gloria to trudge now with her becoming ridiculed by snickers and looks of disdain all the way to her chair.

Mrs. Cramer's appearance in the classroom was well-received by her students, especially Gloria, who just wanted to put an end to her dismal day with the hopes to leave any innuendos of her torment behind her. Staying focused in class was nowhere near an easy thing for Gloria to do, but Mrs. Cramer's lesson lightened her burden a bit with her presentation of the proper way to write a short story with the use of illustrative creation.

As the evil-spirited attention she was receiving was slowly removed, Gloria tried her best to stay focused but found it extremely difficult not to ponder on the outlook of her possible indiscretions. She wished the hours would go by quicker in order for her to meet up with Malala to get the vital information she needed. For now, however, Gloria was forced to endure the amount of torment she faced until the anticipated time came.

Just when her thoughts finally settled in to the lesson being instructed, a movement in Gloria's pocket suddenly caused her to lose the concentration she worked so hard to achieve. Gloria wanted to leave the device alone, but she knew that the vibrating wouldn't stop if she didn't attend to it immediately. When Gloria managed to retrieve the phone to intercept the message that she was getting, it also came to peak her curiosity, since she hadn't received any form of alerts on her phone since the day of the party.

Gloria found herself to be in a state of complete shock at what she came to find. It left Gloria absolutely dumbfounded to see that instead of a simple worded text message, she discovered that a video feed was forwarded to her from a number that she knew to be Jeremy's. The way that Jeremy acted toward her before caused Gloria to feel inclined to view the content of the video feed in order for her to quell the raging amount of anxiety that began to ravage her thoughts.

*****

Gloria took a moment to study her teacher's actions and noticed that Mrs. Cramer was busily writing something on the chalkboard as the class jotted down their notes in obedience. Gloria gulped down the huge lump in her throat and inhaled deeply, when she forced her finger to press down on the button which would allow her to view the hidden footage of the video recording.

After taking the measure to mute the sound, Gloria watched as mindless teens laughed and did stupid pranks to each other while getting themselves drunk. Gloria guessed correctly that the footage was derived from the party at the Sanderson home, as various teens made obscene faces for the delight of the camera.

When the screen went blank for a moment, Gloria assumed that the video feed was over, but her facial features suddenly became ashen from the sight of her own drunken appearance being revealed under the arm of Tommy the Tank as his teammates rooted his action on loudly in the background.

Gloria watched on in horror as she was led to a bedroom while nodding her head absentmindedly along the way with Tommy whispering furtively in her ear. When they reached the bedroom area, the screen went blank once more, and Gloria suddenly gasped at the reemerging sight of Tommy straddling himself on top of her while Gloria just lay there beneath him, exhibiting no emotion.

After he was done, Tommy pounded on his chest in triumph before ushering in his fellow teammates to join in on his conquest. Gloria couldn't resist the tears anymore as she sobbed uncontrollably while in watch of Tommy's teammates eagerly taking turns to have intercourse with her.

Gloria's only consolation came as the number of boys who invaded her sanctity stopped at five as opposed to the roster of the 30-man team. Gloria began feel claustrophobic as though the world was collapsing on her shoulders, and the immense emotion was beginning to stifle her breathing.

Gloria knew that she needed to get out of the room now before she embarrassed herself any further. When she asked the teacher for a bathroom break, Mrs. Cramer became skeptical of Gloria's bleak appearance and questioned her temperament, but when Gloria informed her that everything was all right, Mrs. Cramer instantly knew that something was wrong with the tell-tale signs of tears being evident on Gloria's face, but she allowed Gloria to leave for the moment in the hopes that Gloria would be able to pull herself together, at least until Mrs. Cramer had the chance to speak to her class. Unfortunately… Gloria would never return to the classroom again.

*****

Her emotions led Gloria to be at her present location which was sulking at the train station in wonder of how the aspects of her life became so complicated. Since the morning rush hour had come and gone, the station was desolate and left Gloria with the all-too-familiar feeling of being alone without even a scampering rodent to keep her any company. In weighing out the good from the bad in her life, Gloria ultimately came to the conclusion that the good was in no way a match for the tumultuous state of her current wellbeing.

Gloria could only surmise that the only people who might have an inclining of concern for her at the moment were Ms. Santiago and Malala, although she couldn't be all the way certain of anyone's true intentions with her judgment being clouded in despair.

Maybe they were just like Jeremy themselves in wait for the perfect opportunity to turn on Gloria at the first chance to do so? Whatever it was, Gloria refused to be taken advantage of again.

She suddenly felt the vibration of the train approaching before she could see its headlights in the distance. Then and there, Gloria made the decision to put an end to her life. Why continue on when her dismal problems were only going to get more complicated in the regard of her newly revealed acts of malfeasance? Gloria placed the nail further in her own coffin by replaying the humiliating video feed once more at high volume as the appealing scene of her life became showcased in grotesque fashion on her cellphone.

While the video played on, Gloria came to learn that she was actually used as a sort of sexual sacrifice in order to compliment the final year of Tommy's tenure in high school after he came to be accepted to attend the college of Notre Dame on a full scholarship. The fact that Tiffany and Alexandria had also contributed to relations with the members of the football team on the night of the party brought no form of solace to Gloria's sensibility as she held firm to the decision of bringing a closure to her life as planned.

Gloria thought for a moment about Ms. Santiago's concern and decided to send the guidance counselor a text message that simply read, 'Thanks for everything, Ms. S, but I can't do this anymore,' before hitting the send button on her keypad with a heavy heart.

Gloria became startled when a man entered the station, appearing to be disheveled. They locked eyes for a tense moment, and Gloria wondered if he may have sensed her scheme, but the man took off noncommittally in the opposite direction as though he had something else more pressing to attend to.

The stranger's resignation suited Gloria just fine, because she refused to be deterred in her intent. She became startled again, however, by the feeling of the phone suddenly shaking in her hand in vibration. Gloria quickly moved to put an end to the call that she knew to be coming in from Ms. Santiago calling in raise her concern.

Gloria typed one last message that read, 'I'm sorry, but I'm tired of being the one who has to suffer.' A reply came immediately afterward by text, but that was all that Gloria felt she was inclined to do since she had already gone on to make peace with the situation.

Gloria folded up her jacket neatly and placed it on the bench with her phone on top of it. She then resurrected the video feed once more to allow it to play out in its entire freely.

The feel of the train's intensity could not be denied at that point as it roared in its approach while Gloria took a deep breath to concentrate and clear her thoughts.

*****

As the train neared, Gloria gave a final look to the sky as drops of rain landed on her face. She wasn't sure what was going to happen to her afterward, but Gloria was for certain that she was now destined to go in the opposite direction of where Heaven was located… If there was such a thing. She gave herself one more glance in the man's direction and noticed that he couldn't care less for Gloria's wellbeing. *How ironic,* Gloria thought as she continued to prepare her final breaths.

Gloria faced the direction of her phone as she stood on the edge of the platform to hear the words, "Yeahhhh!!! Do it to her good!!!" from the sounds of the sex-hungry boys yelling and laughing emphatically in the background. The dejection caused Gloria to incoherently mumble the words, "I can't," to herself repeatedly.

When the train finally barreled into the station, Gloria squeezed her eyes tightly before spreading her arms apart and allowing her body to fall back meekly to coincide perfectly with the train's arrival. Only before the train was able to make an impact with her tormented soul, Gloria found herself to be startled once more when the strange feeling of a hand grabbing on to the fabric of her shirt came to be the surprise that brought her back into the disarray that Gloria's life had become.

Gloria's attempt at suicide had been successfully thwarted by the large black man who seemed to be the unlikely candidate for being anyone's savior. The stranger's appearance remained to be more dirty than being covered in filth. In clothing which looked to have been derived from some sort of turmoil that the man may have found himself in. The factor was further proven with traces of blood becoming present amongst the sight of bruises and scrapes on his face.

When Gloria ventured to take a look in the stranger's eyes, bloodshot pupils stared back at her with a perplexing look that could've been laced with either concern or disdain. Gloria couldn't be sure of which at that moment, but for some reason, Gloria felt comfortable enough to break down into his arms and sob.

The stranger was trying to think of what to do. He was tired and had two pistols on him that were empty and smoldering with no extra ammunition available for him to prevent any potential danger he night run into again which would make for a deadly combination under the wrong circumstances.

The stranger also held a sharpened dagger for added protection, but it certainly wouldn't be a match for the type of arsenal that his enemies were known to carry. Now, here, he was with the problem of a sobbing girl in his arms. As the train came to a stop, the stranger knew that he had to get out of there quickly before he came to be discovered by any of his foes, but he couldn't reasonably leave the troubled girl behind with the likely possibility that she would try to take her own life again. Against his better judgment, the stranger held Gloria at arm's length and said, "Let's go."

Surprisingly, Gloria allowed herself to be led away by the stranger toward the exit without any form of resistance on her part. As they walked along together, the strange man came upon Gloria's cellphone which was playing the repeated footage of her deviating circumstance and glanced in her direction. Gloria simply shrugged her shoulders and nodded her head on agreement as though she were answering the stranger's hidden innuendo. He shook his head dejectedly as he gathered Gloria's belongings and ushered her to a car that he had parked in wait which was borrowed illegally.

Chapter 5

Ralph found himself holed up in a seedy motel accommodation where the only questions asked upon one's arrival were the amount of days being requested and whether or not the payments made would occur on a cash or credit basis. The extent of things that could be done by those who chose the cash option were almost limitless and brought about a feeling of sickness to Ralph's stomach in knowing the amount of atrocities such as rape, sodomy, prostitution, and even murder could be induced without a tinge of remorse from the owner who would go on to conduct the premise of business as usual, but Ralph had far more pressing problems of his own to deal with at the moment.

Ralph regretted not preventing some of the egregious acts that he's come to witness over the years. Like the time he stumbled upon a suspicious-looking white man who tugged on the arm of a young Mexican girl, who appeared to be no older in age than ten, with her eyes widened in the utter fear of hopelessness as the man forcibly ushered her into an inconspicuous vehicle before driving off from a motel that was no seedier than the one Ralph currently found himself in.

He very much hated not putting an end to the shady man's scheme with a bullet to his head, but, at the time, Ralph was forced to use his deadly skills to complete a job he was given at the behest of a client before the chance evaded Ralph in a way which would leave him to be on the receiving end of someone's gun barrel for failing to finish the task he was given.

Ralph had always regretted his decision of leaving the young girl in the hands of whatever evil that awaited her, and he still had visions of the helpless girl's fearful expression pop into his mind from time to time. Now, here Ralph was, faced with the problem of his very own dilemma.

The drive to the motel had been uneventful. Ralph's consciousness continued to bombard him with the overwhelming thoughts of worry, guilt, and scorn. Contemplations of a next move were as confliction as the battle between good and evil as he wisely decided to get some time to rest in the motel to think more clearly about the predicament that he found himself in. Ralph's passenger didn't even show any signs of apprehension. She just simply gazed out of the window until her exasperated soul was caressed into a blissful slumber by the rumble of the vehicle's engine.

Ralph remembered driving up to the main office to check in and handing over his money to an overweight black woman who didn't even bother to look up from the magazine she was reading. When she handed him the keys to his room, Ralph retrieved the sleeping girl from the car and entered the small room that his money afforded and noticed that it was sparsely furnished with a queen-sized bed that left little space for the nightstand, reclining chair, and simple television set which were all included in the rate.

Ralph originally intended to get a room with double beds but opted to be less conspicuous about his motives in the attempt to negate any form of questioning about his underage guest.

Though he was an aging black man, Ralph was professional at being undetected. Leaving a witness to positively identify him just simply wasn't an option, so he either eliminated such a threat with a show of force, or he used the skill he possessed of transforming into a slew of the characters that he liked to emulate to make himself seem less discernable.

Identities such as the look of a vagrant, which happened to be the one he stumbled upon the problematic girl with, or maybe the appearance he hated the most as an actual senior citizen who made use of blinder shades and a walking cane in furtherance of the goal he was set to achieve. Though the role of a senior citizen was one that Ralph detested the most, it came to be the most effective for him.

Ralph suddenly clutched one of his weapons tightly as while conveying emotions similar to a movie scene from the old assassin flick *The Professional* which starred a young Natalie Portman, where the brave hitman of the film held a gun to her character's head as she slept in contemplation of ending her young life in order to rid himself of having the troublesome girls as a burden.

Ralph would only be kidding himself with that form of rationale, since he was never in the business of hurting females, much less innocent teenage girls. Ralph placed the pistol he had in his lap instead and took to reclining in the chair he was seated in to stare out of the room window until he was able to

doze off eventually for a short moment of fitful sleep that was very much
needed.

*****

From one of his many haunting dreams, Ralph awakened as though he were
ready for war. After relieving the initial disorientation swirling about in his
eyes, Ralph glanced in the direction of where the girl was laying and was
surprised to find that she was still sleeping peacefully. The girl only stirred a
bit in her state of deep rest as Ralph watched the breathing of the life he helped
to save rise up and down.

After taking the liberty to order some Chinese food from a number he
found in the room, Ralph picked almost everything he could from the menu
since he didn't know what the girl might like to eat before going into the
bathroom to freshen himself up. Leaning on the sink, Ralph shook his head
from side to side on contempt at the telling reflection he saw of himself in the
mirror.

Examining his age-hardened face, which was accompanied by salt-and-
pepper hair, Ralph sincerely wondered how much longer he would be able to
keep up with fulfilling the contracts he managed to acquire from the less than
sociable to help rid the world of its degenerate lowlife.

At times, Ralph truly loathed what he did to make a living, but then there
were the moments that he was called upon to dispense of the lowest form of
criminal element that society had to offer which happened to bring upon Ralph
a sense of worth to add to his moral sanctity. A factor that kept him functioning
on a professional level.

Ralph's thoughts were broken up by the sound of someone knocking on
the front door. His hunger immediately became intensified with the perception
that the person knocking was the delivery man bringing him the food he
ordered. When Ralph made his rapid exit from the bathroom, however, he was
met first by a young woman who was trying in vain to retain the remnants of
her sleep through glazed over eyelids.

As if they were highflying acrobats in sync, Ralph managed to move
himself off to the side just in time for the girl in his company to hurry in to the
bathroom and slam the door behind herself. He stared awkwardly at the

bathroom until the repeated knocking at the front door worked to successfully snap Ralph out of his state of perplexity.

After arranging the food for consumption, Ralph heard the bathroom door open and close as he waited patiently. Due to the carpeting in the room, Ralph couldn't hear the girl's footsteps approaching, but he became aware that she must've been nervous by the way she slowly tiptoed into his view on her bare feet.

As though a nap was exactly what she needed to come back into her senses, the girl now showed signs of fear and alertness that she hadn't done before in the car. First glancing in the direction of the bed where she had slept, then over to the area where Ralph was eyeing her intently, the girl made use of a wide-eyed stare to survey her surroundings before she hung her head low and began twiddling her thumbs together.

"Where are we?" the girl asked nervously without raising her head to meet the stranger's gaze. "Well… At the moment, we're in a drive-in motel, but don't worry, you're safe here with me," Ralph responded with a nervous smile of his own in understanding of the amount of resignation that his unexpected guest must've been experiencing.

Ralph knew that the girl in his care had to be frustrated from trying to put an end to her life one minute, to waking herself up in the presence of a total stranger. A slight moment more passed before she allowed herself to speak again. "Why did you save me?" she asked in a tone so straight forward, Ralph came to find himself at a loss for words for anything to say in return. When he finally recovered his bearings, Ralph's stammered response was a simple one. "I guess it was because… Well, it looked like you needed to be saved."

The tension became thick when the girl asked Ralph if he was going to hurt her. A wave of anger automatically entered into his psyche as Ralph considered her inquiry of concern in the context of sex and violence. "I just wanted to help you out! If you don't want that, then you can just go ahead and try to kill yourself because I won't be coming to your rescue again!!!" Ralph lamented in a tone and demeanor that he instantly came to regret.

The words hung in the balance a moment before Ralph meekly took to saying, "Look… I just want to help you with whatever it is that you're going through and return you to your home and family safely. What's your name anyway, kid?" When the girl finally looked up and saw the intensity in Ralph's eyes as he stared back at her in watch of her emotions, she decided to make the response, "My name is Gloria, and I don't have a family to go back to."

*****

With introductions made as formal as they were ever going to get between the two, each person became a bit more comfortable in the presence of the other. Ralph didn't want Gloria to start closing up to him now, so he suggested that they take the time to settle down and put something in their stomachs before the food got cold. He watched in silence as Gloria ate and instantly surmised that the kind of hunger she was exhibiting could only come from one being rescued from the throes of death's tightening grip. And, Gloria was lucky to have had the fate of her life saved by mere inches thanks to Ralph's fast-acting intuition.

While Ralph took witness of Gloria tearing through the meal with the intensity of a rabid jackal, he wondered how a body of no more than maybe 90 pounds, soaking wet, could be capable of ingesting such a feast the way that she was.

A humored smile swept across Ralph's face when he came to remember that he was even younger than Gloria was when someone took him in and showed Ralph the ropes of being able to survive in a harsh world when the drug addict he had for a mother would never be able to do so, during a time when the foster care system didn't provide the funding needed to be an enriching option for the care of abandoned children aside from the select few it chose to bundle.

Ralph continued to reminisce to a time when, as a young boy of about nine years old, he was intercepted by a white man during a chance encounter who became his mentor by the name of 'Loanshark Jack.' The first person to teach Ralph to shoot a gun. The moniker of a Loanshark came to be attributed from Jack's actual profession of lending people a set amount of money and expecting a high interest payment in return on the funds he lent out. A form of cunning that people also refer to as 'Shy looking.'

Chapter 6

The days of post war were a simpler time when all fashions of the criminal element were able to thrive on the sole premise that anything could be accomplished at will, as long as the proper contributions were made to the authoritative powers that be on a daily, weekly, or monthly basis. In other words, a payment made to the coffer of whoever the officer was in charge of working in any of the crime-ridden areas they were assigned to.

Loanshark Jack made sure to have his payment on time every time himself, however, with a little something extra to fill the greedy palms of the many policemen who eagerly took it in order for Loanshark Jack to have the free reign he required to conduct his illicit activities the way he saw fit.

Jack's philosophy was simple… He took you at your word. If a person chose the service that Jack provided, he expected them to make the proper restitutions at the rate he set, on the exact day specified by the borrower. If any term of the agreement was broken, such as the amount not getting paid on time… Well, then bad things could always begin to happen to good people.

In order for a person to not upset him, the young men under Jack's employ, who helped him run his numbers, wisely kept their own records of the transactions memorized on paper to greatly reduce the risk of losing vital information. Something which, in turn, always helped to add a few more fruitful years to their lives.

Jack, on the other hand, didn't need to keep records of anything. His mind functioned the way a computer system did where he was always able to recall, analyze, calculate, and memorize any information he needed to in an instant. He tolerated the use of record keeping amongst his employees, but after all of the monthly accounts were tabulated, Jack insisted that all traces of the damning transactions were destroyed.

It provided Loanshark Jack a sense of solace in knowing that none of the receipts could be traced back to him, since the records only contained an array of confusing numbers along with the initials of the person who borrowed the money without any mention of Jack's criminal involvement in the matter. In any event, Jack detested anything that could potentially inherit him some jail time.

Loanshark Jack especially liked the fact that his business and form of record keeping successfully worked to keep his mind sharp as a razor, which was a very good thing for him, but not so much for those who may wanted to take his form of wit as a sign of weakness.

Jack meticulously maintained a distinct memory of who he lent his money to, and who owed him money in return, along with recognizing the type of pain he should inflict when someone threatened the validity of his reputation meant to him. As such, anywhere from five dollars to currency reaching in the thousands of dollars could mean the difference between a few fingers becoming broken to quite possibly the last breaths one may take, coming to fruition sooner than expected.

Loanshark Jack had watched the progression of the chase unfold as though a movie were playing, as the boys scattered about wildly in opposite directions. The man who was giving chase was overweight so, naturally, he stayed on the path of the boy he presumed to be the easiest for him to catch.

The chubby man's chance finally came when one of the boys he was after made the mistake of running down an alleyway full of garbage bags and litter that offered him no possibility for escape other than to go back the way he'd come, but, by then, it was far too late to do so.

The man gasped for much-needed air but became elated nonetheless that the chase was over. He just couldn't be sure of how much longer he would've been able to move his chunky legs into a sprint before succumbing to a wave of exhaustion.

The stranger hunched over and placed his large hands on his knees in order to inhale as much vital air he could possibly get to sustain his breathing without ever removing his raging eyes from the sight of his frightened prey. As the man gathered his bearings, a wicked smile suddenly emerged on the exterior of his face from the evidence of desperation in the boy's demeanor.

When he made his approach, a garbage can was flung in his direction unexpectedly which forced him to narrowly dodge its impact by making use of his forearm as a shield to block it out of the air.

The man's anger rose immensely from seeing the young boy trying to regain his courage by getting himself set into a fighting stance with his hands clenched tightly. As the chubby stranger took a step closer to his target, he seethed with vehemence, "I got you now! You little ni—" Before he had the opportunity to finish his hate-filled epithet, however, a tiny fist was rapidly hurled in his direction.

The blow was intended to land on the man's face, but it meekly struck on the shoulder blade of the target's rotund body instead. An evil-laced chuckle escaped the stranger then at the thought of the young boy's feeble attempt to defend himself, before the large man, in turn, used the force of his backhand to make a hard slap across the boy's face with an impact that sent its recipient sprawling helplessly into a heap of trash bags. The robust man suddenly took on the appearance of someone possessed as he gleefully watched the boy squirm around on the floor strewn with garbage, trying to regain his composure.

The stranger's next reaction was most uncanny in maliciousness as he groped himself to an erection while displaying a crude smirk that he wouldn't be able to explain under normal conditions. "So, you like to stare at white women, huh?" were the callous words that escaped his mouth in contemplation of a next move.

Before the ailing boy had the opportunity to gather his wits properly, the stalking man pounced with an overweight body that kept his quarry pinned to the ground. The boy started thrashing his arms and legs about in the desperate attempt to flee, but his efforts failed miserably under the man's immense girth as he began to panic from the feel of the stubby man's hands trying to remove his pants.

Tears began to stream from the boy's eyes with the sound of the man's husky groans reverberating heavily amidst his rising fear. The boy wanted terribly to fight to protect himself, but he knew he was powerless at the moment to derail the stranger's vile intention from happening. He wanted to remain strong and defend his honor no matter what, but what more would the boy do?

The helpless boy opened his mouth to scream for help, but his words never came. As he began to sob uncontrollably from the thought of what was to come next, something strange and unexpected happened... Suddenly, the boy felt totally crushed by the man's overwhelming weight as the body of his captor went limp on top of him.

*****

Positioned flat on his stomach with his pants halfway off of his body, the trapped boy knew he had to get out of there and fast. Hoping to put an end to his nightmare, the young boy forced his hands underneath his body in the attempt to push himself up off the ground to escape the stranger's weight, but his arms only strained from the intense pressure in a way that caused him to collapse once more under the hefty bulk.

Using the will of all of his might to get the task accomplished, the harried boy made another try to free himself once again from the man's weight, and, surprisingly, he was able to lift the body of his attacker more easily on his second attempt. The boy suddenly felt powerful for the strength found in his innocuous ability, until he remembered the gross failure of his previous attempt at freeing himself which instantly caused him to be suspicious of his current circumstance.

The first thing the boy cared to do when he finally squirmed free of the chubby man's immense weight was pull up his pants. It may have been a bit too far over his waist afterward, but the boy didn't mind at all as long as he managed to avoid being violated by the stranger's evil intention; he felt extremely gratified. It was then in the midst of his revelry that the boy did come to realize that he was in the presence of someone other than the unconscious man sprawled out on the ground.

When the perplexed boy took the chance to glance behind himself, his became locked into the eyes of another man who exuded an intensity about him that could only be described as that of a man with power. The boy then examined the stern man from his neatly trimmed hair, to the fibers of what he presumed to be an expensive suit.

When the boy's nervous gaze landed upon the gun that the man gripped tightly in his hand, the boy's fear came to overwhelm once more, until he noticed the bloody gash located at the back of his attacker's head. At that moment, a smile began to emerge on his face that the boy couldn't even think about holding back to escape his emotional distress.

Jack had seen enough. His intentions at first was to wait until the fat man doled out the punishment he saw fit to the young black boy who was probably accused of stealing something before demanding an apology for the man's disrespect toward him.

What Loanshark Jack had come to see instead of an inert infliction of punishment brought about a feeling of absolute disgust in the pit of his stomach that instantly made the pupils in his green eyes turn crimson red with a form of rage that he never experienced before in his life.

The audacity of this guy to think that he could just get away with the sodomistic display of behavior he was intending in public, with a child no less, was enough to warrant the stranger's death at the hands of Jack and his gun, but he had something else in mind that felt more proper.

The sound of the gun initially slamming down hard on the back of the chubby stranger's head was a loud one. As blood began to seep from the gash inflicted at the area of the mastoid process, Jack gave a momentary wonder for whether or not he killed the guy, but an answer soon became apparent from the man's wayward breathing rising and falling slowly as he lay in a heavily induced slumber. Jack then took watch as the terrified boy wiggled himself out from underneath his captor's hold while shaking his head in disdain.

*****

The chance encounter first happened when the boy and his friends were returning from the park and decided to take the long way back home. They enjoyed the sights and sounds of an environment that slowly changed from a ravaged décor to the outlook of a much more upscale element.

The dirtied, second-hand clothing that the boys wore were obviously out of place and clashing amongst the clean-cut attire of the well-heeled inhabitants surrounding them. Some of the people began to stare at their ragged group as though they were appalled by the presence of the young black boys with wandering eyes of tourists who said things like, "That's mine," as they innocently pointed to pricey items in store windows as if the mere words could inherit them with the valuable entreatments.

The boys were simply just being kids at play while looking at the fancy cars and touring the tall buildings, so on one was outwardly offended, until the pretty woman appeared.

Who the mesmerized boys referred to as a pretty woman was one many a grown man could easily find themselves fawning over in an instant. The woman truly exhibited a gorgeousness about her that could cause men to fall in love with her at first sight. The same type of woman that could constitute a war of nations or tame the most savage of hearts at merely her beckoning.

One such woman came striding along on the very sidewalk that the group of boys were on, with an enviable haughtiness about her that one knew married women were warned to guard their men against. Horns sounded off erratically while flirtatious whispers were blown in the direction of a woman who didn't seem to notice the many men vying to gain her attention. There was one man, however, who became too persistent.

The large man appeared from out of nowhere, sweating profusely in the all-too-tight white suit that he wore. He had to be absolutely delusional, because, for some reason, the man had himself convinced that he would be able to get the affection of the beautiful woman he should've known he could never have.

From the moment he laid eyes on her, the fat man's delusion forced him to make some obscene overtures as he tried in vain to court the woman of his interest with cheesy pickup lines and even making attempts to grab her by the hand as she walked. The woman decided to ignore him the best she could in the hopes that he would take a hint and just move on, but the pesky man kept trying to pressure her into something that she wouldn't be caught dead doing. Suddenly, the man caught up in the foolhardy idea of ensuring a gorgeous woman to be his own and did something unprecedently stupid.

Instead of being fully aware of his surroundings, the chubby stranger absentmindedly walked himself straight into the path of a lamppost which slammed into his body hard from the impact while he was in the midst of a sleazy come-in attempt. The man became beet red with embarrassment and experienced immense anger from the sound the boys made when they erupted into a fit of hysterical laughter from the sight of the mishap.

Even the pretty woman joined in on the banter by way of causally smiling and winking in the direction of the admiring boys before she ran her hand along the face of one lucky kid all while continuing on to her destination without breaking her stride.

The large man instantly gave up on his infatuation with the woman at that point and focused his attention instead on the group of young black boys who dared to ridicule him with their mockery. With the use of racial slurs to aid him along, the chubby stranger worked up enough vexation to give a chase that he would soon come to regret.

The act of racism was unfortunately high during this period of time, and although the Negro participation in the balance of war lessoned the burden a bit, the truth of the matter remained to be that people of color were still being lynched, burned out of their homes, and treated with all other forms of malfeasance one could think of to keep them marred by degradation.

Loanshark Jack found himself to be a cynic with such matters of the heart. As a telling characteristic of such a factor, Jack's ideology remained the same as it always did with racism and anything else in life's intricacy. He firmly believed that everyone and everything was meant to experience some sort of struggle for survival on the premise of overcoming such tribulations in order to have a more-determined will to live.

From the ignorance of racism, to such things like a woman getting mugged for the contents in her purse, amounted to be a question of vulnerability in Jack's mind. Where, if a person or entity happened to be somehow weakened by a pejorative state of negativity instead of struggling more so to fight for what they believed in or desired, then such a fate would be rightfully the one deserved.

The very thought came to strike a chord with Loanshark Jack even then as he examined the state of the young boy before him who had dried tears around his eyes and splatters of blood on his mouth from where he was brutally hit. The one thing that Jack didn't see was a weakness.

Amidst the boy's desperation bellied the will to fight back, and Jack could see that courage burning brightly now in the boy's eyes as the kid stared back at him with the sort of veracity that Jack could truly admire.

*****

"What's your name, kid?" Jack inquired with the form of nonchalance that was meant to dissuade any reservations that the boy may have developed about him. "Ralph, sir," was the nervous response made from a boy who was understandably jittery from the circumstance of his present dilemma.

"Tell me, Ralph. You ever shoot a gun before?" Jack asked without any hint of emotion attached. The young boy in his presence seemed to be at a loss for words from the context of the question, before he managed to respond with a simple, "No, sir," as Ralph took to looking in his empty palm to ponder upon the possibility of firing a weapon for the first time. Jack let the response hang in the balance while nodding his head mindlessly in contemplation on his true intention.

"Did you like what that man was trying to do to you?" Jack inquired with fire returning to his eyes. Ralph quickly shook his head in retort as he came to remember the amount of discomfort he experienced at the hands of stranger's vulgar assault.

Jack saw the immense hatred residing in the boy's eyes for what he was forced to endure under the man who berated him and knew that what he had for young Ralph to accomplish would be more easy to do with little prodding on his end. Jack wished for a mere moment that he had a camera on hand to capture the look on Ralph's face when he shoved the small-caliber pistol into his tiny hand.

As if he were a teacher in the midst of a tutorial with a promising student, Loanshark Jack clasped his hands behind his back and asked once more in a stern tone of voice, "I'll ask you again… Did you like what that man was trying to do to you?" Again, Ralph shook his head dismissively while feeling absolutely perplexed by the weight of the weapon in his hand.

"Wait here!" Jack commanded before going to survey the surroundings for any signs of a potential threat. Satisfied that there were no wandering eyes of witnesses about, Jack returned to a waiting Ralph and said, "I want you to shoot that man over there for the harm he tried to cause you."

"You… You want me to shoo…shoot him?" Ralph stammered nervously while eyeing Jack in disbelief.

"If I were you, kid… I'd shoot that fat pig right between the eyes, but it's your choice to make, not mine," Loanshark Jack replied with the sort of casualness that seemed as though he were preparing grocery list. Ralph became startled from the man's sudden movement on the ground. "You better make up your mind quick, because it looks like he's about to wake up feeling really upset," Jack added matter of faculty as the injured man began to moan from the pain he was experiencing.

Ralph became overwhelmed by an intense anger that he never experienced before as memories of the grotesque actions flashed across his premature mind in regards to the chubby stranger's callous assault. He could easily remember the sickening sounds of the man's husky groans in his ear, amid the way that his attacker tried to forcibly remove his pants in a crazed act of depravity in a way that caused Ralph to raise the barrel of the pistol he possessed in the direction of the man who offended him. What happened next came to be totally unexpected.

Ralph couldn't believe what he was about to do. Even his young mind could clearly process the fact that if he didn't take action now, then the man lying on the ground might very well come back to get him or another kid somewhere along the line.

With that very thought in mind, Ralph took a deep, calming breath and squeezed his eyes tightly, since he didn't know whether or not he should keep them open or just drop the gun and run away instead, but he made the conscious decision to stay by way of clearing his thoughts and bracing himself for the consequences of his next action.

Ralph then outstretched his arm and tried to keep the balance of his aim steady as he pulled on the trigger with all of his might. The sensation that Ralph felt after he pulled on the trigger was tantamount to the way any boy his age would feel about igniting a firecracker without anything happening to show for the effort.

When Ralph squeezed the trigger mechanism and heard nothing but a clicking sound in return, he examined the weapon with a dumbfounded look attached to his face before he began to shake it in the fleeting hope to get the gun working again.

"Whoa! Whoa! Don't go blowing your own head off, kid!!!" Jack bewailed while grabbing onto Ralph's hand before he did something crazy to himself. "Lesson one, kid… The safety is on, and this is how you turn it off. Now, shoot this fat pig before he gets away!" Ralph nodded his head in consent to Jack's command and took aim once more. When he squeezed the trigger the second time around, the force of the impending blast sent Ralph's unprepared body spiraling to the ground.

*****

If the man wasn't awake before, he sure was now. Ralph's aim was initially intended to strike the man somewhere on his body, but the force that the shot had on his arm sent the bullet careening instead into the dirt mere inches away from the man's head. The shocked expression that came to the chubby stranger's face from the sight of the young black boy he accosted with a smoking guy in his hand, as he stood next to a person whom the fat man presumed to be a gangster, while both of them stared at him with looks of hatred, was the stuff made from legend.

The stranger was obviously shaken by the current state of his predicament. His mouth began to move in a motion that was meant for him to speak, but no sound emerged as he found himself desperately trying to contemplate the extent of what he was going through at that moment.

"I think you owe my friend here an apology, buddy!"

Jack interjected forcefully on the man's concerns. The stranger frantically stared between the gangster and the tiny black boy with gun in hand before making another attempt at moving; a sound came from the chubby man to deliver an apology while Ralph raised his aim once more to level it in the direction of his target.

"No! No! Pleaseee!!! I'm so very sorry for what I've done!!!" the stranger shouted in fear and regret. He then placed his hand on the throbbing in fear and regret. He then placed his hand on the throbbing at the back of his head and was mortified to see the telling result of blood on his retracted palm.

"His apology is good enough for you, kid?" Jack inquired without ever removing his eyes from the sight of the fat man before him. Ralph nodded his head slowly in response, and Jack immediately exploded with, "What I tell you about that? I want to hear you say it by manning up!" Ralph's arm started to go numb from holding the gun up for so long, but he kept his aim nonetheless and said in a sharp tone of voice, "It's good enough for me, mister."

Jack could almost be heard sucking his teeth in the disappointment he felt with Ralph's decision, but it was the kid's to make, so he kept his feelings close to the chest. The scornful look that Loanshark Jack gave to the fat man forever could've easily worked its way to burn a hole straight through the groveling man's soul. Jack drew in a deep breath of his own, in dismay, before reluctantly saying against his better judgment, "Get the hell out of here. But, be warned… If I ever catch you doing something like this again, you're a dead man walking! You got that!!!"

The chubby stranger nodded his head vigorously is utter compliance, although it may have been done a bit too eagerly in advance, since he instantly became lightheaded from showing little concern toward the wound inflicted at the back of his head over being granted his life back once more. None of that stop the stranger, however, from rapidly getting to his feet and scurrying away past his persecutors with the full speed and thankfulness of someone lucky to still be alive.

"Lesson two, kid… Don't ever waste your bullets, unless you intend to use them. You might not get another chance," Jack opinioned as he patted Ralph on the shoulder and began to walk away.

"Your gun, mister!!!" Ralph shouted in the attempt to return the weapon back to its owner.

"It's yours now, kid! You earned it!" Jack replied without breaking his stride.

Loanshark Jack remembered that he wasn't that much older than young Ralph was when he came to receive his first gun. The lesson may have been a harsh one to receive but one Ralph would certainly need to feel safe in a world where constant survival was of the utmost importance amidst the throes of a menacing society where others may seek to do him unprovoked harm. Jack left his perplexed pupil staring at the gun in his hand with amazement. "Wow," was the only thing that Ralph managed to say in parting as Loanshark Jack disappeared from sight.

*****

Ralph found himself laughing hysterically at the matter even now as he sat across from Gloria who must've been thinking that he was going insane while Ralph's mind flooded with memories of how he could've gotten his face blown off that day if Jack hadn't stopped him from shaking the gun in his hand.

The encounter wasn't the last time that young Ralph would come to see Loanshark Jack. After the incident occurred between them, Ralph found himself to be forever in Jack's gratitude for the type of kindness that he exhibited. Ralph pondered upon the factor for hours on end as he slept on a makeshift bed inside a room or his mother's dilapidated apartment where she sold her body for drug money.

Ralph even stared at his prized possession until the lids of his eyes became weary. He then took the gun that Jack had given him and stuffed it under a jacket he used as a pillow just in case one of his mother's 'friends' came looking for their entertainment in the wrong room.

Chapter 7

Ralph welcomed any opportunity to leave from his torrential household, which was fairly easy, since his mother was either too high to notice or heavily enthralled in an act of coitus with one of her many paramours to care. Ralph found it refreshing just to be able to escape the moans and groans which always threatened to permeate his tender mind throughout the majority of the day.

Whenever visions of the fat man's terrified expression flashed across Ralph's mind, he instantly became elated. He could easily recount how he'd almost come to being violated by the man's evil intention just before the images of his savior emerged.

Ralph just knew that he had to find Jack again. He wanted to look Jack in the eyes and properly thank him for saving Ralph's lift the way he did that day. With that in mind, Ralph made certain to track Jack down the best way he could think of… By retracing his footsteps to the alleyway where it all began.

When Ralph reported back to the alleyway where he first met Loanshark Jack, he maintained a vigil for hours on end for any signs of his savior's appearance. After two days had gone by, Ralph began to give up his hope on the concept by way of assuming that Jack was probably just a stranger passing through town on a whim.

On a lonely walk back to the very home he dreaded, Ralph happened upon an intense commotion which instantly worked to pique his interest. There was an injured man screaming wildly in the streets in the attempt to plead for his life to be spared.

A crowd began to form as the hulking man inflicting punishment with a baseball bat in hand threatened to break the large stick across the screaming victim's head if he didn't come up with the money that he owed. It was then that Ralph saw a familiar figure who stood with his back turned in the midst of the melee, seeming as though he were the one providing the hulking man with his orders to inflict pain.

Ralph scanned the man's attire to see if there was some sort of resemblance to toward the man he was in search of, and Ralph noticed that, indeed, the suit was made of the same tailored fashion as the one Jack wore previously, only it differed in the variation of its coloring.

When the prominent figure standing with his arms folded across his chest spoke, Ralph instantly came to know that his desperate search was over. "And, let this be a lesson to anyone who thinks that he can just up and disrespect me and get away with it! My act of vengeance will not be deterred!!!" Loanshark Jack shouted to anyone within earshot in order for them to fully understand that he was not a person to be reckoned with.

When Jack took in the area in order to command the full attention of those surrounding him, Ralph thought for a moment that Jack may have caught sight of him and smirked in his direction before Ralph tried to hide behind a parked car to keep his watch, but maybe he was mistaken.

*****

When Ralph suddenly heard his name being called, he thought it to be a figment of his imagination at first, until he came to see the presence of the hulking man with the big stick in hand glaring over him with menacing eyes. "The Boss would like a word with you, kid," the giant brute said calmly in a deep tone of voice that caused Ralph to shudder deep in his bones.

Ralph's steps carried him shyly over to where Loanshark Jack stood in wait. When he approached, Ralph heard the slight resonance of jeers and racial slurs, but the sounds immediately dissipated when he ventured closer to a smirking Jack as those in attendance provided their full attention for Jack's appeasement.

"Long time no see, kid. You all right?" Jack inquired in Ralph's ear with a muffled tone of greeting as he pulled Ralph closer to be by his side. Ralph nodded his head in ascension, but after quickly remembering Jack's insistence on hearing him speak as a man, Ralph cleared his throat and said, "Yes, sir," with a hint of pride attached to his voice.

Jack smiled broadly and made a declaration to everyone listening, "This, here, is a buddy of mine who goes by the name of Ralph! You don't have to like him! He doesn't have to be your friend! Heck… You can even hate him if you want to! Whatever you do, however, just make certain that you give him the same respect as if he were me!!!"

There were many looks of shock and awe as Loanshark Jack continued in with his rant of, "Make sure that you treat this boy as though his eyes are my eyes! His breaths are my breaths! Because, trust me, if one hair on this boy's head so much as feels threatened or harmed, I will show in retaliation! I hope I've made myself absolutely clear on the matter! Anyone who cares to show any opposition to my demands, feel free to speak now!!!"

Ralph found himself to be in just as much astonishment as the onlookers were of the statement that Jack revealed. His inside were dancing in pure glee from knowing what the context of Jack's announcement, but Ralph knew that he had to be a man and maintain the face of his composure for the newfound dignity that Jack bestowed upon him.

The only things to permeate the awkward silence that came afterward were the clipped whispers and grumblings which accompanied hard stares, but no one dared to outwardly express their showing of discontent. Ralph glanced in the direction of the man who was being savagely beaten and suddenly developed a tinge of remorse for his troubles, until Ralph became overcome by fit of rage which forced him to abandon any feelings he may have had for the man's wellbeing as if the injured victim had done something to offend Ralph personally.

"Forget about him, kid. He'll get what's coming to him soon enough," Jack proclaimed as though he were reading Ralph's thoughts. Jack looked at his young friend once over and candidly asked, "Where you from?" After Ralph answered the question, Jack responded, "Tough neighborhood, kid. Your mom okay with you being out here like this?" As the inquiry hung off in the balance, Jack could clearly see the amount of turmoil occurring in Ralph's demeanor as his young new friend simply shrugged his shoulders in reply and said, "She's probably somewhere getting high or having sex with one of her 'friends.'" Loanshark Jack flashed a meager smile for the extent of Ralph's straightforwardness before saying, "You look hungry, kid. Let's get something to eat."

To say that Ralph was happy to be in Jack's company would be a complete understatement. Ralph began to walk a bit taller, with an air of arrogance to his stride that couldn't be deterred. When their party walked into a diner and sat down on stools, however, Ralph was met at the counter by the owner of the establishment who was wearing a food-stained apron around his sternum.

The man's fierce demeanor changed rapidly in the presence of Loanshark Jack who equally met the stare that Ralph was given with contempt. When Jack made use of a head motion to prompt the man to follow his gaze, the man instantly looked in Jack's direction; his eyes were no longer on Loanshark Jack but focused more intently on the hulking figure standing quietly behind him who came to be introduced to Ralph by the name of Sal.

The tension in the air was thick enough to cut with a butter knife, but the man behind the counter was the one to wisely cave in as he went about hiding the contempt of his resignation and turned the prejudicial sign around so that the letters could disappear from sight. "Good. Now that that's settled, what would you like to eat, kid?" Jack asked in the midst of becoming famished himself.

Ralph tried his best to forget about the extent of what he just came to witness, but he could do little to hide his smirk of gratitude. "Come on, kid, make up your mind quick! I'm getting hungry over here!" Jack urged while inquiring about his henchman. "What about you, Sal? You hungry?" Sal took himself a short pause before replying. "Sure, Boss. I can eat," he said calmly without wavering from the intense stare he had on the man behind the counter who visibly began to grow nervous.

When Ralph simply asked for a hamburger, Jack called his choice nonsense. "Whenever you're with me, kid, you got to make sure that you eat good in order to keep your strength up, so you can grow up big and strong." Jack then looked at the man behind the counter before lamenting, "Let me have a round of burgers and fries with some large vanilla milkshakes for me and my boys, kind sir," with his mood rapidly cheering.

After the food was prepared, Jack and his entourage ate their meal in a booth while he kept Ralph laughing with stories about some of the wild and fun times that he and Sal had together. Ralph found himself putting away the food then, similar to the way now, 50 years later, he was privy to watching Gloria ravage through her meal. Ralph vividly remembered how Loanshark Jack took him under his wing and showed Ralph the ropes of running numbers, until he grew into a hardnosed teen taking over some of the duties that Sal left for him to attend to.

Sadly, Jack and Sal both came to be murdered later on in the years from an assassination attempt by members of the mafia in retaliation for Jack's role in torturing a mob consigliere who owed him a huge amount of money. The torture that Jack inflicted on the man was justified by criminal standards, but the mafia decided to seek their revenge against him anyway in order to save face amongst their watchful constituents and enemies alike who many have thought of what transpired as a sign of weakness that they wanted to challenge. What the mafia didn't bother to account for, however, was the vengeance of a determined angry black teen who would come calling on their heads. A horrendous oversight on their part.

Ralph's cunning awarded him the ability to seek out the revenge he so desperately craved to have. He avenged the wrongful deaths of Loanshark Jack and Sal the Bruiser with a wrath of fury that was unprecedented. Ralph almost accomplished the impossible of decimating an entire crime syndicate on his own. Wisely, the crime families of the city had gathered themselves together to inside upon a peace treaty with the young man at the time who seemed to have the movements of a ghost, and, in turn, Ralph became the most sought-after hitman of his era.

As Ralph sat before Gloria now, he saw in her what Jack must've came to see in him years ago. Only the course of time had changed dramatically since Ralph was a boy growing up. Where he had to be taught the brash ways of being a brute, Ralph would now make use of the modern day demographic to provide Gloria with a life that had to be, in the very least, more promising than her trying to end her own life for a mere moment of indiscretion.

Ralph watched her intently as he pondered upon the seriousness of giving Gloria vital life lessons in the ways of her being 'Gloria like a dove but wise as a serpent.'

Chapter 8

Gloria finished her meal with a hearty belch in the aftermath, and Ralph laughed in the mirth of her fulfillment. His demeanor suddenly evoked a grim outlook, however, as he considered the ramifications of what he had to propose to Gloria. The extent of it alone could be enough to have Gloria either running for the hills or leave Ralph entirely exposed for the authorities to discover, and he couldn't allow that to happen. The more he thought about it, however, Ralph came to wonder if there was a way for him to maybe be a bit more subtle with his approach of the subject.

When Ralph became conflicted with his thoughts about the proper way to broach the subject matter he intended, Ralph decided that a straightforward form of communication was the best way for him to address anything that he needed to get across. As such, Ralph removed the weapon that was hidden in his waistline and placed it next to his paper plate of half-eaten food, to be in full view of an unsuspecting Gloria while he waited to gage her reaction.

After her hunger was finally satiated, Gloria began to feel a lot better emotionally. Her mind was still a bit cloudy from the effects of her indiscretion, but Gloria was felt adamant about not returning to the life she once knew. She was convinced that her circumstances were beyond repair, but Gloria wasn't so sure about committing again by making another suicide attempt.

But what was Gloria going to do? Ralph seemed to be nice enough, and he kept her safe for the moment, but how long was that supposed to last? Suddenly, Gloria's thoughts were interrupted by something strange occurring in her vision.

When Gloria looked in Ralph's eyes, he stared back at her intently but gave away about his true regard until his arm disappeared behind him. When he retracted his arm back, Ralph revealed a dull metal object that Gloria couldn't readily identify at first, until her wide-eyed expression gave way to Gloria's fearful recognition of the item. As she looked from the gun to Ralph, then from Ralph's piercing gaze back to the gun he displayed, Gloria became immensely paranoid while trying to fathom the culpability of Ralph's action.

Ralph took in a deep breath as the tension hung itself thick in the air. Before he was able to speak, a glimmer of light on the corner of his eye worked to disturb the purpose of his intention. When Ralph took a glance in the direction, Gloria's wide-eyed expression followed, and they both came to see a continuous flashing light emanating from…Gloria's cellphone.

When Ralph looked to her, Gloria hung her head dismissively in guilt. "You're going to have to answer it at some point or another. It might as well be now," Ralph insinuated as he got himself up to retrieve the phone.

"No, I don't!" Gloria implored as she hopped to her feet and folded her arms in front of her chest with discontent as Ralph was left with the phone in his hand.

While she fought to stop any tears from streaming down her face, Gloria couldn't bear the thought of ever looking at her phone again while memories of her imprudence were readily accessible as a constant reminder in the phone's hardware. When Ralph checked the number on the I.D. screen and informed Gloria that the caller was from a Ms. Santiago, she squeezed her eyes tightly and whispered, "I can't," in a repeated chant.

Ralph fully understood what Gloria must've been going through, but he also didn't want the entire police force coming out to arrest him on some kind of kidnapping charge for Ralph simply trying to save the life of a girl who seemed to be desperately yearning to rid herself of it. He placed the phone down again after sending the caller to an already-full voicemail box, but Ralph fully intended to convince Gloria to face her demons for the sake of her livelihood.

Without turning around to face him, Gloria interrupted the volitive speech that Ralph prepared to make by coyly asking, "Why do you have a gun?" Ralph found himself taken aback again by the bluntness of Gloria's query, but he recovered quickly by simply replying, "In a harsh world… It's a necessary requirement." Gloria turned to face Ralph then, but her look of dejection was now gone and replaced by one of sheer skepticism as she appraised him intently.

The presence of a theorem formulating in Gloria's mind gave her the insight to assume that a person in possession of a deadly weapon was one who hailed from either side of the judicial spectrum. As her eyes scanned ascertain that Ralph was in no way associated with the authoritative powers of law enforcement.

With that vital detail correctly determined, the only thing that was left now for Gloria to decipher was the resolve of just exactly what kind of criminal did Ralph amount to be? Gloria figured that she already knew the answer with a very good assumption coming to be etched in her mind.

The next thing said by her was, "Can you teach me how to shoot?" The question was so off kilter that Gloria couldn't believe herself that the words had escaped her mouth. Ralph tried to keep his emotions in check, but a smile betrayed the attempt he made. Sure, there were a million positive things that Gloria could've requested to learn at that point, but Ralph was happy just to discover that there was a glimmer of hope in her will to live. His face suddenly hardened while Ralph narrowed his eyes to make the reply, "I can show you anything that you want to know, but we have to do some serious talking first."

*****

Their conversation lasted for what must've seemed like hours. If Ralph hadn't been toughened by the hands of time, he might've been able to shed to tear for the struggle of Gloria's plight, but he absolutely understood the type of turmoil that she endured. From what Gloria implied, Ralph was able to gather the fact that her mother was also into the heavy use of drugs and alcohol, but unlike his circumstance, Gloria also had a father whom she gave a description of as being a morphine junkie.

After being brutally beaten, Gloria's mother, Angels, was left on the stained carpet with her frail body desperately gasping for air as her husband screamed out her name with their daughter standing in watch, too shocked to move.

Gloria's father, Julio, forced himself to his feet from the chair where he was being held and shoved one of his tormentors to the side as he landed a hard punch on the face of the other. When he took a step to comfort his ailing wife, a loud blast suddenly stopped Julio's motion in a way that forced him to stand stiff.

Making use of a hand to scan over his chest in search of damage, Julio felt an immense pain radiating from a hole in his body that could only be made from the destructive force that a bullet could achieve. After raising his hand and seeing the result of a pool of blood on his palm, Julio dropped his arm in defeat as his blurred vision looked to see a smoking gun in the possession of someone he couldn't readily identify at the moment.

The last thing that Julio saw before the darkness took hold of him was the shocked expression on Angela's face while his eyes rolled to the back of his head as his lifeless body dropped to the floor with a loud thud.

Gloria recounted her story while using some sort of rapid hand motion to wipe at her face. Instead of wiping away tears, however, Ralph came to determine that the action was actually Gloria reliving the vivid tale as though her younger self could once again feel the blood that came to be splattered on her face from her father's mortally wounded body on the day that he was killed.

The only other person privy to the information that Ralph was receiving was Gloria's counselor, Ms. Santiago, and she was only lucky enough to read the dismal details from a police report that was stuffed into Gloria's file.

When she first encountered Gloria and tried to delve into the circumstances of her father's demise, Ms. Santiago was met by a young girl who was extremely defensive and refused to recollect any memories of the traumatic day until later on in her teens, and, even then, an entire account of the incident wasn't forthcoming. Now, here Gloria was, fully able to recall the amount of torment she endured as she spilled the truth about her troubling past to a complete stranger.

Ralph's look of concern was a genuine one. It took a moment for Gloria to gather her bearings, but as she continued on with her account, Ralph found that he came to sympathize with Gloria's strife with the sort of connection that he never experienced with anyone else before.

Gloria remembered how her mother's woes continued on even after her father's death. Although Angela knew the identities of her attackers, any thoughts of filing charges against them were consciously negated by the common street sense that there remained to be a 'No snitching rule' that was violently enforced in the neighborhood where they hailed from. Any infringement of such a rule could easily result in the penalty of death. In an environment where one could possibly get themselves savagely beaten for a mere buck, Angela wasn't tempted to leave their fate to chance.

Angela's addiction to drugs only increased while she suffered immensely from depression. She just didn't know how she could make it through life without the loving support of her soul mate and resorted to the use of illicit substances in the attempt to escape her pain. Gloria's health even began to decline as a result of her mother's callousness where she became malnourished and often remained sullied from her mother's constant neglect.

Gloria was able to survive most days thanks to the concerned neighbors who offered their support, but once her mother succumbed to fatally overdosing on a bad mixture of heroine, the support for Gloria's welfare stopped abruptly, since the neighbors couldn't fathom taking on the responsibility of having another mouth to feed to go amongst the kids and obligations they already had with solely the minimum wages they received each month. It was then that Gloria was forced to live by the guidelines of a foster-care system which only seemed to add to the many problems she faced.

Ralph was overwhelmed with emotion from what he heard of Gloria's torrid tale of circumstances. So much so that he shared with her the account of how his own mother was also a junkie of any narcotic she could get her hands on. And, how, instead of getting a regular job to pay for their food and rent, Ralph's mother went and sought the company of men who paid her cheaply to fulfill their sexual desires while she, in turn, used what she made to fuel her needy addiction.

Through gritted teeth, Ralph also managed to reveal how he returned home one day to find his cherished mother sprawled out on her bed naked as the day she was born, starting at him with bulging eyes. Ralph screamed out for her attention as loud as his young voice would allow for it, but it was done in a fleeting attempt to bring her spirit back from where Ralph was certain she was too far away from the reaches of the living.

*****

Through it all, Gloria never said a word to interrupt him as she sat on the bed with her legs crossed and her arms propped up beneath her chin as she listened attentively to the words of Ralph's dismal circumstances. She felt a tight bond with him then. As he did with her, and they both understood that it was the perfect remedy for establishing the best kind of friendship.

Something which they both sorely needed at the moment. Ralph saw Gloria watching him expectantly, and before the question could leave her mouth, he went into telling her about the saga of three men. One of whom she already knew of, but the stories of Loanshark Jack and Sal the Bruiser would soon prove to be great fodder for the type of life that Gloria was about to be a part of!

After Ralph concluded his tantalizing effect on Gloria's psyche, she remained mesmerized and bombarded Ralph with a flurry of questions in regards to the lore he told. Gloria wanted desperately to know the length of time it took to fire off the perfect shot, while in the midst of a full sprint, to go along with any instruction on how to decimate the attack of three or more men without sparing breath between a two-minute time period. Ralph had to finally throw up his hands in surrender in order to stop Gloria's onslaught of questioning.

Gloria's life was obviously reinvigorated from what Ralph came to instill in her mind through the usage of storytelling, with the desires of hope, confidence, and trust lingering on the horizon. Ralph also felt as though the weight of the world was finally lifted off of his shoulders with every word he uttered.

After all of this time, Ralph was able to come to grips with the tumultuous fact of finding his mother dead… Chocked to death by the bare hands of one of the Johns she so endeared. And, Ralph was able to face the demons of his torrential past, all thanks to the company of a teenage girl who only had to lend him an ear.

Knowing that his time was wearing thin from old age, Ralph now yearned to share the knowledge of everything he knew with someone who wouldn't let it all go to waste. Ralph viewed Gloria as the perfect pupil for a tutorial with him as the patient teacher, the way Loanshark Jack had sought to do with him as a young boy growing up.

Sure, the significance of the subject matter would come to be a harsh lesson to learn, but it also entailed the necessity for being responsible. Something that Ralph was for certain Gloria would be able to adjust to well under his precise tutelage, but there was a huge hurdle to overcome first.

Chapter 9

The smile that Ralph wore only seconds ago had since disappeared and been replaced by a stern look as he watched Gloria intently; her hand shook after the phone was practically shoved into it. She toyed with the mechanism in her fingertips with the contemplation of remaining on the defensive in her mind, but Gloria already knew that she wouldn't be able to avoid Ms. Santiago forever. She just hoped to put it off for a little while longer until Ralph's urging prompted her to make the call.

As the phone rang on the receiving end, Gloria found herself to be nervously biting her fingernails as she waited. In order to give her some form of privacy, Ralph tried to move as far away from earshot as the room would allow, but he only found himself back to where the small metal table and chairs were which held the cold food that was left over. Ralph decided to check his weapons of cleanliness, but he couldn't help but to keep an ear open in curiosity for what Gloria might say.

Gloria didn't notice the tears that began to stream down her face when the call was answered. She found herself at a loss for words when the person on the other end of the line began shouting, "Hello!!! Hello!!! Gloria, is that you!?!" There was an air of awkward silence before Gloria whispered to a concerned Ms. Santiago, "Yeah, it's me, Ms. S."

"Oh my God!!! Gloria, are you all right?! What happened to you?! Are you in any kind of trouble?!" Gloria couldn't even get a word in edgewise amongst Ms. Santiago's bombardment of questioning, but her inner child smiled warmly in remembering all the times when Ms. Santiago was there for Gloria during the course of her many struggles.

Ms. Santiago was actually the one who talked Gloria through her first phase of the menstrual cycle that Gloria experienced at a time when she thought that the symptoms she was feeling was the result of a baby dying inside of her.

As the role of a guidance counselor, Ms. Santiago also gave Gloria valuable lessons about the intimacy of sexual intercourse. And the ways of protecting herself from sexually transmitted diseases to go along with the use of any other planned contraception that she would need if Gloria ever became pregnant. All the advice a young teenage girl might need to properly adapt to a life as a child of the foster system.

"Gloria?!?! Are you still there?! Please speak to me!!!" Ms. Santiago pleaded as she became concerned once more.

"Yeah, I'm still here, Ms. S. And, I'm okay, but there's something that I got to tell you," Gloria responded while trying to gather her thoughts for what needed to be said.

"What is it?! You're not hurt, are you?! Oh my God!!! Are you in some kind of trouble?! Do you need me to come and get you?!" Ms. Santiago asked in deep worry as she began to fear for the worst.

"No! No! It's nothing like that. It's just… I…I'm not going to be coming back," was Gloria's response as she went on to become concerned herself when no reply came in return. It took a tense moment, but when Ms. Santiago provided her response, it was one done with a more sullen tone of voice when she simply replied, "I understand."

Gloria was left in an utter state of disbelief by the sudden change of Ms. Santiago's temperament. She became offended while wondering if that was all it took for Ms. Santiago to diminish any feelings she had for Gloria's welfare. At the very thought, Gloria whispered, "You do?" Ms. Santiago was a stern one when she came back with the response, "You're not selling your body, are you?"

The question raised by Ms. Santiago was one that threw Gloria for an absolute loop before her anger helped her to recover quickly with, "Is that what you think?! That I'm out here selling my body?!" in a tone of disgust as her skin began to crawl at the mere thought of it.

"Oh thank God!!! At least that isn't what's been going on with you! But, Gloria, if that's not it, then what's the problem?! I'm sure we can work out any problems that you've been having. Was it those Bennings?! I've had numerous complaints against them in the past. Just say the words and I'll have them investigated and get you into a new home with a better family at the touch of a button!!!"

Ms. Santiago was adamant about her position, remembering the time that Gloria spent trying to conceal the fact the bruises she carried once before was something other than the abuse she suffered at the hands of the creepy drunken spouse named Dan who inflicted them. Ms. Santiago was determined not to allow another episode like that to happen again under her watch.

Gloria felt a lot better now that she knew Ms. Santiago's care for her never wavered. Still feeling a bit uneasy and insulted by her counselor's last inquiry, however, Gloria asked, "Why did you ask me if I was selling my body?" as she wrapped her arms around herself, feeling a bit cheapened by the insinuation.

Gloria breathed in a deep sigh of relief when Ms. Santiago explained to her that it was far more normal, then not, for a teenage girl of the foster system to run away and fall into the clutches of a vulgar pimp who would then do everything in his power to make use of his ruse in eventually having the girl turning tricks only for the deceptive support or his own financial gain. Ms. Santiago even went so far as to run down a list of girls Gloria actually knew, who all fell hard for such a form of deceit, along with the details of whose stories faired far worse than the other.

Ms. Santiago even explained how teenage runaways from the foster-care system became so redundant in occurrence that she was often forced to be very insistent that the police be in the lookout for Gloria after the investigating officer laughed and referred to the circumstances jokingly as, "Oh no. Not another one gone to the streets." The officer and his partner even began trading sarcastic jibes at the concept while nonchalantly recording the information they were given into their logbooks which, Ms. Santiago correctly surmised, would go no farther than being placed onto a file on the station's outdated computer system.

Gloria was thinking of how easy it could've been for her to be forced into a life of prostitution when Ms. Santiago interrupted her thoughts by asking, "Gloria, honey. Where are you? Please come in so we can talk." Gloria shot a glance over to where Ralph was trying his best to act as though he wasn't listening in on her conversation before she made the response, "I'm in another state right now." A reply which captured Ralph's attention in a way that forced him to eye her curiously just a warming smile came to his features.

*****

As if looking to him for inspiration, Gloria continued on with her conversation as Ralph carried on with cleaning his weapons. When she gave a false account of how she paid to take a ride across the country on an Amtrak train in the hopes of getting herself to California to become a famous actress, Gloria thought for a moment that she could hear Ms. Santiago trying to stifle her tears over the phone with sniffles and wiping herself with tissue.

Gloria couldn't believe the tale that she's spun. She instantly started feeling guilty about lying to Ms. Santiago the way she had, but Gloria couldn't see herself going back to a life where she would always be susceptible to whatever detestable circumstances that society had to offer, especially with Ralph proposing a better way for her to live as a strong willed woman of independence. Gloria viewed the foster-care system as a reoccurring cycle of bad happenings that she no longer wanted to be a part of anymore.

Before Gloria concluded her call with Ms. Santiago, she tried to assure her counselor that she would be back one day so to see her once again. Gloria wasn't sure if Ms. Santiago believed anything was feeling a bit distraught about losing the power of supervision she held over Gloria's wellbeing.

Gloria stayed on the line a little longer while Ms. Santiago tried fleetingly to offer her parting advice, which was intended to save a young girl from the dangers of what the real world had to offer, in order to shield Gloria from the many falsehoods that a life of glamour and glitz could create.

Gloria was left misty eyed when the call ended, but she felt upbeat about the opportunity presented to her. Remembering the daunting memories that the phone held, Gloria quickly shoved the mechanism back into Ralph's hand and watched intently as he disassembled the parts before her eyes.

"Lesson one, kid… Always remember that your phone calls can be traced right back to you." Ralph would've prompted her to end the call sooner, but Ralph overheard it when Ms. Santiago informed Gloria about the lack of regard that the police had shown for discovering her welfare.

Although the founding circumstances of their chance encounter was extremely unusual, Ralph found himself feeling a bit giddy about the prospect of treating Gloria like the daughter he never had. He could clearly see the amount of grit that Gloria probably didn't even know she had and vowed to bestow the entirety of his knowledge on strengthening Gloria's psyche for the instances of life as he knew it to be, no matter how harsh the lesson may become. And, Gloria was going to need that grit if she never expected to be around Ralph for much longer.

Chapter 10

"Look into my eyes," is what Ralph said to her next, but it was a statement of redundancy, since Gloria was already watching his every move intently. Watching the way Ralph effortlessly maneuvered with the amount of confidence that she could only dream of; Gloria just knew she was making the right choice.

When Ralph continued on and asked Gloria if she was sure that she wanted embark on the journey he proposed, Gloria was hoping that she didn't offend him with the condescending chuckle that escaped the motion of her consent as she nodded her head in agreement, but Ralph just smiled and proudly proclaimed, "Okay!!! Well then, we're blowing this joint! So, lesson two, kid… We wipe down the place for any fingerprints we might've left behind."

For her third lesson, Gloria came to learn of the intricate necessity of being able to steal a vehicle on a whim while only making use of a wire hanger and a screwdriver to do so in a hurried form of maneuvering.

Gloria never knew that committing crimes could be so much fun, but Ralph remained adamant about informing Gloria that she had to exude the utmost responsibility for the type of things that he was going to show her. Ralph reminded Gloria that whatever she did in life, she should make certain that it be completed with the purpose of not ever endangering herself or the lives of those deemed to be innocent.

Along with the circumstances surrounding injury, death, and incarceration, just to name a few, Ralph also instructed Gloria on constantly remembering the fact that the fun she so innocently detailed always had the looming potential for incurring the many consequences which associates itself with the criminal activities they were bound to engage themselves in.

*****

Over the course of the next few weeks, the intimate bond between teacher and pupil, companion and friend, became strengthened tenfold. Ralph didn't know Ms. Santiago personally, but he would certainly go on to praise her and the Gods daily for not having to be the one to give Gloria an explanation about the inner workings of what goes on with a teenage girl's body. Hell… Ralph couldn't even begin to account for what made a grown woman tick, let alone a mini one.

As Ralph stood in a checkout line, recovering from a shiver of disgust which shook him to his very core that came by way of what the feminine products he held felt in his hands, Ralph wondered about what kind of father he would have been to a daughter of his own rearing.

Ralph came to the conclusion that he would've made for the perfect absentee father. He certainly would've tried his best to stay at arms' length of sorts from his daughter's affairs unless they managed to luck up and she just happened to grow up to be a tomboy who showed an interest in what he had to offer.

Otherwise, Ralph wouldn't make an effort to shield her from the type of life that he lived, only to appear when times called for him to wrap his hands around the throat of any man, big or small, who dared to threaten his precious daughter with any form of verbal or physical abuse.

In consideration of Gloria, who must've been wondering what was taking him so long to come back, Ralph thought of how perfect it would be for a girl like Gloria to enter his field of work to professional assassin. Ralph wouldn't have intended for Gloria to actually kill someone, but this is the real world we're talking about here, and it's full of shady characters who wouldn't hesitate to kill on a whim if one didn't take the necessary precautions to get to them first.

One of Ralph's tutorials consisted of teaching Gloria how to be virtually invisible of any form of detection. A trait which can be carried out perfectly by a woman of intrigue who wished to be proficient in the chosen profession of contract killing.

The professionals who Ralph had come across whether in life, or brought to him on television and movie screens, were femme fatales who could easily get close to a mark of their choosing with sheer ease by way of offering anything from a warm embrace with a meager touch of the hand to the engagement of intense acts of coitus, in order to carry out their intentions of delivering a sudden death with the sort of intensity that most men would never be able to accomplish. Exactly the kind of thing that Ralph had in mind for providing instruction to his young pupil.

*****

On his many jaunts to complete any given task, Gloria was left to be herself in whatever hotel or motel establishment they found themselves in, until Ralph made his return. Where any normal teen would instantly find themselves becoming bored within minutes of spending time alone, Gloria experienced the exact opposite.

Although she was given specific instructions to remain in the rented room for reasons of safety, Gloria bided her time well with the effects that were tailored for her to study in the ways of being homeschooled but which gave her the uncanny ability to learn and experience subjective materials that traditional institutions would never be able to teach her properly.

Aside from the food, feminine products, and any other necessity that may be needed on their travels, Ralph always thought to obtain a variety of learning tools which would be of help to heighten Gloria's awareness to the ways of the world around her. Gloria's current favorite thing to use was the Rosetta Stone program in order to learn different languages through the use of translation which varied in the selections of Spanish, Italian Russian, French, and sign language.

Or perhaps something more physically challenging, such as the intricate usage of dining etiquette onto the harsh methods associated with hand-to-hand combat, was all done with the purpose of furthering Gloria's way of thinking to introduce her mind to a world that she never knew existed outside of the foster-care system.

Replaced by the new hunger she possessed to gather information, Gloria dispelled any thoughts of suicide away from her mind. Ralph became her coed of sorts, since he not only assisted Gloria with her studies by way of quizzing her on any of the subject matter she learned, but he was also able to absorb much of the information as well which allowed them both to communicate on a level neither of them had ever before experienced.

A different language was explored daily by the duo, which caused Ralph and Gloria to acquire the linguistic capabilities of even the most discerning of tourists, but the pair chose to articulate in the language of sign as their personal favorite to converse in with each other. It became so natural for them to learn something new that Gloria found herself not caring much for the television she came to desire anymore.

Ralph began instructing Gloria on how to properly disassemble weapons then put them back together again as he timed her progress and was constantly left impressed by how rapidly Gloria improved with each attempt she made. It became so easy for her to accomplish the task that Gloria could've completed it blindfolded. Exactly what Ralph had intended when he initiated the lesson.

The training for hand-to-hand combat consisted of teaching Gloria how to break limbs with her hands or feet or by knocking the wind out of a potential attacker by implementing the use of strategically placed blows before any such attempt could be made to endanger Gloria's welfare. Since Ralph was raised in the ways of a street brawler and wanted Gloria to become more proficient in the ways of fitness, he made plans on enrolling her into martial arts training in order to broaden the variation of Gloria's skill set.

Gloria also received valuable information on the care of administering first-aid treatments whenever Ralph made his way back from one of his many crusades in need of medical attention which he wouldn't have been able to receive from a hospital without garnering the security of authorities. One such incident occurred when Ralph returned on a particular night and Gloria immediately came to notice something strange about his demeanor.

Ralph's spirits weren't always cheery whenever he made his return, but it didn't take him long to calm himself and be rid of the troubles he encountered before reassuming his teaching duties with Gloria.

On the night that Ralph came back and wasn't responsive to any of Gloria's attempts to greet him, she immediately noticed that he was suffering from some sort of immense pain. She couldn't be exactly sure of where he was hurt, until Gloria realized that Ralph was trying to keep himself composed by using his hand to cling onto a coat that was not a part of the attire he had on when he went out.

Gloria noticed that Ralph carried with him a shopping bag, but that wasn't her main concern at the moment. She hurried and retrieved a bed sheet from the closet while grabbling the first-aid kit on her way back. As she spread the sheet on top of the small couch that the room afforded, Ralph found his voice to say

"That kit won't be necessary… At least, not yet anyway."

Gloria stared absent mindedly for a moment before she placed the first-aid kit on the nightstand and awaited for further instructions to come.

*****

"Got the coat from a Bum on the street," Ralph revealed as if he could read the hidden question coming from Gloria's stare. He groaned loudly in pain as he shrugged off the coat and placed it on the floor near the bag that he held. Gloria could clearly see that the contents consisted of a tall bottle of some kind of liquor, a box of gauze pads, medical tape, and something metallic which Gloria couldn't readily identify at the moment.

Gloria gasped and became utterly concerned from the sight of the blood that oozed from what appeared to be a hole in Ralph's shoulder area. He placed his hands on top of hers as if to assure Gloria that his condition would get better soon before muttering, "Help me out of his shirt."

After Ralph's shirt was removed, Gloria could see the amount of damage done to a wound which still held the remnants of the piercing slug that got trapped within. Studying Ralph more intently, Gloria noticed that his body was marred with scarring which either didn't heal well or came to leave ghastly reminders of the amount of carnage that was once inflicted upon him.

In agony, Ralph tried his best to reach for the bag to no avail until Gloria offered him her assistance. "The bottle," he said simply while pointing in its direction. Gloria complied and handed Ralph the bottle he requested as she made a grab for the metal object that previously caught her attention.

Gloria toyed with the metallic tongs in her fingertips until the realization of what needed to be done with the claw like clasp at the end of the utensil caused her to shoot an inquiring look to Ralph in search of his confirmation of what needed to be done.

Ralph put forth a weak smile and said, "Lesson… Ahhh, forget the count! Just get this damn bullet out of me!!!" The remark was made in playful jest as Ralph removed the top off of the bottle that was clearly marked 'Whiskey' in bold lettering. Gloria watched as Ralph took a plentiful swallow of the liquid, then cringed as though she could feel for herself the amount of pain that coursed throughout Ralph's body when he attempted to pour the contents within the bottle over his wound that caused him to release a roar of agony, as the liquor burned into his flesh to sterilize any threat of an infection.

After a few tries and enduring some of the most profanity-laced insults she's ever heard, Gloria was finally able to grab ahold of the ever-elusive slug casing with a firm clamp of the tongs she used. Ralph then nodded his head on contention after Gloria looked to him for reassurance.

Ralph gripped the bed sheet tightly as Gloria gave a tug on the object in her hand. When the bullet was finally removed, Gloria stared at it as though it were an extraterrestrial from outer space before giving Ralph a condescending look from the sound of him moaning and groaning in immense pain.

"Ugggh! Ahhh!" Ralph groaned loudly before creasing open one of his creased eyes to see if Gloria was still watching him. The false act caused her to laugh hysterically at Ralph's display of humorism.

"Man up!" Gloria joked in return as she hit Ralph on his arm playfully.

"Oww, that really hurt!!!" Ralph lamented in jest through gritted teeth as an actual pain coursed through his weakened body.

"You did a great job with getting that bullet out of me, kid. That was just an example of how you take care of yourself without the need for conventional methods," Ralph informed her, but Gloria couldn't believe what she'd just heard.

"You mean to tell me that you did all of that just to teach me a lesson?!" she asked in disbelief.

"Well, not by shooting myself, if that's what you thought. But, what better way to teach you something than for you to learn it through personal experience?" Ralph's response said, but Gloria still wasn't convinced.

"But, you almost got yourself killed," Gloria implored while still trying her best to fathoms the extent of Ralph's rationale.

He nodded his head and said, "You're right; with the way you were sticking them tongs into my shoulder, I thought I was going to be a goner for sure!"

The sentiment brought a smile to Gloria's face as Ralph ended his pained dialogue with, "This is definitely far more easier to remember than shoving a book into your hands and telling you to simply read it. Now, help me clean up this wound a little better with that first-aid kit of yours." Ralph was still trying to recover from his gunshot wound, but for an aged man, he kept himself together well through the usage of callisthenic workouts and scouring the city for the enemies he sought to do combat with.

"Pack you your stuff! We're getting out of here!" Ralph started with enthusiasm etched to his tone after returning from a day out. Gloria was so used to hearing those very words regularly that her emotions became monotonous as to whether or not they stayed in the same location, but noticing Ralph's upbeat demeanor, she inquired, "You hit the lotto or something?! You're acting really strange." Ralph smiled with a boyish grin in return but gave away nothing about his true intentions.

"We're going sightseeing," he exclaimed as Gloria eyed him suspiciously.

The scenic drive the pair took this time around didn't consist of any preserved pastures and the expensive acreage of fine homesteads where fawns and other sorts of exquisite wildlife scampered about as it happened when they first encountered each other. No. On about this particular route, the views that came to witness both all too familiar with already.

Where decades-old sidewalks, which were littered with filth and debris, all combined to support the worn heels of the streetwalking prostitutes and the other shady characters who all roamed the area of terrain as though they were actually the wildlife of the night's landscape.

Chapter 11

Ralph parked the vehicle they were riding in and began his tutorial. He instructed Gloria on the intricacies of being able to implement integration as a resource instead of seeing those she gazed upon in a state of loathing. "But, they're prostitutes!" Gloria remarked dejectedly. "Yeah. And, conmen, stick-up kids, drug dealers, and pimps amongst the other forms of lowlife out there, but your goal should always be to learn the reasons why each live like they do and how to use anything that you come to derive from them to your advantage," Ralph replied sternly.

Gloria pondered upon Ralph's response for a moment before raising the question, "Is that why you had me acting like a lot of different people?" An inquiry, Ralph merely nodded his head to in agreement.

At times, Ralph called upon Gloria to assume the identity of someone they've maybe seen or had come across and was always left surprised to see how well Gloria effortlessly carried out the task once she got over the initial bout of nervousness she experienced which threatened to stifle her performance.

Ralph often asked Gloria to don a wig, or fix up her hair into an array of styles, in order to be able to emulate the many different characters needed to give off a false impression as to her true intentions. Something Gloria began to enjoy doing, since it acquainted her with experiencing the thrills of suspense and intrigue on a whim.

Gloria's character assimilations consisted of emulating the part of a teenage tourist visiting from the United Kingdom while exacting a flawless accent to match. Making use of drugstore spectacles with her hair straightened into pigtails in the attempt to compliment the look she initiated, Gloria was able to fool countless passersby and the minds of the concierge from the hotels and motels they visited which always found Ralph basking in awe from the sight of Gloria's many well-played performances.

Gloria was also able to make spot-on impressions of any person Ralph requested just by merely pointing in the person's direction. Anyone form an overweight man yearning to know the exact details listed on an establishment's dining menu, in order to adhere to his very own sort of 'strict diet' on to something like a pretentious socialite who continuously stroked the hairs of her toy poodle as though it were an extra flab of skin while demanding only the best of services to accommodate her extravagant tastes was nothing of consequence for Gloria's imaginative impersonations to accomplish.

Gloria's overall favorite characterization, however, had to be her portrayal of a rock groupie for a heavy metal band such as 'Gwar.' Donning the group's signature tee-shirt and wearing heavily applied makeup to look the part came with ease, since Gloria derived the sort of persona she needed straight from the memories Gloria had of Malala.

Gloria missed her friend dearly, but since the circumstances of their last encounter was dismal and remained soured, Gloria wasn't so sure she had a friend in Malala anymore, but she also wasn't ready to relinquish the hope she for saving it either.

*****

After a bit more driving, Ralph finally parked the vehicle on a desolate street and simply said, "We're here!!!" with that boyish grin of his emerging once more. Gloria couldn't be sure of where 'here' was exactly, but witnessing the cats being chased away by the even bigger rats, she immediately began to wonder if Ralph might've been trying to furtively get rid of her after all.

It wasn't as though Gloria was afraid to die at this point. In fact, it was the exact opposite. Remembering Ralph's constant speech of, "Danger is a fear, but 'fear' is a choice," epithet, Gloria was determined to remain headstrong and face any imminent death she came to encounter with her chin held high.

Gloria couldn't believe for a second that Ralph would actually try to kill her after literally saving her life the way he had in the first place. So, with not waiting to seem prissy in regards to any hidden concern she may have had, Gloria asked, "Why are we here?" After looking along the forlorn streets and thinking, *No one could possibly want to live under these conditions,* Gloria became warmed by the sound of Ralph suddenly exclaiming, "We're home!!!" For the life of her, Gloria couldn't understand why.

"Come on, Mrs. Upright, and allow me to show you where we're going to be making our bones!" Ralph said excitedly while existing the vehicle. Gloria was left dumbfounded by Ralph's showing of enthusiasm. Something she'd never come to see in him before, so out of curiosity for the words he left to hang in the air, Gloria reluctantly stepped herself out of the car in order to see exactly what all the hype was all about. A factor which made Ralph extremely happy, or delusional, for as far as Gloria could tell at that moment.

*****

A gust of wind threatened to send Gloria scurrying back into the comfort of the vehicle, after it delivered a powerful shiver that reverberated throughout her entire body, seeing Ralph breathe in a deep sigh of relief, however, as though he were a prospector in discovery of a perfect parcel of land, Gloria found herself to be beyond intrigued to see what the end result of Ralph's surprise would be, since from what Gloria gazed upon so far, it would take a lot of creativity on his part to impress her at this point.

The darkened environment allowed Gloria views of its dejected surface to go along with the dormant buildings which occupied it. The location was centered near an industrial area that contained large warehouse catering to the making of anything from appliances. There was even wholesale fish distributions near the water which catered to the demands of shady characters who, the world would find themselves relieved to know, were only interested in the fresh catch of the day.

The area was completely a realtors' nightmare, with its cracked sidewalks and withering trees, but, for some reason, Ralph couldn't be more happier with his find. "Well… What do you think?!" he asked. Gloria began to think that Ralph may have bumped his head a bit too hard or something, because she still couldn't come to imagine what he was trying to convey to her. Sensing Gloria's doubt, Ralph pointed in the intended direction as she allowed her eyes to follow with skepticism.

Adjusting her eyes to focus in the darkness, Gloria came to see the traces of a structure that screamed a melancholy of spirits with its shuttered windows and walls of gray brick which gave the building a haunting like eminence amidst the darkened clouds that surrounded it. Its levels consisted of two floors with possibly a basement for more accommodation, but as Gloria watched while Ralph fiddled with a steel door in guard of the structure, she allowed her doubts to allow heavily in her mind once more.

"What are you waiting for?!?! Come on! Let's go inside!" Ralph exclaimed cheerfully. What Gloria was actually waiting for, she thought, was for the feel of a large hand wrapping a cloth of chloroform around her nose just before she came to awaken a short time later to the sound of a buzz saw whirring in rotation at the area of her gut, but she politely refrained from voicing her apprehension and followed in Ralph's footsteps instead.

Gloria guessed right. Maybe it was from watching too much television late at night, but the entrance to the foyer area was totally reminiscent of countless horror movie scenes where the pretty blonde starlet became the first casualty of an Axe-murderer's blade with its grim and dreary interior that was only missing the thunder and lightning needed to compliment its eerie effect.

Watching Ralph attempting to make his way through another locked door provided Gloria with all the time she needed to contemplate upon whether or not she should stand her guard or go bolting back out the way she came, until Ralph was finally able to gain entry into the room he desired and flicked on the lights which caused Gloria's clenched jaw to drop open in… Amazement????

*****

The accommodations weren't five star, but the ambience of the above provided a homely feel that no hotel establishment could offer. Maybe it was because the place was something that they could both call their own, but the comfortability within the recessed walls of the former plumbing-supply company became instantly inviting to them as they surveyed their surroundings with awe and glee. Gloria smiled at the nostalgia of it all as she stepped across the shag carpeting and glanced at the furnishing which must've been recovered from an era that has long ago passed.

Ralph watched Gloria silently while smiling at the feet of his accomplishment. He felt pretty proud of the fact that he was able to acquire the property for pennies on the dollar from an overenthusiastic sales broker who only became all too happy to be rid of the listing after not being able to sell the property for over two years due to lack of any gentrification happening in the area anytime soon.

Gloria came upon a retro picture of dogs playing poker and shot a questionable glance in Ralph's direction. He simply shrugged his shoulders in return and said, "I think it gives the place character, don't you?" Gloria shrugged her shoulders mockingly before playfully doling out a disdainful look toward the old leather couch which was accompanied by an overstuffed matching ottoman that was all situated in front of an old box-television set. Something still in need of its bulk in order to make a change to the channels properly. "I'll get a cable box put in as soon as possible, but, overall… How do you like it?!" Ralph inquired while feeling extremely giddy about the prospects of his find.

"I picked out the furniture myself from a secondhand store not too far from here," Ralph stated with the pride of his decorating prowess beaming in joy. Gloria nodded her head in agreement from the plain thought of knowing that Ralph could only be so brave as to pick out furniture which should've been burned to cinders at the turn of the century.

Gloria ran her finger along the length of the couch with an upturned lip movement that caused Ralph's smile to turn upside down. "You don't like it?!" he asked, fearing the worst in her response.

"No," Gloria responded shockingly. "I love it!!!" she declared loudly while leaping onto the furnishing to start bouncing up and down on the balls of her feet in elation.

Ralph was skeptical for a moment, but after seeing the genuine smile form on Gloria's face as she feigned coughing from the imaginary dust of old age in the air, he instantly warmed himself to the extent of her humor.

"It's comfortable, isn't it?" Ralph asked her, wanting Gloria to be totally at ease in their new home. Gloria smiled only halfheartedly, since she didn't want to inform Ralph about the spring in the couch that was currently digging into her thigh, but she felt no less pleased as Gloria made her best attempt to maneuver herself away from being stabbed to death. "Well, don't just sit there! Come on, and let me show you the rest of the place!" Ralph said emphatically as he took Gloria's hand into his and led her on a tour of the abode.

The furnishing was sparse, but everything consisted of the necessities needed for them to survive. A kitchen was converted out of the supply company's old break room, while the former offices were turned into either the bedrooms with makeshift walls or cleared out for the use of storage space.

Gloria also had sufficient heat which was a vital resource that some of the foster homes Gloria's been in couldn't afford to have.

The bedrooms were of the same size, only Ralph's was painted a dark forest-green texture, while Gloria's was placed with a lavender hue. Something that amounted to be a good thing too, because if it was done in anything pink, she might've just gagged before painting it over herself. Suddenly, Gloria began to feel a bit queasy about the thought of actually liking the way Ralph chose to decorate but tried to shrug it off as just being a part of her imagination.

Ralph felt comfortable with just slumbering on a simple twin mattress, since his sleep pattern wasn't too forthcoming much anyway, but he was able to score Gloria a queen-sized bed that instantly earned him a big hug of gratitude from his grateful student and friend. Watching Gloria bounce around happily on her new bed then playfully measuring the spaces on the wall where she could potentially hang pictures, Ralph found himself seriously wondering again, the 'what ifs' of why he truly never bothered to have children of his own.

Ralph warmed to the sight of Gloria's smile and knew deep in his heart that he made the right decision by saving her precious life. The question of whether he should be teaching Gloria the lessons he had in store came to mind, but Ralph immediately quashed the sentiment since he figured that if he was going to care for Gloria as though she were of Ralph's blood, then he would go on to do so by preparing her for whatever harshness the world had to bear.

As a contingency plan, maybe the contactor who entered the layout of the building doubled as some sort of assassin, or perhaps an accidental genius who initiated the complex art of architectural science in order to develop the perfect means for an escape. But in whatever probability one decided to choose, Ralph was thankful to whoever thought to make the hidden hideaway he first discovered when he purchased the property.

*****

Located on the second-floor landing between the two bedrooms was a steel ladder leading to the roof area which was bolted into the wall. If needed, Ralph explained to Gloria that she would be able to make her escape easily by moving across the adjoining rooftops until she could make her own way down to safety at a designated building about two blocks away. Although the next option would have to be implemented quickly, there was another means of escape for Gloria to flee, should her life ever depend on it.

The reason Ralph selected which room was suitable enough for Gloria to stay in was because after inspecting the property while being shown around by the hopeful sales agent, Ralph came across an anomaly that was barely visible to the naked eye. As the broker babbled on about something incoherently while walking to where the bathrooms were located, Ralph took one more look over his shoulder to make certain his escort was gone before moving in to get a better glimpse at what caught his attention.

When the sales agent doubled back to check on him, Ralph asked, "Can you give me a moment? I would like to make this important decision without any interruption." To which the broker replied, "Ah, certainly. You would like to be alone. I can assure you that this is an absolutely ghost-free environment, so there are no spirits lingering around anymore." The broker added with a smile so wide, Ralph would've thought it hurt if the fake expression wasn't one the agent made use of so many times before in order to secure a deal.

After a moment of awkward silence while staring into Ralph's unrelenting gaze, the broker informed him that he would be patiently waiting for him downstairs before nervously spinning on his heels to give Ralph the privacy he requested. Remembering what he'd seen while inspecting the makeshift closet in the room, Ralph went and retrieved the metal pole he found to be oddly out of place, resting almost indiscernibly at the base of the closet floor, gathering dust.

Maybe it was the reason he came to notice the anomaly in the first place, but the steel, two-foot rod, with a slightly curved tip in resemblance of a hook, fit itself quite nicely into an indentation in the room's ceiling. Ralph's theory came to fruition when he tugged on the pole in his grip, and the ceiling gave away to reveal a collapsible stairway that led to what appeared to be a storage attic.

Ralph climbed the stairs for a peek and was surprised to find that although he was forced to stand in a semi-crouching position, the area was quite roomy within. The space was like any other attic with its reinforced beams and wood flooring in order to support weight in the excess of a thousand pounds. *This must've been where they kept all of their old storage,* Ralph thought to himself, which was a factor still very much evidenced by the few boxes left behind, covered in an overlay of festering cobwebs, labeled with titles such as 'invoices' and 'tax receipts' stenciled in with the ink of a black marker.

"Sir? Sir?" Ralph heard the sales agent calling nervously. He hurriedly secured the stair casing and brought the hideaway to a close once more before returning the metal rod back to its indiscernible position on the closet floor. When he met the broker's smiling face again, Ralph asked the question of, "Are there any passageways I should know about?" For a moment, the sales agent seemed to be at a loss for the words to say for something before responding. "No. But, there aren't any ghost from the beyond either, right? Or do I need to call someone to perform an exorcism?" he added in a condescending tone that made Ralph want to smack some reality into him.

Ralph affixed his stone-faced gaze on the broker before the sales agent asked in worry, "You don't like it?" Ralph remained pensive for a moment before creasing a condescending smile of his own and commenting, "What's not to like? At least it's not haunted with apparitions, right?" The sales agent chuckled absentmindedly, hoping that there wasn't another punch line coming. When there wasn't, he escorted Ralph to an area where he could sign the purchasing papers with the use of the alias he prepared in exchange for a cash transaction.

*****

Afterward, Ralph went and retrieved the metal rod from its restful position and held it in front of him. Intrigued, Gloria stopped what she was doing and asked, "What's that for?"

Ralph looked his student impassively and replied, "Tell me if there's anything you might find to be strange in your room where you might have to use this." Gloria quipped for a moment, "You mean besides you?" before coming to stand next to him to see if she might be able to figure out what he was talking about.

Gloria crouched low in order to look under the bed at first, then scanned around the sparsely furnished area to see if she could pick up anything odd but saw nothing out of the ordinary. As she looked up to see if she could formulate more ideas, Gloria squinted her eyes toward the ceiling in contemplation. She took another look at the object in Ralph's hand, then, without uttering another word, took the metal rod from his grasp and began to walk in the direction that caused Ralph's smile to emerge brilliantly.

Gloria's surprise was tantamount to Ralph's when she used the metal rod to reveal the hidden attic. Ralph tried to inform her to only use the hideaway when necessary, but Gloria was feeling too enthusiastic about going exploring at that moment to listen, as she darted up the steps gleefully. Seconds later, Gloria was dashing down the steps as fast as she could to seal the attic behind herself. "Spiders," she said simply as Ralph nodded his head knowingly. He made the effort to get rid of the old boxes and their contents after inspecting them, but he decided to leave the harmless spiders around, since, technically, it was their home before he and Gloria ever decided to trespass on their sanctuary.

Chapter 12

Ralph's look was stern as he considered his next course of action. Gloria saw the sincerity in his gaze and asked with only a tinge of concern in her voice, "What now?" Ralph scratched his chin in mock contemplation, since he already knew the answer. He intended for Gloria's anticipation to build, so that the intensity of what he had planned could take on its optimum effect when he surprised her. Without any further hesitation, Ralph simply said, "Follow me," leaving Gloria to follow in his footsteps.

The walk to the basement was swift, but in Gloria's anxious mind, it took them forever, since she was trying her best to figure out exactly what Ralph was up to. The dimly lit hallway led to a heavy steel door that seemed intimidating to her. Ralph turned to Gloria and asked with all seriousness, "Are you sure you want me to teach you this sort of lifestyle?" since the inquiry held the reservation of broad implications; he opened the door to the darkened room beyond.

After Ralph found the switch to illuminate the room in a stark luminescent glow, Gloria gasped at the sight before her. Her thoughts became so enthralled at that moment that she began shaking uncontrollably. The space itself was obviously where the former company kept the bulk of their plumbing supplies for distribution. It seemed vast, with its dimensions leveled at about a hundred feet in both length and width along with a ceiling height of about 12 feet.

Not allowing her to focus on anything else, Gloria's attention was instantly grabbed in a firm stranglehold by the look of the bulky noise-cancelling headphones which were arrayed on a thick wooden table alongside two black pistols that were harmlessly unloaded with full clips of ammunition at the ready to turn the innocent-seeming weapons into deadly over in an instant. Gloria was besides herself and at a loss.

It seemed like shooting was the only thing that Gloria had asked Ralph to teach her ever since they first encountered each other when they had their initial talk months ago in the seedy motel room. Ralph glanced at her from the corner of his eye and asked once more, "You sure you're ready?" Gloria's wide-eyed stare was gone now and replaced by a more intrepid look as she simply replied, "Like I was born to do it."

Gloria didn't shoot anything that day, to her dismay, but when she got her shot, if you will, she made sure she came ready. Gloria placed the noise-cancelling headphones over her ears and the soundless distortion that followed caused her body to quiver nervously in wait. Ralph had already explained to her the intricacies of checking the slide, firing pin, and trigger of any weapon before usage, but as Gloria peered down at the metal objects before her through the protective eyewear, she found herself trying to quash the rising fear she felt lingering.

After setting the targets just right on their cables, Ralph motioned for Gloria to assume her position and commence firing. When Gloria raised the weapon to the side, as though she were in some gangster video, Ralph was glad she had the headphones on to evade the expletives that escaped his angered temperament. Over by the time she removed the headphones, Gloria was lucky enough to only hear the question, "Just what do you think you're doing?"

After being berated for a long five minutes about not firing her weapon like someone cast in the sequel to a *Scarface* movie script, Gloria stepped into position once more, this time assuming the more proper two-handed shooting stance with her weapon held firm. The weight of the pistol felt like a ton of bricks in Gloria's palm now as she took aim at the targets taunting her in the distance from 20 feet away. She wasn't sure on how to go about attempting her first shot, which is exactly, so Gloria simply took aim and pulled on the trigger.

Gloria's first shot attempt went wide and missed the target altogether, striking nothing but dead air and landing high in the wall at the opposite end of the room. Even with the protective eyewear shielding her vision, Gloria still managed to close her eyes before firing the projectile at its intended destination while only feeling the imminent recoil in her loosened grip. *At least I know what the feeling is like now,* Gloria thought, but Ralph was besides himself. He slapped a heavy hand on his forehead, aghast by the failed success of Gloria's attempt and simply uttered, "Yikes," in a monotone of disgust as his facial features took on a look of horrified dismay.

Ralph reigned in his emotions long enough to teach Gloria the method of simply squeezing the trigger, rather pulling at her entire arm in order to perfect at her entire arm in the process in order to perfect the accuracy of her shot. He informed her that a shooter never thinks of a shot as easy while insisting that every shot requires maximum concentration and effort to avoid the innocence of any bystanders, should Gloria ever find herself in a real-time life situation.

"So keep your eye open!!!" Ralph lamented in a tone that caused her to smile as he instructed Gloria to make her attempt once more.

Gloria felt proud of herself the second time around. She surprised herself by actually following through with the shot and not feeling compelled to close her eyes in order to do so. Her shot went wide again, but, this time, she saw the target flapping in the breeze as though she nicked it. So, at least figuratively, she came close to striking her mark, right? As Gloria looked to Ralph for confirmation, his impressive gaze screamed the words, 'Not even close,' as he came over to offer some more advice to help her along.

Ralph watched as Gloria squeezed off another round. He instructed her to take aim once more, then reached in to help by way of adjusting her grip, feet, and elbow positioning in order to create the perfect power triangle with the use of her arms to strengthen the form of her shot. He reminded her again to concentrate on the target, then squeeze the trigger while implementing the power stance Ralph had shown her to maximize her chances for success.

Gloria did as she was instructed, only this time around, she started to feel a lot more comfortable with the weapon in her hands, especially since she was learning how to handle the ensuing recoil more effectively. Just before taking the shot, Gloria removed her aim and closed her eyes as she inhaled a deep breath slowly. She released the breath as it came and opened her eyes once more to focus on the task at hand.

The kickback was hardly felt as the bullet rocketed toward the mark in the distance. The resulting impact caused Gloria to jump for joy after seeing the amount of damage that was inflicted on the destroyed target. Ralph finally nodded his approval, then slanted a grin, which only added to the gee that Gloria felt, as he reached up and pressed the switch to reel in the target for closer examination.

"Pretty good," Ralph muttered while only allowing a tinge of the pride he felt to escape his sentiment as Gloria beamed with joy from ear to ear.

Gloria didn't know it, but Ralph was actually surprised to see that not only did she happen to hit the mark, but she did so with a precision that would've landed with devastating accuracy to the center of the vital organ pumping throughout the best from 20 feet away.

With the powerful feeling of being able to control the weapon she now commanded, Gloria now had a yearning to make every shot better than the last. As the days went on, she was able to hone her abilities more actually with the sagacity of a professional marksman, but Ralph informed her that it took a lot more than merely pulling a trigger in order to handle a weapon effectively.

"D.N.A. is like God. It's everywhere!" Ralph lamented as he instructed Gloria on the vital usage of being able to leave little to no evidence at all in order to evade any form of capture. Lessons included teaching her how to load weapons with only the use of her bare knuckles and making ready use of disposable silencers when necessary to aid in avoiding detection after discharging her firearm.

Further instruction came in the form of teaching Gloria the lifesaving method of counting the amount of rounds that may have been discharged from a weapon. Ralph was impressed by the way she was able to rapidly asses the correct number of shots released from whatever automatic or semiautomatic weapon he fired, with only the use of sound or assistance after being blindfolded. Pretty soon, Gloria was able to discern the model of weapon used, even though her senses of sight were severely restricted.

*****

There was even the time when the two enjoyed one of their long drives together, and Ralph happened to turn off at a juncture, which led to a huge forested area, then stopped deep within its tract of lush green landscape. Gloria held a cynical gaze as Ralph cut the engine and got out of the car to retrieve a suitcase from the trunk.

"We going hunting or something?" she asked quizzically while following Ralph into the vast expanse.

When they reached a designated spot, Ralph went into the suitcase and dug out a bulletproof vest for Gloria to put on. Hesitant, she stared at the bulky garment for a moment before taking it and murmuring, "I knew it; we're going hunting, aren't we? What are we going after, bears? Buffalos? It has to be something big if we need the bulletproof, right?" Ralph loaded the nine millimeter in silence, with his back turned to her, as Gloria rambled on. His heart was heavy with the thought of what he was about to do, but it had to be done. He breathed in deeply, then, without another thought, turned and fired.

Gloria absorbed the impact with the shocked expression of a frightened fawn who found itself caught in an automobile's horrifying headlights with no chance for escape. She landed harshly on the ground and was forced to gasp for air as she heaved and coughed in an effort to regain herself. Ralph hurried over to comfort her as Gloria's eyes raged at him in contempt.

Gloria wasn't sure if she was imagine things or not, especially seeing as how she wasn't thinking straight after being shot at pointblank range, but watching Ralph amble over to her with the look of sorrow-etched areas his face, she couldn't sworn she saw the glistening of tears in his eyes as he scanned her body for any excess signs of injury. Gloria didn't think she was bleeding, but there was definitely a pain to her ribcage that hurt like someone in Hell was trying to burn a hole through her body from the inside out.

From her position on the ground, Gloria looked down to see the slug that embedded itself in the armor of her vest. Ralph couldn't bear to look her in the eye with his face awash in guilt, but he shuffled over and undid the straps of the protective garment anyway in order to get a better look at the amount of damage that was inflicted on her. After instructing Gloria to raise her shirt to expose the wound, Ralph was able to breathe in a sigh of relief when he saw that the bullet didn't pierce her skin and only left a blotchy reminder of its impact with no telltale signs of broken or fractured ribs to account for.

"I can't believe you shot me," Gloria said flatly after the extent of her initial shock subsided.

"But, you understand why I felt it was necessary, right?" Ralph asked, maybe a bit more to comfort his own conscience than he cared to admit, but Gloria nodded her head and said, "Yeah, I think so," which was true since after perfecting her shooting skills, the question always arose for what would it be like to actually be shot or be shot at. Gloria began to feel a bit invincible and smiled now that she survived the shot attempt until she noticed Ralph reapplying the straps on her vest.

"Why are you putting the vest back on me?" Gloria inquired nervously. Ralph didn't answer the question; he just held his hand out to her and asked if she could stand. Gloria didn't know why, but she nodded that she could and reached at to grab Ralph's hand, so that he could pull her to feet. She almost didn't hear what he said next, or maybe she chose not to, but when Ralph asked again, "Can you run?" Gloria stared at him for a moment before asking a question of her own, "Why?" Ralph said nothing more. He just raised the pistol and fired once again with a smirk this time around.

Gloria saw the weapon being raised once again and closed her eyes as she braced for impact. When the pistol discharged, she felt her bowels loosen in fear while wondering why she was still standing there alive. When she creased open her eyes open slightly to see what happened, Gloria found herself staring down the barrel of a smoking gun, with Ralph's smirk radiating through the fog. "That one must've to take that chance?" Ralph asked as he raised the weapon once more.

Gloria wanted to ask if he was serious, but she felt no need to question the menacing glare in his eyes as she took off running in the opposite direction. The sound of another blast confirmed that Ralph fired off another round, but he taunted, "Oops… That one was a blank too!" as he began to give chase. The next round resignated as loud as the last, only this time, a patch of dirt and grass was lifted into the air, right where Gloria's left foot had been only a second ago, which immediately killed her next question before it arose.

Objections either near or around her became obliterated as Gloria ran deeper into the recess of landscape while Ralph fired off rounds at her. Trees splintered and grass exploded as he bared his quarry. The chase ended when Gloria stopped to catch her breath near a thick tree trunk, and Ralph came around the bend with the weapon raised for the center of her chest. This time, however, Gloria managed a smirk of her own as she stated, "You're empty."

Ralph sucked his teeth as though the assumption were preposterous and squeezed the trigger once more. "Huh. Seems you're right," he confirmed after the empty chamber had nothing more to offer than a hollow clanking sound in return. "You get an 'A plus' for the extra effort, young lady," Ralph stated proudly for Gloria's power of deduction under fire. The lesson was a harsh one, but it was initiated so that Gloria would have the ability to control herself whenever there came a time for her to be confronted with the real thing. Famished now, Ralph said, "Let's get out of here, I'm starving."

The drive afterward was done mostly in silence until Gloria reiterated once more, "I can't believe you shot me," with the pain she endured, ruminating as a constant reminder of her harsh studies.

Ralph looked at her from the corner of his eye and said, "I think you deserved it for all of the headaches you've been giving me, but if it makes you feel any better, I just might let you shoot me back."

Gloria smirked as she thought about exacting her revenge and replied, "Yeah, I like the sound of that idea. I would shoot you right in the butt for being such a hard ass," she responded as they both burst into laughter instantly. It was then, as it is now, a lesson Gloria would use to survive at all cost if she needed to.

Chapter 13

Along with the handling of firearms, Gloria was instructed on the finer points of defending herself with a dagger whenever necessary. Ralph often placed her in the basement with a sparring dummy in order to practice striking the vital areas that would kill or be swift at knife throwing but found that she didn't fare too well at the effort. Since Ralph wasn't too familiar with that form of technique either, she didn't have to do it, but Gloria stuck with it anyway since she found it to be entertaining.

Gloria laughed hard every time Ralph tried to instruct her in the classic ways of fighting like a street brawler by baring his teeth and shaking his head from side to side as though he were ripping off someone's ear or lips after chomping into their unsuspecting flesh. Gloria knew that such a particular form of behavior that Ralph exhibited wouldn't be too becoming of a lady, and Ralph must've understood that, since he enrolled her into a karate school to further her training.

After her time in the dojo was completed for the day, Gloria would make a few side stops to see the latest fashions left out for display in store windows, or maybe go to a pet shop to get a glimpse of the puppies and kittens that she knew Ralph wouldn't let her dream of having. When she made it back to the house after taking the clandestine measures through the side streets that Ralph insinuated on in order to evade a potential follower, Gloria found herself faced with the instruction, "Ask me what did you do today."

She didn't know it, but after Gloria asked Ralph the question he requested, he would recount every detail she did after leaving the karate dojo, until she asked the obvious, "You followed me?" inquiry. As it turns out, Ralph had been tailing Gloria ever since she started her karate training and continued to do so until she finally picked up on him one day before trying her best to lose him before he realized it.

Ralph was so proud of Gloria for being able to use the power of deduction in order to eliminate the threat of one of his tails which was no small feat. It happened when she caught sight of him a bundle of roses outside of a flower shop. Gloria herself stopped at the window of a grocery store which allowed her the access she needed to watch him through the glass. When she saw Ralph stand to watch her movements, Gloria continued walking on as though she didn't know he was there. She assessed the amount of time she had to lose him by measuring the distance Ralph was behind her, then quickened her pace a bit.

Gloria swiftly made her move to round a corner where she wanted to encounter a man whom she knew would be predictable enough to be out panhandling as he always was.

"What's up, Eddie? I was wondering if you could help me out with something important?" she asked, hoping that he would go along with her plan. Eddie flashed a magnificent missing and chipped-toothed smile before lamenting in a drunken drawl, "Hey, Maria! Sure, what's wrong? Coupl'a punks botherin' you or something?"

Gloria, wise enough to offer the stranger a fake name when he introduced himself a week prior, replied, "No. No. It's nothing like that. It's just that this guy asked me for directions and I didn't know what to tell him. He's about to come around the corner, so I was thinking maybe you could be the one to point him in the right direction."

Eddie, who scratched at his rough stubble of a beard in contemplation of possibly making a buck in the process, said adamantly, "Yeah! Yeah! I can do that for you! What's he look like?" Gloria smiled, then gave a detailed description of Ralph's appearance before continuing on after saying her goodbyes.

When Ralph finally rounded the corner, Gloria found herself to be feeling giddy on the inside as she hid behind a mailbox, peeking to see the action unfold. As if on cue, Eddie hopped to his feet and yelled, "Hey! Hey! Marie told me you needed some help! You lost or something, man?" Ralph was taken aback for a moment as he wondered what the old vagabond was talking about, and, more importantly, who was what this Marie he was referring to, until he saw Gloria smiling at him from her hiding place before she casually walked away once more.

Ralph had to admit; he was truly impressed by Gloria's spur of the moment tactic as he began to follow her again, but before he could get too far in his steps, he felt the a tug of by an eager panhandler who pulled him back and asked, "Hey, buddy. Can you spare an old man a buck?" After conceding the currency over to his aggressor, Ralph looked to see that he lost sight of Gloria, before murmuring, "Well done, Gloria. 'A plus' for the effort… 'A plus' indeed."

As a new adult, Gloria wasn't going to let anything dampen her mood today. She was already floating in the clouds after celebrating her 18th birthday two nights ago, with Ralph taking her out for a day of visiting museums, going to the movie theater, then enjoying pieces of ice-cream cake while they watched late-night talk shows together. As a gift, Ralph gave Gloria a golden necklace which suspended a matching locket that contained a picture of him sticking his tongue out at her. A keepsake which she absolutely cherished.

Gloria felt ecstatic today, not only because she was now the legal age of what was to be considered an adult, but Ralph cared enough to save her life and take her under his wing; she was able to use the very discipline he instilled in her to attain the coveted black-belt accolade for her distinction of being able to master the art of her karate teachings in a rapid fashion. Gloria wore the traditional karate uniform known as a 'Gi' with pride as she adorned the garment with her awarded black belt and walked with her head held high for the accomplishment.

When she finally made it home, Gloria decided to fire up the Rosetta Stone program to begin learning the intricate dialect of Japanese in the attempt to converse with her sensei in his native tongue. After about a half hour of matching words with phrases, Gloria heard the scuffle of feet and heavy breathing just before she heard Ralph scream out her name.

Gloria was in her room when she heard her name being called. Her smile broadened as she thought about the look on Ralph's face when she informed him of her accomplishment. She even grinned slyly at the thought of him becoming a bit jealous that he wasn't the one to teach her the art. Gloria started thinking that her celebration should consist of something manly, like ordering a big fat sirloin at a reputable steakhouse while sneaking in a hard beverage, although she knew Ralph would rather have a heart attack than have her drinking liquor in front of him.

When Gloria opened the door to her room, she immediately knew something was wrong when Ralph barreled up the stairs with a wide-eyed look of fear on his face. Her smile turned into a look of grave concern when Ralph rushed up to her and said, "I'm so sorry, Gloria! I must've gotten sloppy! I don't know how, but they found me! I can't believe they found me!" He lamented in disbelief. Just when Gloria could ask him to clarify what he meant, they both heard a loud explosion that rocked the interior of the building.

"Shit! They must've blasted their way in!" Ralph exclaimed in surprise. He pulled Gloria in close and gave her a tight hug before quickly shuffling her back into the room and quickly revealing the hidden attic. Ralph held Gloria by the arms as he looked deep into her eyes and said, "No matter what happens, I will always love you. Remember that! Now let's get your stuff together quickly, so you can hide before it's too late for either of us!" before he rushed to put all of her things into a pile on the bed.

Gloria tried to fight back her tears as she pleaded, "No! I want to go with you, please!" Ralph smiled meekly before replying. "Not this time, Glor. But don't worry. I'll get rid of these guys, then come back and get you when it's all over. Now hurry, we don't have much more time! I have to get to the roof so I can lead these guys out of here!" he stated as he helped Gloria to make her way up the steps for the hidden sanctuary.

Gloria was skeptical, but she said nothing more than, "Please come back safe."

Ralph nodded and said, "Don't worry. These guys are no match for me," with a wink that seemed a bit too forced. In a last ditch effort that surprised him, Gloria turned and hugged him tightly once more before whispering, "I love you, Ralph." No more was said as Ralph closed the hidden attic with Gloria's fearful expression gazing down at him. Just before fully closing the ceiling tile, Ralph yelled, "Don't forget to wait until everything is over before you come down. I'll come back and get you!" Although valiant, the promise would be one that Ralph wouldn't be able to keep.

Chapter 14

Ralph knew his time for creating a diversion had ran out when he heard the voices approaching from the bottom of the stairs. The intruders had made a full sweep of the floor below and were now making their way up to find him. To somewhat make up for the promise he made to Gloria, Ralph bounded for the ladder leading to the roof anyway. Just before he could complete the climb, however, a burst of shots echoed and tore through his leg with an intensity that caused him to stumble backward and yell out in agonizing pain.

Ralph already had an idea of how this was going to end. The quest for vengeance was for too great for any man to resist, a circumstance he knew well. So, Ralph came to terms with the fact that it was now his turn to be the one on the receiving end of someone's smoking gun. Another burst of fire caused Ralph to taste his own blood, as the slugs penetrated his shoulder and sternum areas with blows that sent him sprawling to the ground. He could feel his life beginning to slip away now, but before he died, he wanted to be a little closer to Gloria. With all of the strength he could muster, Ralph barreled himself through her room door and awaited for the inevitable to come.

Gloria heard the shots being fired off and immediately dropped down low to get a peak of the action from her perch above. When Ralph came crashing through the door and fell weakly to the floor in pain, she gasped as her eyes widened in horror. Gloria was tempted to scream out his name, until she saw the muzzle of an automatic weapon sweep the room just before four men barged in and converged on Ralph with their weapons aimed for his chest.

How did they find me? Ralph wondered once more. For a sunny walk to the fish market, he didn't feel the need to carry any weapon other than the knife he had since the area was so desolate, hardly any people moved about, much less actually live there, but now he felt helpless. Just then, it occurred to Ralph that the very fish market he began to frequent may have been the factor which played a role in his undoing.

Whether heavily influenced by some kind of political connection, or simply mafia sanctioned, the wholesale fish market stood as a pillar of shady dealings which had the potential to wield great power for the upper echelon of the criminal element who stood to gain from it. Who was Ralph to not relish in the catch of the day like everyone else? He would be one to haggle the best purchasing price for fresh sea bass, jumbo shrimp, red snappers, or any other delicacy of the ocean in order to prepare him and Gloria a meal that was as close to restaurant grade as they could get.

Ralph guessed correctly when he assumed that someone must've put out a citywide alert to be on the lookout for him which, in turn, had him on the verge of being hunted. He would've detected any such attempt, easily, but since the best cunning requires careful planning, Ralph was for certain that whoever decided to conspire his death proved to be wise enough to realize who they were dealing with and thought to take the required precautions before engaging him as a target.

The four enforcers who were elected to dispatch to Ralph only had the chore of watching him from afar after he was first discovered. They managed to bring themselves closer and closer to their quarry as the opportunity arose for them to do so, but, even then, they made no attempt to intercept him, since they wanted the force of their strike to be perfect when they did. After the location of where Ralph was staying became apparent, the enforcers only had to just watch and wait.

The strongmen immediately came to realize that Ralph wasn't living alone. They didn't know of their connection, but it appeared that he and the young girl he was always seen with were of no blood relation. The enforcers could only assume that the girl was no more than a mere teenager of no consequence, but when the call was made to report the circumstance, the reply replayed a harsh message to ensure that no survivors were to be left standing in the aftermath.

When they chose to strike, the enforcers made certain to trail Ralph from a safe distance in order to monitor his movements just in case the potential for him to become a threat increased. The four were excellent at what they did, so it proved easy for them to spread out then blend into the crowd as Ralph went shopping for nonessential housing supplies for plumbing needs as well as enough food products to stock up the pantry for about a month.

The strongmen wanted to engage Ralph in the parking lot, but since they had no idea of what kind of weaponry he was carrying at the time, the enforcers didn't want to risk the chance of a messy gun battle ensuing, which had the certainty of leaving them all too exposed for the authorities to discover, so they decided to take Ralph at home.

After existing the car on his way back, Ralph discovered that he had followers. He saw them and instantly took on a look of fear as he thought about Gloria's safety. Ralph dropped whatever he held in his hands and made a mad dash for the building in order to keep her out of harm's way before it was too late to do so. He looked back to see his pursuers walking at a leisurely pace while loading their weapons with mischievous smirks coming to their faces.

The type of surveillance that the enforcers implemented missed the whereabouts of Gloria, since she decided to sleep in a little late before heading out to continue her teachings in karate. Everything was going well for her until this point, especially after she was awarded the coveted black-belt distinction, but, now, here she was, looking at Ralph as he lay dying on the floor below.

When Ralph caught a sight of his beloved Gloria gazing down at him, he creased open a weak smile. He hoped that she would be able to stay out of the way long enough for his death to play out, and before any of the men realized what he was doing, Ralph used his remaining strength to raise the three finger language sign for 'love' and held it close to his chest. Gloria couldn't fight the tears that began to flow her face as she helplessly watched in horror.

The four men made use of plastic explosives in order to make their entry into the abode, which they knew for certain was secured by locks, after Ralph made his way inside. They moved in unison to sweep the floors quickly before making their way up the steps to further the hunt for their prey. They caught sight of Ralph trying to make his escape for the ladder leading to the roof and fired a burst of shots to stop his attempt. The enforcers weren't even sure they struck him until they heard Ralph scream out in pain.

"He's here!" the lead man shouted after the four men cleared the previous bedroom and found their prize lying in a pool of his own blood, dying.

"He's still breathing. Let's follow Mr. Ciccarrelli's instructions to the letter and finish this," another said as all four men readied their weapons to tear into Ralph's flesh one last time.

The sounds were nearly deafening as the enforcers emptied their ammunition into Ralph's writhing body. "No!!!" Gloria screamed as she watched the carnage unfold.

"You hear something?" one of the strongmen asked the others who were all shaking their heads in response.

"Not unless you're talking about the sound of this guy talking his last breaths," one quipped, as another snickered and remarked, "Yeah, Vinny C is going to be real pleased. Now let's blow this joint and celebrate by getting some pussy at the strip club." Another sentiment that caused them all to laugh wholeheartedly.

Before leaving, one of the men crouched low over Ralph's carcass and removed an old ring that he wore on his index finger which belonged to his mentor, Loanshark Jack, so many years ago. The ring was a keep sake that Ralph kept after Jack's untimely demise and was often used as an instrument in exacting his revenge killings, since he branded the flesh of his enemies with the ring's insignia embedded with an eerie skull. The ring was requested specifically by the person who wanted to ensure that Ralph was made to become a forlorn memory by exacting his own form of revenge.

"Hey! Wasn't there supposed to be a girl around here somewhere?" one of the brutes asked contemptuously.

The other shrugged as one remarked, "Don't worry about it. If she's not here, she's just not here. Besides, Mr. Ciccarelli only wanted this guy dead, anybody else was just extra."

"You think she was a whore? She sure looked a bit too young to be, but you never know," another interjected, then added, "She should consider herself lucky; she could've been laying right next to this guy."

"It doesn't matter where the girl is now; the head man date tonight." As a parting joke, the other three talked about how they didn't think the whale of a girl the brute was dating could fit into his car as they all left with huge grins on their faces after completing their task, although they still had one more thing to do first.

It was like her father being killed before her eyes all over again. And in a sense it still was, as Gloria thought about her relationship with Ralph. No more tears were shed as she simply gripped the two, three eighty-caliber pistols tightly. It was upon Ralph's insistence that the weapons were to be left in the attic for safekeeping in case of an emergency. Gloria couldn't think of a better emergency to use the other weapons than now, but she knew it would be unwise to go into battle with these four men, especially now that she knew who was responsible for the attack.

Gloria knew the name of Vincent Ciccarelli well. Leader of the Ciccarelli Cosca, 'Vinny C' as he was known, inherited the prestigious title of Mafia Don from a long ancestry of Ciccarelli's who ruled the lands of Palermo in Italy for centuries. The modern day Ciccarelli had just been released about a year ago after a lengthy 14-year term in a federal penitentiary for extortion, racketeering, and other related charges associated with being a kingpin.

It wasn't immediately known, but when one of Vinny C's top consiglieres turned state evidence against him, no one knew that it was actually Ralph who was pulling the strings. Maybe it was his way of confessing his sins to her, but Ralph explained to Gloria that, in war, often times consequences were doled out harshly. As such, he informed her that in order to turn a top aide to the mafia don into a police informant, one had to threaten the man's family with malicious intent, since that particular type of man would consider a threat to his own life a laughable joke.

Ralph detailed how he kept tabs on the man's family for about two months by monitoring the school schedule of his kids and his wife's weekly visits to the beauty salon for her styling needs. Ralph even gathered information on the man's elderly mother, which scared him the most, as Ralph recounted the mother's recent doctor appointments and Bingo-playing times with ease. The final decision to betray his boss wasn't a simple one, but it was accomplished nonetheless where his family's safety was at issue.

The man did as he was told, with every bit of disdain he could master for Ralph's wellbeing. When the task was completed, with Vinny Ciccarelli receiving the maximum time allowable under the guidelines for a first-time felon, the man involved with Ralph's endeavor declined any form of witness protection whatsoever for him and his family and went to pay his former don a visit to discuss the extent of what transpired between him and the black assassin.

As a result of his forthrightness, the don ensured that the man's family would be spared any ill-will while granting the man's wish for an honorable death to atone for his sins committed against the mafia's rule of 'Omerta.' Without any form of torture, the man's death was received quickly with a gunshot to the back of his head before being taken out on a boat to rest in a watery grave.

Vinny C bided his time in incarceration well by reading ancient history books of Italian, Greek, Rome, and even African affairs. He kept his body fit by physically engaging in a strenuous workout regiment daily while issuing orders to ensure that the criminal enterprise he was still very much involved in stayed running like a well-oiled machine. In the back of his mind, however, the don intended to introduce the black assassin named Ralph to the true meaning of a vendetta. The likes of which he had never known.

As the story goes, Vinny C was one of the mob bosses who commissioned the death of Loanshark Jack along with his trusted companion, Sal the Bruiser, for Jack's role in torturing a mafia consigliere in return for a substantial debt that was owed to him. Ralph learned Vinny C's involvement while on his quest for blood. Apart from the others involved, Ralph raged his silent war against the mafia but decided to spare the don his life in the attempt to weaken his enemies both physically and financially, by keeping one of its prominent figure heads incapacitated.

It was unprecedented that any one man could possess the amount of skill it took to severely weaken the structure of the mafia, but Ralph was able to do so, as Vinny C was forced to bear witness from the guise of his concrete jail cell. He was contemptuous but remained patient as he savored the thought of Ralph's demise somberly. Now, after asking certain the affairs of his life were attended to during the year of his release, Vinny C would find himself pleased with the work of his enforcers, especially after they bought him the token of a job well done that he requested, which would truly ensure that it was indeed the black assassin who was slain, although there still remained a factor that they should've accounted for but will now regret since they neglected to.

Gloria wasn't for certain if they were gone or not, but after the men left the room laughing at Ralph's expense, she took the chance to make her escape from her hiding place. Gloria wanted to do anything but look at him, but her eyes became tear soaked once more as she caressed the locket on her necklace while looking at Ralph's bullet-riddled body. The sight was almost too intense for her to look away, but Gloria knew the death of her teacher, mentor, friend, and surrogate father had to be avenged the way he would do it for her, if their roles were reversed, so she forced herself to get out of there the way he would've wanted her to.

Chapter 15

Now, Gloria understood why Ralph always made certain that she packed light. Any traces of her in the home were gone now, stuffed into a book bag, while others were placed into a small duffel bag. Both of which were manageable enough for her to make an escape in a hurry. Inside, the bags held clothing, her laptop computer, 25-thousand dollars in neat stacks of five thousand prepared by a bank teller, along with the different identifications Ralph prepared for her to make use of.

Of course, there remained the two pistols she acquired from the attic, along with spare clips of ammunition, but there was still something in Ralph's old bedroom that Gloria remembered would provide for great assistance should the need arise. She dashed into the room and recovered the metal object and carefully placed it into one of the bags. She wanted to look for more weaponry in the basement and possibly figure out what to do about properly disposing of Ralph's body until a strange scent attached itself to her nose.

Gloria exited the bedroom and began to sniff the air like as stranded mutt for food. The smell became stronger as she made her way toward the stairs. As she began to descend the steps, Gloria picked up the distinct smell of gasoline in the air as well as voices conversing on the floor below.

"This is going to be one big explosion. Putting C4 on the side of the stove like that while the gas is in the air is going to take hours to extinguish," one voice commented, as another replied, "Yeah. The fireball from this thing is going to be able to be seen from miles away," which was accompanied by sinister chuckles that caused Gloria's skin to crawl.

At the thought of an impending explosion occurring, Gloria scurried hard to gather her belongings and make her escape the way Ralph had instructed her to do. Not able to resist the urge for too much longer, she went to see Ralph's body once more before she made her departure. Gloria stared at his corpse for a moment, just before blowing a kiss and whispering, "I'll miss you, Ralph.

Save a place for me in heaven." *Or Hell*, she thought as she made her way up the ladder to the roof and gang planked her way across the strategically placed plywood to safety.

About five minutes after making her way down to safety, Gloria heard the sound of an explosion that shook the ground beneath her feet, which sparked a fireball in the air that was indeed impressive to everyone except Gloria. A few moments later, Gloria was still clothed in the traditional 'Gi' she wore, indiscernible amongst the other spectators of the forming crowd who were gathered behind the yellow tape barriers the police raised, watching as the flames burned the building to cinders. The fire that burned in Gloria's eyes was not only a reflection of the inferno but a desire to avenge Ralph's death by any means necessary.

The following month was not laid in waste. Gloria resorted back to rooming in hotels and motel accommodations which resided on either side of ritzy or seedy. Only this time around, she was all alone to fend for herself. The death of Ralph took a huge toll on her psyche, but her determination for a redemption proved to be stronger. The choice for whatever establishment Gloria chose to stay in revolved around her being able to track the movements of Vinny Ciccarelli and his men which, often times, led to strip clubs and gambling holes, but one place in particular remained constant.

'The Cove of Palermo' was an upscale Italian eatery owned by one other than Vinny Ciccarelli himself. The fine cuisine involved was prepared as a four-course meal affair which was served on handmade flatware imported directly from the shores of his homeland. Exquisite selections of vino were chosen from a menu of their own accord and served from chilled crystal decanters, which would cause any wine enthusiast to salivate for a mere swallow, at prices beginning from a 150 dollars to monies ranging in the thousands.

In true mafia fashion, Vinny C kept a separate area in the restaurant which was curtained off and secured by a steel door that was not so far refined as the rest of the establishment. The area which led to an alternate entrance of its own served the purpose of being able to thwart the unwanted gaze of praying eyes and federal surveillance alike from the don's connection to the place than the adjacent dining-hall serving gourmet well swallow would ever allow.

The alternate entrance was where Gloria chose to begin her strike, but in order to ensure that her level of safety remained sound the way Ralph had taught her, she decided to indulge herself in a few of the exquisite tastes the restaurant had to offer to properly assess all the possibilities available for an emergency escape.

After making a reservation and fashioning herself in the ways of a young socialite, Gloria was seated at a table where she was served and entrée of lobster fettuccine coupled by a side dish of sautéed shrimp. The food was absolutely divine in Gloria's mind, and she made sure to shower the staff in acclaim for their efforts. No one chose to question her when she placed an additional order for dessert in the form of a crème Brule to be accompanied by a tall vanilla milkshake topped with a cherry that would cause any rich girl to scoff at such a fattening combination, since they figured she would be making a beeline for the bathroom at any moment to throw it all up anyway.

Instead, Gloria allowed her food to digest as she enjoyed the classic stylings of Bach's concerto, which wafted melodically in the air through the establishments speaker system, as she tried to appear self-absorbed while wearing a tight dress, heavy makeup, and round designer sunglasses that covered half of her face with her hair pulled back in a tight ponytail. The look complimented the other dining patrons well who also accentuated their gaudy attire with jewelry and the heavy odors of different fragrances.

In order to kill a bit of the time she needed for assessment, Gloria found herself in a pickle of trouble when she caught the attention of some of the older male patrons, then smiled seductively in their directions as the men received the brunt of the scorn she received from the wives or mistresses in their company.

With her reconnaissance completed, Gloria asked for the check and was surprised to see that it totaled 285 dollars for a similar meal she could've received at 'Applebee's' for less than 50 dollars, including the customary tip for the service. She now understood the possibility for why a niche in the wholesale seafood business wouldn't be such a bad idea for a profitable endeavor.

Gloria paid her tab in cash and left a suitable tip for the attentive waiter just before sauntering toward the curtained area where she was immediately intercepted by the hostess who politely admonished her by inferring, "This is a restricted area, Madame. For staff only, if you can understand," in a feigned dialect of accented Italian. One, Gloria knew for certain that the Rosetta Stone program would be able to fix in no time. She was close enough to the curtain now to catch a glimpse at one of Vinny C's goons stationed in a seat outside of a black steel door leading to the adjoining room beyond as she smiled apologetically at the hostess before excusing herself to make an exit.

Gloria departed the dining hall in the high-heeled shoes she loathed but wore exceptionally well. She made her way about a block over from the restaurant to a hotel which spirited away its grand suites for starting rates at a paltry 350 dollars for a night's sleep. There, after already checking in under an the assumed name of Maritza Sanchez, she entered her room and headed straight for the shower in order to wash off the heavy makeup that had her feeling as though she was gaining weight solely on her face.

After she was done, Gloria ordered a bowl of Crunch Berry cereal from the hotel concierge, which was to be drowning in ice-cold milk. It was delivered in what seemed like seconds, and she ate her cereal while gazing out into the glow of the night's skyline. When she was for certain that the shift change of staff had occurred, Gloria dressed in a more casual attire of jeans, sneakers, and a hoodie before making her way over to a motel where she also held reservations for a room that was in more of a squalor condition than the establishment she previously existed would ever knew existed.

Chapter 16

The motel Gloria found herself in now held traces of rat droppings and housed roaches who were intent on making their presence strongly felt. There remained no need for her to use an alias, since only a cash deposit and a scribbled name on a contract detailing the rules and regulations of conduct was required to reserve a room at 40 dollars a night. No questions were asked for what Gloria intended to do with the sparse room after she secured the mediocre accommodation for a week in advance, but it certainly proved to be why a few prostitutes were able to flourish freely.

It wasn't ideal, but the reason Gloria asked for this particular sort of room was that it allowed her the opportunity to gaze at an indiscernible storefront with awning and dark-tinted windows from her third-floor perch. This was where Gloria intended to implement her attack, since the storefront was the adjacent space connected to the prestigious 'Cove of Palermo.' A storefront leading into the throes of what is also known as 'The Ciccarelli club.'

There was movement when Gloria saw one of Vinny C's goons step out and light a cigarette in the shadows of the night. She watched as only the tip of the cigarette glowed its bright orange hue. A sight which instantly made her remember the added help she intended to use when she decided to strike. When a dark van approached and parked a few buildings ahead, Gloria hurried to her bag and dug out a pair of small binoculars to increase the magnitude of her vision.

The lenses of the binoculars may have become steamed in a fog as Gloria stared at the men walking from the sports utility vehicle toward the storefront of Vinny Ciccarelli's club. She came to know the men a bit too well by now, from their gait of nonchalance to their resembling snide demeanors and mischievous smirks. Gloria didn't need to know their names, since she knew something above all… She hated all four of them immensely.

As others came and went, so did the four men of Ralph's demise who came back to check in with their boss during different times of the day to either report the success of their assignments or to receive them. After about 40 minutes inside, Gloria caught a glimpse of the four enforcers leaving the club and entering the S.U.V. they arrived in before driving off.

Moments later, a limousine pulled up to the front of the club as two goons emerged from the entrance with their eyes darting from left to right, trailed by the don himself who slid into the backseat of the vehicle for the ride home. Gloria watched as a third goon pulled down the security gate and secured the locks before joining the rest of the entourage in the stretched limousine, and she knew that she could wait no longer to make her move.

The night was a restless one for Gloria. Not only because of what she had in store for the day ahead, but she also felt like she couldn't sleep in a bed that looked like it was crawling with bedbugs and the stains of countless one-night stands in it, so she was forced to try to get some sleep in the comfort of a rusted bathroom tub. Her back ached a bit harshly, but Gloria awoke with a start as she formulated a great way to begin attaining the retribution she sought.

She wasn't for certain if her idea would work, but after remembering that Vinny Ciccarelli maintained a vast family structure to compliment his namesake, Gloria decided to take a big chance. Although she was now the age of an adult, Gloria looked even more the image of a girl in her early teens with her hair separated into two bushy ponytails, a makeup-free face, and an attire wielding the ability to raise a few eyebrows.

As she approached, Gloria saw the enforcers' S.U.V. parked at a random spot a few buildings away. She wore an expression of indignation, disdain, and downright tiredness as she hauled the small duffel bag that she carried, that was open with clothing spilling out at the top as though it were the heaviest thing on the planet, until she reached the front door of Vinny C's club. This was the sketchy part. What was she going to do now…? Knock on the door? Shoot her way in? As her options began to wane, the door she sought entrance to suddenly opened on its own accord.

Stepping out of the club was the smoker who Gloria often saw talking the time to puff away on a cigarette, although it wasn't immediately known why. Maybe it was because the man ironically wanted to get a breath of fresh air as he indulged in his habit, but after Gloria watched him more closely over a period of time, she came to notice that his eyes often darted from left to right in the attempt to detect any form of surveillance that may be lurking from either the threat of enemies or the ever-watchful gaze of the authorities.

Before the man could light up his cigarette this time around, he became distracted by the sight of a young girl dropping her bag down in front of him like a ton of bricks on the sidewalk. She was old enough; it seemed to be his daughter, but the smoker gazed over the girl's petite frame salaciously as she stood with a hand on her hip while wearing tight jeans and a cropped top. An act which all illustrated the curvature of her body perfectly, with erect nipples that were pointing at him like sharpened daggers. The man began to wonder if the merciful Gods had just dropped the offering of a cute hooker into his lap as he started to lick his anxious lips in need.

The sentiment was short lived, however, as the man tried to regain his senses after the girl before him inquired, "Is Uncle Vinny around?" After hearing that she may be one of the don's nieces, the smoker almost suffered a stroke as he struggled with the words, "Yeah, sure. The boss is in," with traces of sweat beginning to form on his forehead.

"Well, don't just stand there! Take me to see my uncle!" Gloria lamented excitedly as the bag on the ground instantly became lighter when she hoisted it up again. She sensed a problem when the man was ready to comply but narrowed his eyes and gazed at her more intently instead.

Of a Spanish descent, Gloria's skin tone was a bit darker than the average olive complexion of an Italian, but it seemed as though the smoker was trying to recall her from somewhere in his memory but found himself unable to place her. Ever since the don's release only a year ago, after serving a long stretch, his reintegration back into society became a security nightmare with the threat of his potential enemies increasing tenfold after he fully reclaimed the reign as a high-ranking mob official.

The same could be said easily about the fact that there seemed to be influx members sprouting up from everywhere, to the point where even the don would find himself confused as to who was who, so his man positioned at the door wouldn't have been able to discern the girl before him now from the countless young females he's seen at all the parties, weddings, and family reunions the don was privy to since the time of his release.

The idea may have been a big misconception on her part, but Gloria came to surmise that since most women who descended from an Italian ancestry were named either Maria or some other rendition of the name such as

Rosemarie or an Annamaria, she decided to make an attempt at using it to work in her favor. Before the man could ask any questions, Gloria stated, "I can't believe my mother, Marie, just kicked me out of the house like that. Is he busy? I hope he isn't going to be too pissed off. My name is Tiffany, by the way. What's yours?"

The man was already skeptical about how comfortable things should be between him and the boss's niece, especially after the way he already reacted to appearance, but he sheepishly replied, "Danny's my name. It's a pleasure to meet you, ma'am."

Gloria smiled flirtatiously and touched his hand before saying, "Well, Danny. I hope that maybe we can get to know each other a little better later on, but, for now," while pouting out her lips in feigned dismay.

The man belted out a nervous chuckle in answer as if to say, 'Not even on my best day,' as the sweat on his forehead began to trickle a bit more profusely. Feeling even more uncomfortable with the awkward situation he found himself in, the man simply forget all about his habit for the moment as he responded, "Follow me," not realizing that he just allowed someone with a malicious endeavor to follow him inside.

Gloria wasn't sure what to expect on her way inside of Vinny Ciccarelli's club. Lucky enough, the walkway leading to the main area was a long one, at 30 or more paces on an incline. With her chaperone leading, Gloria moved swiftly to remove her weapons from the bag as she placed it on the ground discreetly. She had already equipped the two, three eighty-caliber pistols Ralph had left for her with silencers as she took to sliding the one behind her back in the waist of her jeans.

Gloria gripped the remaining pistol tightly in her palm with her aim centered on Danny's spine as voices stared to become audible from the area coming into view. She brought her other hand up while trying to maintain her aim and began fiddling with the metal object she brought along for support as her escort took to mumbling something about hoping the boss doesn't kill him for this. *If only he knew,* Gloria thought to herself as she allowed only a sly grin to escape her now-serious demeanor.

Gloria could see them now. Seated at the head of a long table was none other than Vinny Ciccarelli himself who was in the midst or sinking his fork and knife into what appeared to be a succulent steak. Excluding the smoker, Danny, Gloria counted ten more men in her peripheral vision, most of whom were engaging a game of cards while the others watched sports on a wall-mounted television as their boss ate his meal.

"Aye, Boss! Look who I found standing outside. It's one of your nieces!" Danny exclaimed in what appeared to be an attempt at saving face. Gloria thought she could hear the garble of, "Which one?" as the don chewed with a mouth full of meat. Before anyone had a chance to react, she tossed the metal object toward the table and prepared herself to do battle.

No one seemed to notice Gloria in the room, but the fragmentation grenade which was inscribed with Ralph's name in bold lettering around it commanded a much more attentive audience than Gloria could achieve on her own, as eyebrows were raised in shocked and fearful expressions. Danny's eyes widened in fear as he watched the grenade land on the center of the table with a dull-sounding thud. As he turned his gazed to see if the boss' niece was seeing what he was seeing, the last thing Danny remembered was the swinging of her arm as the girl he came to know as 'Tiffany' brought down a pistol hard on the top of his skull in order to use him as a defensive shield.

The sound of the resulting blast was deafening and shook the walls of the building tremendously. As the splatters of blood and gore began to settle, Gloria looked to see that Vinny Ciccarelli's face now resembled the sight of chewed meat. Without any further thought, she pumped two shots into Danny's heart, then removed the second pistol she carried from behind her back as she set out to search for more survivors.

The five men who were seated at the opposite end of the table, playing poker, became pulverized by the force of the blast as well. A similar fate to the one their boss was forced to endure. The others who were lingering around were now writhing in immense pain from incurring life-threatening wounds which were the result of the fragmentation shards impaling their flesh after the metal pieces found their mark wherever they landed. Aside from Vinny Ciccarelli, Gloria knew none of the other men who were seated at the table, but all of that was inconsequential at the moment as her emotions danced in glee at the sight of those writhing in pain to be none other than the four enforcers responsible for Ralph's death. They were probably watching the details of their latest conquest as they all huddled around the television set which had just been channeled on the local news station.

There were leather lounge chairs scattered about, as well as a pool table that was used for recreation, but it seemed the enforcers were more intent on standing in order to pay close attention to whatever was being broadcasted as they drank beers which explained why they suffered such an impact from the blast. Eyeballs were gouged. Lungs became punctured, with faces badly burned, as groans of agony became apparent while emerging from defeated souls.

Gloria realized that she was running out of time for her window of escape to be clear, but she decided that she was determined to see things through to the end. When she neared, one of the enforcers made an attempt to reach for his weapon but was met with a slug that penetrated the base of his skull right between the eyes. The others found themselves in despair with injuries too extreme to allow them to make any sudden movements.

As another enforcer gazed from the remaining eye he had left, he came to realize the girl standing before him, holding two smoldering pistols in her hands, was the very same girl they discovered under surveillance as they kept watch of the black assassin they were to kill named 'Ralph.' It painted him at the moment to do so, but the enforcer managed a weak smile with the thought of going out in a hail of bullets in the same fashion that he forced so many others to meet their marker. Suddenly, it seemed as though the room became dark when the enforcer saw Gloria raising her weapons to commence firing.

As the impact of the shots landed, the enforcer could've sworn he saw the image of the slained assassin smiling directly at him through the muzzle flash as though he were firing the shots himself from the pits of Hell. Gloria spared no one from her wrath as she hurriedly made her way toward the exit she sought. As she was leaving, Gloria heard a banging on the door leading to the adjoining restaurant. She noticed the arm bar on the steel door that could only be opened from the inside and surmised that it may have been the alternate goon that was stationed on the other side trying to make his way in to check on what just occurred.

Gloria heard the muffled sounds of someone lamenting, "Hurry up with the fucking keys!" before hearing the dangling of meal and the person fumbling with the keys dropping them on the floor. She decided that she couldn't risk being seen by waiting any longer, so she went and pulled a bottle of water out of her bag to douse her hair with in order to turn her two bushy ponytails into a straight one before slipping into a hooded sweatshirt and making her way out.

Surprisingly, the explosion was well-contained with only cracked windows evidencing the blast that occurred within as gawkers struggled to figure out where the explosion originated from. Gloria made her departure from the scene as though she were one of the others in fear of another drew nearer. Deep down inside, however, Gloria relished in the fact of achieving the vengeance she so desperately sought.

"I love you, Ralph. That one was for you; just make sure you give them all Hell when you see them," Gloria whispered sincerely as she caressed the locket on her necklace. Not a thought more came to her mind as to what transpired only minutes ago, but, suddenly, a sly grin came to her face as Gloria's hunger began to crave for the taste of a succulent steak. An indulgence she just might partake in in order to contemplate the steps of her next endeavor.

Chapter 17

Gloria couldn't believe how quickly the last ten years had passed since she dispatched of Vinny Ciccarelli and the enforcers who were responsible for Ralph's death. Now, at 28 years of age, she had long since blossomed into the confident young woman that she was today from the insecure teen that she once was, by transitioning herself with the incentive she possessed to do so.

After reeling from the rush of bringing a demise to the Mafia Don, Gloria soon discovered that she harbored no guilt or remorse whatsoever from achieving the redemption she desired. In fact, the instance seemed to peak her interest in the craft all the more as she took the time to delve into her mind as though analyzing the entire situation in three dimensions while trying to troubleshoot and project alternate outcomes should she have done anything differently.

Gloria even laughed to herself at times when she recounted the shocked expressions on the faces of everyone in the room after she tossed the fragmentation grenade resembling the shape of one of the pears in the fruit bowl it landed in before exploding. As she thought about the movements that followed, Gloria instinctively caressed the locket which hung around her neck while remembering how she effortlessly maneuvered as though Ralph were whispering the instructions in her ear, allowing her to easily dispose of their enemies with brutal efficiency.

The turmoil should've proven to be taxing on the soul of a beginner, but instead of deterring her, Gloria chose to hone in her newfound skills more intently as she sought to broaden the level of her training by implementing methods most women wouldn't have thought was available to them. Starting with what was considered to be the sport of 'eight limbs,' Gloria immersed herself in the art of Muy Thai for a time which incorporated the heavy use of elbow and knee strikes.

As though she were one of the actors cast in an old karate movie, Gloria was now able to implement any one of her acquired fighting styles from jujitsu and Muy Thai, to her expertise in the standard karate she learned at the New Moon school Ralph insisted on her attending, in the attempt to dispose of any threat she may come to face. As for her shooting capabilities, well… Let's just say that Gloria no longer felt the need to squeeze her eyes close anymore while pulling on the trigger.

Gloria didn't know if she was just being nostalgic or not, but on a monthly basis, she found herself to be at the secluded area of the woods where Ralph had first taken her in order to continue his unorthodox form of training. As if on cue, she always found herself rubbing on the exact area where the bullet Ralph fired at her landed hard on her ribcage. Gloria smiled even now at the memory of remembering the look of guilt and concern that was etched across Ralph's face when he thought to comfort her after his veiled deception had the potential to truly end her life. Gloria furthered humored herself a bit by thinking that she should've played dead, but the pain she endured that day left no room for any playacting on her part as she struggled to regain her breath while convulsing.

To perfect her aim as a markswoman, Gloria made use of an assortment of weaponry, all while trying her hand at being ambidextrous with the use of both hands, but her weapons of choice remained to be the two, three eighty-caliber pistols that Ralph bestowed upon her for her safety, which seemed to be what she handled the most expertly anyway.

Gloria made a point of suppressing any weapon she fired to the best of her ability which only seemed to scare away the birds who were playing amongst themselves in the trees. On many occasions, she heard the thundering sounds of rifles and rapid-fire munitions being targeted at the many elk, boar, and deer who roamed the area which originated from them being in the crosshairs of a hunter's scope.

Gloria didn't mind the intrusion so much, since she was able get the privacy she needed, but the way most of hunters who scoured the land left behind the destroyed carcasses of their prey's bullet-riddled bodies was enough for her to want to deliver the same form of treatment to them in return, for turning what was considered to be a sport into their own killing field just for their own personal amusement.

Although there was little solace in the effort, Gloria felt at ease with the thoughts that maybe one day, the hunters would get mauled by a bear, or maybe suffer the bite of a rabid creature when the animals decided to attack, but she had to keep herself focused on the more pertinent matters at hand.

Although she managed to overcome her tumultuous experience with the dexterity needed to thwart her ever-present flaw, Gloria couldn't begin to fathom what made her give in to the thought of gyrating herself on the length of a stripper pole in the presence of gawking of their approval, but in the back of her mind, it was all done in the nature of the business that she found herself in.

"That's it right there, Babyyy!!!" Boris lamented with his deep Russian accent. He and his comrade, a fellow expatriate by the name of Yuri Shvetovish, were enjoying the sight of watching an attractive young woman gyrating her body on a steel pole as though the pole possessed arms of its own to caress the curvature of her body along with rhythmic movements she made which were in tune with the sensuous music that blared melodically throughout the club's speaker system.

Boris was much too intoxicated at this point to notice when another scantily clad woman had eased up to them from behind but not that too far gone to mistake hearing her when she sensuously whispered, "She can be all yours for the night if you'd like. Along with me and two other girl friends of mine." When Boris and Yuri spun around in their seats to see who it was that accompanied the erotic voice addressing them, their jaws immediately flopped open with wagging tongues from the sight of the voluptuous female smiling mischievously at them.

Speechless, the two were forced to only nod their heads in agreement to the proposition their gorgeous enchantress detailed. She giggled coyly at their display of resignation before making a head motion to the women performing onstage to end their act. The female on the stage displayed one more showing of grace on the pole by managing an acrobatic pirouette in the air which brought about a round of applause upon her descent. She gathered whatever currency laid scattered about around her feet and left nonchalantly to meet her friends in the dressing room.

"Wait here, gentlemen. We'll be ready for you in a few moments. Just sit back and enjoy the next performance," their enchantress commanded as she sauntered off toward the back of the establishment. Boris and Yuri wanted to follow her instructions to the latter but immediately found themselves distracted by the thoughts of what was yet to come. They began to conspire a night of unrelenting pleasure they were promised with the four women as they sat patiently in wait.

In the dressing room, the woman who was expertly working the stage and now erasing traces of the clunky makeup she wore to enhance her appearance was none other than Gloria using the name of 'Sky' as part of her stage act. The moniker suited her well for the talents she came to display while performing on the pole. As she began to put on a more casual ensemble for their trip with the fawning Russians, the other women involved with the scheme followed in suit, starting with the removal of their own makeup and wigs.

The enchantress who first encountered Boris and Yuri employed the stage name of 'Genie Powers' which ironically was derived from her actual name of Genevieve Powerstone. She used the moniker spectacularly when it came to enticing men as though her talents were conjured by true gypsy magic. Genie's figure could only be described as voluptuous, with a body that could barely be contained by the turtle neck and jeans she squeezed herself into.

Amongst the other women in the room, Gloria and Genie both heard a burst of laughter that they knew could only have been generated from one person's direction. Still chuckling, Dawn asked, "Hey, Genie! What's the difference between a woman and a computer?" She waited a moment as the expected dumbfounded looks of silence and contemplation came, before continuing on with, "The computer accepts three-and-a-half inch floppies!!!" Dawn laughed again hysterically at the funny anecdote she discovered while reading through a Nelson DeMille novel as a few of the confused women in the room began to chuckle amongst themselves as they started to catch on to the jokes 'hidden' meaning.

Dawn actually liked to have her real name used during her stage presence, since it made her feel sexy on a personal level, although she hardly needed the extra incentive to define her sexuality with a body which could rival that of any video vixen in the genres of rep, rock, or anything else in between. Her given name of Dawn Frantangello was the way of a family whose descent resonates back to the shores of Italy, the way the infamous Vinny Ciccarelli's did.

"Is everything a go?" Lauren, a sultry black woman who resembled the appearance of Kelly Rowland of Destiny's Child fame, asked in anticipation after she came from working the room full of lustful admires.

"Sure is, Baby doll!" Genie acknowledged gleefully in response while trying to cinch her jeans close around her waist. Lauren was also a stage moniker used by the beautiful girl whose name was actually Shanda Goines. She once found herself in a relationship with a successful rapper, but her seemingly status of joyful bliss became her worst nightmare when the man she came to profess her love to turned into a violent monster who began to treat her as though she were nothing more than garbage for disposal. Something similar to what the other ladies in attendance could relate to.

Genie herself had once been married to a husband for over five years who, for some reason, was adamant about not having any children with her but did find the time to smack her around about almost as much as he cheated on her. She endured years of the abuse until, one day, she just finally became fed up and simply left without taking any of her things. Genie soon found herself cowering in the homes of friends and neighbors as her deranged husband came hunting for her with fake sobs and pleas for her safe return.

Maybe he really did love Genie after all, since after not being able to have her present in his life on a daily, overbearing basis was the cause of him committing suicide by placing the bullet in his head which splattered his brain all over the walls of the former bedroom they shared together. Genie didn't know how to react to the turmoil after she received the news of his death, since the bad her husband had done to herm far outweighed the good, but she did take the time to honor his memory with a small 'Rest in Peace' tribute to him which was tattooed on her thigh, helping to bring a close to that tumultuous chapter in her life.

Chapter 18

Dawn, on the other hand, was forced to endure a much harsher circumstance, since her transgressions came about by way of meeting a man who introduced himself to her as 'Steve' on a chance encounter when she was on her way home from hanging out with friends at the mall. Everything appeared to be normal at first, as 'Steve' took to wining and dining her while going on to tell Dawn everything that she wanted to hear. A factor which only proved to add to his deceit as he lured her further into the guise of his truly evil intention.

In a short amount of time, Steve had not only convinced Dawn to move in with him, but he also deceived her into secretly depleting almost all of the savings in her parents' bank account with the ruse that his life was in danger because of unpaid gambling debts to the mob. Her bond instantly became tighter with Steve in Dawn's mind after her parents came to disown her when her role in the apparent theft became revealed.

Dawn soon felt extremely guilty for what she had done, especially when her father succumbed to a massive heart attack from the stress of not being able to keep up with the payments of the mortgage amongst their other financial responsibilities. In turn, her mother suffered immensely from the loss of her husband, and although she survived a life-threatening stroke, she found herself to be placed into the care of a nursing home against her will anyway since she soon diagnosed with a bout of dementia afterward which would soon work to overtake her mind completely. Of course, Steve was there to comfort Dawn throughout her time of need, until the time came for him to ask another favor of his beautiful and ever-faithful girlfriend.

Dawn became astonished once Steve informed her that they were along the lines of being flat broke. She had to admit to herself, however, that she never really did bother to ask what Steve did for a living, as he took her out to dinner at expensive restaurants and buying her the type of clothing with pricey purchase tags still on them. He even came to produce several months' worth of overdue notices for the lack of nonpayment in rent on the apartment they shared which was soon accompanied by a final notice calling for their eviction.

If she thought she felt she was astonished before, Dawn became absolutely shocked by what Steve had to propose next. Suggesting that she should sleep with a bunch of random guys for money was just simply something Dawn couldn't see herself doing, but Steve was just so damn convincing about being there to protect her if anything ever went wrong while trying to make every attempt to have her understand that she would only be doing it for a short time, until they were able to get back on their feet. In hindsight, Dawn came to hate herself for going along with Steve's plan no matter how disgusted she should've felt by it.

As the days went on, Dawn began to question her loyalty and love for the man she came to endure. She could only surmise that they were asking money, since she never saw a dime of it, but her major concern at that moment was why she was still being asked to subject herself to the demands of sexually needy men while the one she was supposed to be having the affair with seemed as though he had lost interest in her altogether.

After hearing for about the thousandth time, "We're almost there," whenever she managed to ask Steve how much longer before they stopped living the way they did, Dawn decided on her own that she was through with having sex for money in musky motel rooms and refused to do anything more. It was then when Steve revealed to her the true person that he really was with a violent showing of force.

Where she once enjoyed the liberty of being in a relationship with someone she cherished, Dawn had now come to fear for her life after being severely beaten and threatened on a daily basis. On a few occasions, she was placed in the care of emergency workers when Steve just happened to drop her off with her entire body blemished by cuts and bruises consistent with someone being physically and sexually assaulted. Dawn even suffered the injuries of fractured ribs and a broken arm but never dared to implicate Steve in any of the happenings whenever she came under the scrutiny of the police, because of the constant reminder he would put into her mind of the retaliation he would inflict on her should she become tempted to do so.

Dawn also came to develop a bad cocaine habit at the advice of Steve who suggested that she use the substance in order to stay alert just in case any of the Johns tried their hand at doing something funny. The only problem was;

Dawn came to finally realize that the only one doing things to intentionally hurt her was Steve. She started to lose weight and not care much about her appearance until the day Dawn decided to fight back.

Dawn finally opened her mind to the fact that Steve was nothing more than an uncanny pimp, using her body just to make an extra buck for himself. In another form of absurdity, when he became comfortable enough with Dawn being under his control, Steve actually had the audacity to subject her to the outlandish surprise of introducing her to the two other woman he had hidden under his employ. She was astonished, to say the least, that the man she had was a conman and thief hailing from a small town in Kansas.

Of the two females introduced, one was an older and much more seasoned broad by the name of Mary who was the one to fill Dawn in one the blanks she knew of Billy's life. She gave a firsthand account of his true attributes, since she was the one who happened to escape that small town in Kansas along with Billy in the hope that they were going to live life by their own rules and not by the way the law demanded for them to do so.

It was supposed to be a glamorous life of traveling the country, experiencing new people and things, but it ended up with Mary having to volunteer the innocence of her body in order to support their endeavor, as Dawn had been first led to believe, until she was placed in charge of supervising the other women he finally recruited over the course of time.

"Some life, huh?" Mary murmured more to herself than to anyone else with her aspirations of being a famous movie star shot to Hell, but she seemed to be content with herself at the moment with an outlook which forced Dawn to shiver down to her core with contempt.

The other girl was even younger than Dawn was at that time and just as paranoid, with the telltale signs of bruising to her face and arms from no doubt incurring the wrath of 'Wild Bill,' as Mary referred to him. Seems as though she was thrown for a loop, just as Dawn had been and herself enough of Steve, or Billy, or whatever his name was.

Dawn was allowed to carry a stiletto in her purse when Billy forced them to start street walking for customers. On the day she became insolent to his demands and he raised a hand to strike her, Dawn was able to strike first as she plunged the dagger she had just above the collarbone of Billy's neckline. An attempt which barely missed the vital windpipe organ by mere inches as Billy gasped in horror while trying in vain to put a stop to the blood that began to gush from his throat. Dawn made a slash at his face for good measure as Mary appeared with a shocked expression etched on herself when she came to see what was happening. Suddenly, a smile bloomed on her face before she said, "I always told him that something like this was possible by some who'd be brave enough to stand up to him." Dawn saw when Mary pulled out a cellphone to call for medical assistance and didn't want to be around when they arrived.

Dawn ran up to the other girl who was named Ashley and shook her by the shoulders as she yelled, "Now's your chance to escape him! He can't, but the time is now!!!" The girl seemed to be a bit unsure of what she should do as she took back at Billy laying wounded on the ground, but when she brought her head back around, she nodded her assertion to Dawn before asking, "But, where can I go? I don't have any money." Dawn didn't think much of that aspect either and only had enough money in her purse to make it through the night, but suddenly both girls heard the words, "Here…Take this."

When they both looked in the direction the voice emanated from, they came to see Mary holding a hand out with a wad of money toward them, with a sly grin forming on her lips. "Don't worry about it. Especially since it was made from the sweat of you ladies working on your backs," she said as Dawn palmed the money in her hand and mouthed the words 'Thanks you' before grabbing the hand of Ashley to lead her away as the sound of sirens became apparent in the distance.

Mary was right. The money Bill had come to amass over time was from him coming to the minds of the many young women he'd come across over the years into doing his bidding, until he grew tired of them and deserted them just as fast as he had come to meet them.

The money she had given to Dawn and Ashley amounted to be about five-thousand dollars which was held in the event that should any of the girls came to be arrested for solicitation of prostitution, they could be bailed out quickly in order to work the street again in some other city.

"I hope you've learned your lesson from all this, Billy. Now, maybe we can get started on that family we've been talking about," Mary said as she caressed his face in her hand. Billy looked deep into her eyes for a long moment before nodding his head in consent as the tears began to well up in Mary's eyes. She was able to slow down the flow of blood that was coming from his wound by cinching the torn fabric of her sleeve around his throat, which helped him immensely to breathe, as they waited for the paramedics to arrive.

Sure, Billy had lied to her more time than she could count over the years, but Mary knew deep down in her heart that he was going to make good on his word this time. Especially since he had no choices, Mary thought, as she rubbed on her growing belly in glee. When the ambulance came, Mary kissed Billy on his forehead and whispered, "Don't worry, Baby. Everything is going to be okay from here on out," with the thought of their resurgence resonating loudly in her mind.

When they exited the cab at the train station, Dawn gave Ashley her portion of the money and asked her what her intentions were. Ashley remained just as uncertain as Dawn was of her own plans as they both stared at the destination board for locations near and far. Dawn had considered the option of finding her way in the cities of the east and west coasts and everywhere in between except of Kansas, she thought with a smile, but deeded to head east in order to experience the bright light and sounds of New York City.

When Dawn shared her travel interest with Ashley and asked if she would like to come along, Ashley took the time to consider it for a long moment but decided that she was going to head out west to try her hand at acting. After her mind filled with all of mumbo jumbo that Mary was always telling her about, Ashley wanted to see for herself if there was any validity to what she was saying.

The women embraced in a long hug, which appeared to be the bond of two sisters who knew of the turmoil each other had been through, before departing to be on their separate journeys in life. Dawn could have only hoped for Ashley to take care of herself but was glad to see the girl that she once came to know only briefly had often appeared on the television screen marketing an assortment of merchandise for different companies in broadcast commercials. As for Dawn? Well... Let's just say that her path took on a rather more interesting turn than the path of stardom.

Dawn may have had the worst kind of story to be told, but she was glad to have the bubbly personality which helped her to pull through the turmoil of her tumultuous experience. As Genie, Lauren, and Gloria could attest to, Dawn refused to be taken advantage of again without doing something about it. The four of them together could've easily been mistaken for the modern age version of 'Charlie's Angels' campaign with their very own 'Charlie's' to boot.

Chapter 19

"Hey, Genie! There's two guys out there practically begging to see you guys again!" a girl by the name of Chelsea said when she poked her head into the dressing-room door. Before any other word could be spoken, the door flew all the way open as Yitzy made his entrance. "That's right, ladies! It is I, your leader!" he lamented in jest before continuing on. "I hope to God that you are all going to spend as much time out there making money as you are in here sitting on your lazy butts!" he added in an attempt at sincerity as the ladies filed out of the room in hurry before coming to lose the job that helped them to put food on the table.

As the ladies made their way out the room in their skimpy attires, or those with naked breasts roaming freely, the four women with stern looks to their appearance remained.

"Do we need to hold hands together and pray, or do you ladies still remember how to get things done?" Yitzy joked in a way that only he could, with a sly grin that made everyone smile.

"That's why you pay us the big bucks, Yitz," Genie remarked as the other women chuckled.

Yitzy Hammond was the proprietor of the gentlemen's establishment artfully named 'The Pink Lotus.' A cunning and spirited individual from the sunny island of Barbados, Yitzy had personally selected his batch of angels to work simply for the common goal of making money. There wasn't much of a discrimination in his process of choice, just as long as those natural features of skin tone, height, breast size, and beautiful smiles, accompanied by the occasional wig and costume, remained to be effortless, Yitzy could care less about anything else. The four who stayed behind, however, remained to be by far his most interesting and favored of his employees.

"Okay, ladies! What's our motto?" Yitzy inquired as he scanned the faces in the room. Even if the ladies had an inclining of what he was yammering about, they wouldn't have indulged him, so he continued on, "Be polite. Smile brightly. And, most importantly, remember to come back without getting yourselves killed in the process!" he added with an emphasis which received the round of applause that made him blush. "Wise assess," Yitzy murmured, just before Dawn shot a hand to her forehead in salute while lamenting, "Yes, sir!!!" as though she were acknowledging his begrudging sentiment.

"Okay! Okay! Enough lollygagging! Get out there and make Daddy some money!" Yitzy commanded before adding for good measure, "And, Sky. I don't want any mishaps like the last time." To which he received the reply, "Anything for you, Yitzy baby," coming from Gloria whom he knew had a propensity to be a bit too instrumental in how she produced results. Satisfied that his directions were well-received, Yitzy departed after giving each woman a tight hug of support as he brought the phenomenon of his perceptible demeanor to play the gracious host to his room full of praying customers.

*****

"This is a night that I will cherish for years to come. I am truly honored, my dear," Boris implored, in an attempt at chivalry, as he grabbed ahold of Genie's hand and brought it to his lips in order to place a kiss softly above her knuckles. Genie blushed in return and replied, "I guarantee you; this will be a night that you will never forget."

"Boris!!! Look at this beautiful skin!" Yuri lamented as he started at Lauren's mocha-colored complexion. He was obviously still very drunk, but his demeanor was adorable, she thought, as Dawn chimed in with, "I hope I can get some of all this attention that everybody else is getting." She pouted her lips in dismay but quickly revealed a smile when Boris informed her, "Of course you will. I'll make sure of it personally. What about you?" he asked with a head nod toward Gloria's direction.

"Oh. You know Sky already. She's the one who was doing all of those fabulous stunts on the pole. She doesn't talk too much, but—"

"I'll make all of your dreams come true," Gloria implied as she cut Genie's statement short in a perfect pitch of Russian dialect which made both Boris and Yuri drop their jaws in astonishment. Boris stared at her speechless for a moment before managing to inquire, "What's the price?"

125

When Genie whispered in Boris's ear that the charge would be for him to pay two-thousand dollars for each girl in order to enjoy a night of passion, he scoffed at the notion and implored, "We are only interested in the best. And, since I think that you beautiful women are the best that money can buy, you each get five-thousand American! Don't worry. We have lots of money to spend," he boasted with maybe a bit too much of the liquor influencing his decision. The newly formed entourage piled into the limousine that Yuri reserved for the evening, and they all began to fondle each other on their way to where he and Boris were staying.

The limousine barked in front of an immaculate residential buildings which seemed to be designed for those accustomed to be a more distinguished taste in life. Gloria immediately came to notice that there were no doormen positioned in front of the residence, but an attendant stationed in the inviting interior was there to log in the entry of the guest.

The ladies all managed to keep their heads low as they giggled and huddled amongst Boris and Yuri who were actually telling them stories which were quite amusing. Gloria surveyed her surroundings and noticed that there were surveillance cameras positioned to monitor the comings and goings of everyone allowed entry into the residence and caught the eye of Lauren who apparently spotted them too when she smirked in return. Gloria could only assume that the elevators were equipped with the same sort of surveillance, but it wasn't much of a concern at the moment.

Gloria afforded herself a glance back at the concierge and saw that he was starting at their party with disdain. Not so much from the sight of the women the men found to be in their company, but what Gloria surmised to be the man harboring contempt for the two foreign residents who probably treated him as though he was nothing more than their callboy, similar to the way they just ushered the ladies past him without even acknowledging his presence. Gloria didn't think he would be much of a problem to them.

Just as Gloria presumed, there actually was an all-seeing eye that was able to capture a view of the entire cab which was juxtaposed high above in a corner of the ceiling next to the speaker system resonating the standard elevator music as the crowed metal conveyor made its ascension to the top floor. All of the women tried their best to obscure themselves from view, but all Gloria seemed to be focused on was…the kill.

The party spilled out of the elevator loudly as while soon finding themselves in front of one of the four penthouse doors that shared the floor. The timing couldn't be more perfect, Gloria thought, with the previous details she attained of the wealthy neighbors being away on excursions to travel countries abroad, or, in one particular instance, enjoying a trip navigating the seasoned waters of the ocean, bringing a sense of security to her mind.

Inside of the elaborate abode, the state-of-the-art lighting illuminated a wall of floor-to-ceiling windows which showcased the brilliant stars sprinkled amongst the shade of night. "Oooh!!! Look at all the fishies!!!" Dawn shrieked when she caught sight of the enormous water tank which was littered with bright tropical fish of all shapes and sizes.

"Let's party!!!" Yuri exclaimed happily while grabbing Lauren's hand and beginning to dance with her after pressing a button on a remote control which allowed the club music to blare from the speakers of the pricey home-tech system.

"Money," is what Genie whispered in Boris's ear. He stared at her briefly before emerging the grin that spread wide across his face as he responded sarcastically, "No money. No honey!!! IS how they say it in America, right? Well, not to worry. We can take care of business now," before walking toward the three-foot safe they had positioned in the room and punching in a code on the numbered keypad.

Gloria watched intently as Boris rummaged through the safe with his back turned to them. She was ready to do battle when he rapidly spun around but held fast to the notion after noticing that his hands were filled with her favorite color of green. "You want money?! We have lots of money!!!" Boris lamented in glee as he showered the room in bills, the way one would use rice to celebrate the union of a bride and groom at a wedding reception.

"Yeahhh!!!" Yuri roared as the bills of large denominations cascaded in the air like snowfall. Feeling in need of a 'pick me up,' he asked Lauren, "You like candy? I have some. Hey, Boris! Bring the powder!!!" he yelled out without the need for Lauren's response.

"I think he can read my mind sometimes," Boris confined to Genie as he went back into the safe and retrieved the half kilo of cocaine which he raised high in the air to display while loudly acknowledging, "I have the candy!!!"An announcement which caused the ladies to clap their hands in feigned appreciation.

When Yuri went over to take a seat on the plush leather sofa, Dawn and Lauren shared a wide-eyed glance in each other's directions. When he erected, Yuri came to display a large 45 caliber from the waist of his slacks and set it down on the coffee table. Noticing their trepidation, Yuri remarked, "That's right, ladies! Tonight, you party with a real gangster!" to which he received the reply, "But, I thought that was something else that was big inside of the limo," Dawn implied sheepishly as she did the thing again with pouting her lips in dismay.

It took Yuri a moment to process what Dawn meant, but he burst into spontaneous laughter when the meaning finally stuck him as he responded, "Don't worry. You will see soon that my other pistol is just as big!" Boris came over and poured out enough cocaine on the table to make a snowman, which Yuri wasted no time in attacking with his nose. Yuri inhaled deeply and simply muttered, "Candy," as he allowed his brain the time it needed to entwine with the euphoric effects of the narcotic.

Boris sat down next to Yuri in order to get his fill of the drug, but when he came to notice Gloria still standing off to the side while clutching her purse, he remarked in his native language, "Don't tell me that you learn how to be paranoid like a Russian woman too? No need to be nervous, my dear. We are friends here," just before stuffing his face once more into the pile of cocaine, the way his comrade Yuri had done.

Boris wanted to enjoy the 'Candy' to his mind's content, but instead of allowing the narcotic to take effect, his head was forcefully snapped back by a different kind of element as Gloria replied to the inquiry he raised in Russian, "I'm not paranoid. I just like to take care of business." No one seemed to notice when the unwelcomed sound of compressed air forced a projectile down the muzzle of Gloria's concealed weapon until it was too late as the hollow-tipped bullet found its mark with devastating accuracy.

Chapter 20

Now it was Yuri's turn to implement a wide-eyed look of his own, since he received the surprise of having the remnants of his longtime friend's blood and brain matter splashed across his face. He wanted to scream and yell as he reached for his weapon, but, by then, it was too late to do so, as Lauren plunged her knife deep into his earlobe and withdrew a blade quenched with the blood of its victim.

"And just when I was starting to like them too," Dawn remarked as Lauren retorted with a condescending smirk.

"You always like them." Dawn laughed as she countered with, "It must've been hard for you to kill that crazy one. I could tell you 'really' liked the way he was leaving all of those handprints on your ass," which caused everyone else to laugh as they shared in her humor.

"Damn, Sky! At least you could've warned me before you put a bullet in his head! Now I got his brains all over my new shirt!" Genie exclaimed with a look of disgust plastered across her face as she picked pieces of the vertebrate from her clothing.

"Sorry." She moved to the terrace in order to get a breath of fresh air while the rest of the ladies moved about the luxury residence, trying their best to make the scene seem as though a robbery had occurred.

Gloria took in the magnificent views from the spacious outdoor terrace without a thought in her mind as to what transpired indoors. She did, however, wonder if Ralph would've been proud of the way she chose to live, especially since she decided to follow in his footsteps, but she knew her inquiry would receive a bias response, since Ralph was always proud of what Gloria did, as any father would be of a daughter that he raised. A thought which made Gloria smile. She was now a hundred-thousand dollars richer, as were the other women, for their completion of the task of dispatching of the affable Boris

Ramov and his comrade, Yuri, at the behest of a Russian Pakhan named Nikolai Kroll.

With the collapse of the former Soviet Union, thugs and Mafiosi-like came to rule supreme over the land where corruption remained to be rampant. As a 'Pakhan' meaning boss or godfather in Russian, Nikolai Kroll wielded great heavy-handed power to remain one of the most treacherous Mafiosi in Moscow, as he engaged in the practices of extortion, blackmail, bribery, and pay-to-play type of techniques while forcing legitimate businessmen out of their financial holdings.

As a reinvented mob state, Nikolai was able to earn a vast fortune while plying his tradecraft of instilling fear and intimidation on those who failed to yield to the demands he proposed something which came to be a fairly easy thing for him to do, since, along with his loyal enforcers, Nikolai was able to maintain a beneficial connection to members of the former K.G.B. who still controlled access to all the weapons and spyware needed for him to stay on top of the food chain.

Boris Ramov and Yuri Shvetovich were actually two of Nikolai's most trusted enforcers and confidents until the day they decided that they themselves wanted to be men of great standing instead of living in the shadow of one. They conspired together to steal millions from under the nose of the 'Lion,' as Nikolai was known, from the many cash accounts and bearer bonds he held, before fleeing to the United States in the attempt to live in anonymity.

Luckily, the two were able to escape the clutches of the Lion who very much liked to be instrumental in the inflicting of pain and misery on those who dared to challenge his tyranny, through the use of use of torture methods. Most sessions were brutish and conducted without any forethought or planning, but the act of torture was practiced on a variety of levels nonetheless. Where some insisted the tactics in order to derive information from their subjects, Nikolai implemented the action just simply for the fun of causing immense pain to those he desired as though he were addicted to the torment technique the way a sadist might be, for the delightful joy of feeling the surge of power.

Anywhere from plugging electrodes to a person's body to shoving their faces into a pile of human excrement was all fair game to Nikolai, but the Lion's favorite method, by far, had to be the implementation for conducting what the Russians refer to as a 'Zamochit' which happened to be the term for a symbolic kind of murder by torture that left every bone in the recipient's body severely broken.

Nikolai wanted nothing more than to follow his traitors to the land of America in order to dispatch of them by the force of his own two hands, but he knew that the option was an almost impossible task to accomplish. The Lion knew, for example, that he would find himself immediately 'red flagged' by whatever watchful eye the C.I.A. chose, who so desperately wanted to question him for his role in being tied to an arms dealer under the suspicion for providing arms to the notoriously violent terror groups whose sole intent was bringing an end to the 'Infidels.' Which was a term that roughly translated to America and all of its loyal allies.

Another option for Nikolai was for him to extend the long arm of his power by having the Russian Mafiosi in the States extinguish his troubles for him, but always in true fashion, the Russians were notorious themselves for drinking too much and bringing unwanted attention to themselves by carving out a bloody trail of destruction everywhere their services were engaged. No, Nikolai needed an outlet of his discretion in the event that if anything happened to go wrong, the mishap couldn't be traced back to him by the authoritative powers of America, which is how he came about to seek the help that the female persuasion could provide.

"Got it!!!" Genie announced in satisfaction as Gloria made her way back into the residence. Genie had found what she been searching for in the safe which was concealed in a thick manila envelope. The ladies found themselves gathered around to view the contents of.

"Well, Let's see 'em!" Dawn said excitedly as she rubbed her hands together on anticipation. "Ooohhh!!!" the ladies all crooned in unison as Genie revealed the hidden bearer bonds totaling to be about 20-million dollars of guaranteed funding to its holder.

"So that's what being rich looks like," Lauren commented with an implication that received chuckles of agreement. "No wonder their boss wanted them killed," Genie added in a statement which was only part true.

Nikolai 'The Lion' Kroll felt deeply betrayed by his confidants, but even more so, he came to feel angry with himself for not being more astute to the goings on around him and intercepting the threat of their treachery long before it began. Yuri was actually the brains of their deceit, as he found a way to hack into Nikolai's personal account and discreetly removed five million dollars of the Lion's ill-gotten funds through the use of several wire transfers to shell accounts which were extremely difficult to detect. A tactic that Yuri learned while training alongside the former K.G.B. in order to exact the same form of trickery that was implemented to steal from countless others before the fall of the Union.

Boris played his own part by being the one who dealt with the business end of things where he set up the fences who would purchase the stolen bonds at a reasonable fraction of the cost and providing them with the fake passports and documents needed for them to escape the country. He was also the one who smiled brightly for the broker and tenant board who allowed them residency in the lavish building, especially since they were able to acquire the accommodation being offered at asking price.

The Lion was able to secure the information he needed about his traitors easy enough, although, to his dismay, it took only the cutting of just one finger from the men who sold the pair the forged documents to Boris and Yuri to get the details he required, so Nikolai cut off another one just to make up for the disappointment of not being able to torture the man more fully to his liking. He forwarded the aliases the two were traveling under to a faction of the Russian Mafiosi in the States, with the strict orders to simply monitor the movements of his prey without intercepting them or being detected until he gave further instruction.

When Nikolai received word that Boris and Yuri never even bothered to waiver from the aliases they assumed, and even made the more-egregious mistake of becoming bold enough to lavish themselves in pricey jewelry and clothing, all while making the preparations to move into their newly acquired penthouse with the use of his money, Nikolai knew then that it was where he wanted them to die as he sought for the experienced help he needed to carry out his requirements.

Where the extravagant abode was once immaculately maintained, Gloria now looked to see that the other ladies did an excellent job of leaving things in disarray as though a tornado had passed through, leaving in its wake a trail of destruction, in their attempt to make the surroundings seem a lot more than just a mere assassination. The tables were turned over along with the chairs. Every room in the three-bedroom accommodation was searched, with the closets and dresser drawers receiving the bulk of the attention along with the mattresses being cut open to seem as though someone were looking to find something within them.

Even the two bathrooms and kitchen area were thoroughly checked, as the ladies left nothing overlooked while gathering everything they found to be of value and placing it in the center of the living-room floor to be transported with them.

"What?!" Dawn asked when Gloria's gaze landed on her while Dawn appraised the brilliant cut of a diamond ring before stuffing it in her pocket. "Yuri already know that I have a fetish for diamonds, Sky!" Dawn implored as Lauren interjected with, "Did she forget to mention all of the male strippers who's been leaving her broke?"

Dawn laughed before retorting with, "So what? If they can ogle us, why can't we do it to them? Besides, they're a good return on my investment, and let's not forget who's been accompanying me on a few of those trips to see them," Dawn added with a statement that caused Lauren to blush, as she recounted the few times in her mind.

Gloria smiled at how crazy the girls were, but before Dawn could make her joke about not being some rich millionaire with an envelope full of bearer bonds to purchase her own male servants, she immediately became defensive when she saw Genie hand Lauren a gun and point it in the direction that made her eyes widen with fear.

"No! No! No! They are innocent in all of this!" Dawn exclaimed as Lauren raised her aim in the direction of the large fish tank.

"You're willing to put your life on the line over a bunch of scaly fish?" Gloria asked incredulously with a smirk on her face.

"Yesss!!! They're my friends, and I love them all!!!" Dawn lamented adamantly as she stuck her arms out and turned her head to the side while closing her eyes in protest as though the gun were set to discharge at any moment. A feigned reaction which caused them all to burst into laughter until Genie tried to bring things to order by saying, "Okay, the fish live. Now, enough bullshitting, ladies! Let's get the hell out of here before Yitzy kills us all for taking too long to come back!"

"Take care, lovers," Dawn demurred just before blowing a kiss in Boris and Yuri's direction where they were both still positioned on the sofa with shocked expressions of wide-eyed stares etched across their faces. Or in Boris's case, what was left of his, as the ladies made their way out of the residence. They each donned a pair of oversized sunglasses, after taking the measures to apply just enough makeup to distort their natural features. Genie and Dawn already wore wigs that actually resembled the real thing, as Lauren and Gloria styled their hair to further enhance their anonymity.

Before leaving, however… "What?" Dawn inquired innocently as Genie held out her hand. She knew it was useless to act as though she was naïve to what Genie was requesting for too long, especially when Genie came to imply, "You do want to save the little fishies, don't you?" Dawn gave up the ruse instantly and dug into her pocket to get out the diamond ring she discovered, which was big enough for her to slide two fingers through, and dumped it into Genie's palm while huffing with a disgruntled look on her face.

Genie appraised the ring herself for a moment and simply said, "This could help us out," just before wiping it clean of any prints and dumping it into the water tank to Dawn's dismay. The ring appeared to be in a value of over 50-thousand dollars which may provide the unsuspecting police with an ulterior motive to the death scene when they eventually came to investigate as Dawn hopelessly watched it sink to the bottom.

"Not cool," she murmured until Lauren perked up her spirits by implying, "Don't worry. I'll buy you one for Christmas." To which Dawn responded, "You promise? The same size and everything?" She bemused as they exited the abode to leave Boris and Yuri to themselves.

The ladies kept their heads low in the elevator as planned but made the motions as though they were still just a bunch of girls out having a fun time, as the glare of the surveillance camera stared on. When the ladies reached the lower level, they spilled out of the conveyor as though they were enjoying all of the spirits the night had to offer and were only mildly relieved to see that the concierge who had been stationed at the desk beforehand had since been replaced by an older gentleman who stared at them salaciously as the ladies were making their way toward the exit through the lobby.

Apparently, ladies of the night often made their way in and out of the luxury residence in order to discreetly visit the wealthy men and sometimes women of their choosing with financial gain for a night of passion while their significant others were away. A circumstance which became evident as the attendant continued to follow the movements of the ladies with a lustful gaze in his eyes without inquiring anything about where the women may have been coming from.

Genie and Lauren exchanged nervous glances with each other when they came to see Dawn rummaging through her purse. They began to fear for the worst when she suddenly broke away from their pack and headed straight for the creepy concierge with roaming eyes as though she was going to shoot him right there in the lobby.

"Dawn, get back here," Genie mumbled harshly but only in a whisper, since she didn't want to bring their team any unwanted attention, or to Dawn, who Genie was going to personally shoot herself if she did anything to compromise the operation, but it was already too late for Dawn to be stopped as Gloria just stood off to the side and smiled.

When Dawn made her approach, the concierge tried his best to act as though he wasn't just stalking them with his eyes only seconds ago, as he found a bunch of papers to shuffle around to aid in his attempt at seeming busy. As Dawn neared, however, the attendant couldn't resist the temptation any longer but soon became absolutely surprised by what she did next. No words were exchanged between them when Dawn grabbed his face in her hands and pulled it to her lips in an action which caused the attendant to turn beet red with embarrassment as she planted a kiss on his mouth.

The concierge nervously darted his eyes around the lobby to see if anyone may have saw what happened while Dawn demurred, "If you're ever looking for a good time, handsome, make sure you give me a call, lover boy." She implied just before slowly licking her top lip to further peak his arousal and sliding over a business card marketing an escort service to him across the counter.

The card Dawn gave the attendant was embedded with the signature of 'Amber' scribbled on it in red ink which was accompanied by a phone number at the bottom to contact for the request of services. Dawn whispered, "You can have me and all of my friends to yourself if you want, but don't keep us waiting for too long, or somebody else just might come and snatch us up first."

"We wouldn't want that now, would we?" the attendant found the words to say, and, in reply, Dawn silently shook her head from side to side while mouthing the word 'no' before winking at him and walking to a round of applause from the other ladies who were lying in wait.

While Dawn was away to engage the attendant, Gloria informed the others of her intentions. Gloria told them that it was that it was actually her who came to find the alluring card stuck in the crevice of a telephone booth in a

Laundromat for advertisement and confided to Dawn that she wanted to plant it at the scene in order to throw off any attempts to readily identify them as witnesses while conjuring the name of 'Amber' to sign on the card.

Dawn volunteered to take the deception a bit further by playing her role with the concierge who, most certainly, posed to be a threat to their team as a witness. A factor, which was why the two women decided to leave the calling card which could, in no way, be traced back to them.

The ladies all giggled amongst themselves and waved goodbye to the attendant whom they would never encounter again, as Genie carried the duffel bag of the requested bearer bonds along with everything else they managed to collect, which would be evenly distributed amongst them later as an added tip for a job well done, while they discussed what they should do to celebrate. "I don't know about anyone else, but I usually feel absolutely ravenous for the taste of a well-done steak after completing an assignment," Gloria implied with every bit of a sly grin etched across the extent of her face.

Chapter 21

After taking the standard two weeks needed to disengage themselves from any given mission, the ladies were all once again summoned to Yitzy's office to discuss the terms of their next endeavor. "They're getting younger and younger as the days go by, aren't they, Yitzy?" Genie commented dryly as they all watched the look of a new girl who was trying her hardest to awkwardly straighten the skimpy clothing she wore while making her way out of the boss' office as Yitzy smiled in the girl's wake, feeling satiated.

Pulling the strings on the robe he wore even tighter around his waist, Yitzy remarked, "If they are old enough to work here at our fine establishment and buy drinks at the bar, then, certainly, they're fair game to travel on the road of lust with yours truly," he replied in jest with a statement that garnered sneers and jeers from his team of lady killers who couldn't blame Yitzy all that much for the amount of aloofness he displayed.

Far from the traits of some common pimp, Yitzy actually endeared the many women who ventured in and out of his life over the years, with the utmost respect and admiration forwarded to them. An aspect which, in turn, enabled him to implement those very same mannerisms into literally charming the pants off of the women who just wanted to show Yitzy their gratitude in return, after receiving the caring ways he showered them to be along the lines of a true Casanova. A characteristic Yitzy was able to maintain ever since he was the age of a little boy in his native country of Barbados.

"Come on in and let's talk business," Yitzy instructed to his troops who all crooned, "Yesss, Daddy!!!" in return before piling into the room and finding seats on the comfortable sofa and chairs scattered about in the office. "Always the wiseasses," Yitzy mused in delight as a smile emerged on the exterior of his face despite the looming seriousness of the proposition he had to convey to the women, which hanging on the balance.

"What's up, Yitzy? You paying us for another girl's night out in the town or what?" Dawn asked excitedly with an inquiry that reigned partially true, since the women mostly operated on solo missions until circumstances such as the Boris and Yuri affair called for them to work together as a team. Yitzy happily responded, "You guessed right, my dear. It seems that due to the resulting efficiency by which the last job was completed, the services we have to offer are now being highly sought after. Thanks in part, to the vigorous recommendations of a very pleased Nikolai Kroll who's been praising our ongoing efforts of anyone who cared to listen."

Not a single word of Yitzy's proclamation needed to be overstated, since he suddenly found himself stuck with the daunting task of fielding the many requests he came to receive from an unrelenting slew of underhanded aficionados who required the expertise of his lady killers to tackle assignments which bordered on the mundane to the more outrageous requirements such as the killing of the Pope or the Queen of England.

The women all groaned in unison after learning the details of their next assignment. Dawn took it especially hard after she came to think that all the possibilities entailing her to have a good time were now hopelessly lost.

"So, you mean to tell us that we don't get to shoot anything?" she asked in belligerence in the attempt to salvage some of the enthusiasm she felt prior to hearing the details involved.

"Unfortunately, there may no longer be any need for it on this mission," Yitzy commented with a response that received him a round of 'boos!!!' from the ladies who weren't all too pleased with the information they were being provided with.

*****

The next endeavor the ladies were to embark on, consisted of a simple snatch-and-grab of some computer geek who happened to be in possession of some vital information which was to be extracted or disposed of by any means necessary. Someone was willing to pay a handsome amount of money for his capture, which is where Yitzy and his ladies became involved. Their job was to make the abduction and hold onto their quarry until he would later be transferred into the hands of those who would most likely torture the software hacker for the intelligence that they desired.

"Ha!!!" In a burst of laughter, Dawn's funny bone was tickled pink by the way in which their target's name sounded as it rolled off the tip of her tongue. "Peter Steeber?!?! That's got to be a joke, right?!" she asked with amused skepticism as Lauren interjected with, "It sounds like a 'Noogie' waiting to happen." A statement which continued to bring on the laughter from the ladies who were all trying their best, at this point, to warm up to the prospect of what needed to be done. Yitzy, on the other hand, remained stone-faced as he retrieved a yellow legal envelope and produced a photograph of their prize for examination.

"That's right, my little freaks!" Yitzy began as the trace of a smirk formed on his face. "It's not nice to make fun of effect," as his team of women gawked at the photos they were given with wide-eyed looks of mesmerized awe.

"I saw him first!!!" Dawn lamented with glee.

"In your dreams, Sister, he's mine!!!" Genie countered as Lauren implored. "Why would he want either of you two heifers when he can have all of this here," she admonished them along with the movements of her body to match those of a belly dancer.

Gloria tried her best to remain impassive about the feelings she felt, but she had to admit to herself that the person displayed in the photographs wasn't your typical computer nerd of yore who implemented the use of thick bifocaled glasses to go along with the neatly pressed white dress shirt that his mother ironed to hold firm the over-accessorized pocket protector baring the sharpened pencils and pens of different color variations. No. The man staring back at Gloria now, as though he were posing for a spread in the pages of G.Q. magazine, didn't seem to be in the need for any orthodontic retainer as far as she could tell.

"Peter... Peter... Please be my pu—"

"Hey, young lady!!! This such!" Yitzy implored just in time to cut short the lust-filled diction Dawn was set to convey, which was to be a sort of twisted nursery rhyme, ending with the word of 'eater' at the finish of its catch phrase. Granted that their present place of business consisted of an erotic and sensual nature, but Dawn got the gist of Yitzy's sentiment nonetheless as she smiled salaciously before using a hand motion to stimulate the appearance of her mouth being zipped shut.

The pictures the women were shown depicted a glimpse of their target in his everyday appearance, as he dressed in an assortment of designer threads while sporting a pair of wire-rimmed glasses that seemed to help accentuate the look of his model-like features all the more acutely. The ladies also found themselves impressed by the bright red, imported sports car he drove which appeared to be further illustrating all the makings of the extravagant lifestyle he'd come to lived.

From the corner of his eye, Yitzy could see that Dawn was chomping at the bit to say something, as she coyly bounced up and down on the balls of her feet in the attempt to uphold her end of the promise to remain quiet. When he raised a hand in her direction, Dawn rapidly released a slew of words as though they were freeing themselves from deep within the bowels of her gut. Without daring to pause for a breath in between her words, she blurted out, "I just want every day to know that if I miraculously become a holy woman and began praying to God, I would ask that an exact replica of this man to be the father of my children. And, if that doesn't work, I'll be willing to sell my soul to the devil for the favor."

After the laughs were shared at Dawn's expense, the team became serious once more as they broke down the details of the assignment. Apparently, the man known to them as Peter Steeber was a much sought-after computer hacker who made himself available to the likes of those who were willing to pay him a large amount of money to do what he did best… Create havoc through the use of cyber terrorism and embezzlement by fraudulently pilfering funds from the coffers of government and those established in a wealthy life of opulence and affluence.

The background specifics on their target was surprisingly detailed. A white male of American descent, Mr. Steeber was groomed in the ways of a child prodigy as he became homeschooled in the advanced courses of Science and Mathematics while being classically conditioned to perform as a trained pianist. For a time, a young Peter found it intriguing to perform the stylings of Mozart and Beethoven for the appeasement of family members and friends, but it all changed when, as birthday present at the age of nine years old, he was given his first computer system along with a manual which allowed him to learn and understand the physical representation of binary digits by an electrical pulse to carry out, control, or produce his intentions by the means of a central processing unit.

Converging to be quite the computer technologist, Mr. Steeber could've easily went on to start his very own electronic communications company, similar to the likes of Mark Zuckerberg who founded Facebook, or what Sergey Brin and Larry Page of Google had all gone to establish themselves as technological giants, but after he endured years of being forced to adhere to the strict guidelines his parents had instilled for him to succeed in life, it was natural for young Peter to engage himself in the thralls of teenage mischief as he found a way to illegally hack into his first software system at the age of 15 by using a seemingly innocuous program to download a virus into the government's very own database. An action which, at the time, was enough to disrupt the distribution of payment checks to government employees as high as the president himself.

The practice of computer piracy came to be what made Peter's image. As such, he made use of the codename. 'The Pillager' had been to the amusement of his fellow hackers or those who would eventually come to seek the services he had to offer. The Pillager had been doing quite well for himself until he decided to engage himself in a little extracurricular fun by once again misappropriating the fund he was originally paid to steal from those who had hired him to pilfer the funds in the first place.

The Pillager would, in turn, take a large percentage of the ill-gotten monies he received and rewire them through a slew of bank transfers before he finally used it to make charitable contributions to various associations such as the Children's Aid Society, The Animal Wildlife Conservancy, and The Feed, the hungry-type campaigns. To add further insult in jest, The Pillager would often ensure that a tax-deductible receipt was forwarded to those he deceived which would also include a letter of acclaim from the organizations praising them for their continuing efforts to make the world a better place to live. Something most would find to be a hilarious gesture, while others couldn't find themselves being so amused by the prank.

The Pillager also held sway over the secrets kept by those who thought they were able to protect their most valued information from the detection of spyware capabilities. A heavy-handed power he wielded as leverage after being able to crash through the firewalls shielding the interests which were to remain hidden. The tactic worked well when he wished to hold those he deceived at bay, but there remained the others who could be relentless in their pursuits, which is how the contract arrangement to apprehend The Pillager fell into the lap of Yitzy and his capable team of women enforcers.

For the currency of three-million dollars, most underhanded aficionados would put an end to an entire country in order to attain such a reward, but that was the amount being offered to simply catch and detain the one man who was in possession of information for which someone was willing to pay such a high sum, to never have such sensitive details divulged for the scrutiny of public attention.

*****

To the trained eye, apprehending their subject would be as easy as shooting fish in a barrel, with the amount of information at their disposal having been perfectly detailed to accomplish the task effortlessly. But, to Gloria and the other ladies involved, who were professionals at their craft, the instance would've certainly raised some red flags for them immediately, with the strong possibility looming that they were being baited into a trap by the threat of authorities who may have been seeking to put an end to what they did best.

Yitzy had vehemently expressed the fact that the contract was placed upon him from a reliable source with whom he's conducted decades of business with over the years. The ladies never bothered to question the circumstance any further, since he always dealt with the business end of the arrangement as a 'broker' without any resulting backlash occurring.

"And, besides," Yitzy reiterated. "Need I remind you ladies that this is the very same three-million dollars that I'd be willing to chop my right hand off for?" The team of women were informed that the entire amount of the reward would be evenly distributed amongst them without Yitzy taking his usual 50-percent off the top, but they were also warned to be on guard for the potential threat of a trap despite Yitzy's reservations.

As a decisive measure, Yitzy made the determination that it would be best for Gloria to be the one who took charge of detaining their quarry, Peter 'The Pillager' Steeber, until the time was appropriate for them to make the requested transfer to those who would later extract the information they desired by implementing whatever means it took for them to do so. The designation obviously didn't bode well with Dawn who immediately took to staring at Gloria with daggers in her gaze, as though Gloria may never live to see another day, for the act of snatching her dream man completely out of her grasp.

142

Dawn raised an arm to her face and pointed her two fingers at her eyes before turning the aim in Gloria's direction and mouthing the words, 'I got my eyes on you.' Gloria knew that Dawn's hidden innuendo had the threat of being about 80 percent true, but it was all done in jest, although Gloria felt happy nonetheless that the responsibility for being in charge of their subject was bestowed upon her, before Dawn had the opportunity to jeopardize their entire mission in the attempt to have a big nerdy family with the captive.

Yitzy based his selection of Gloria on the premise that the other ladies were often summoned to engage their targets with the ruse of lust in order for them to get close enough to dispatch of their marks per the requirements of those who arranged the contract, while Gloria, on the other hand, preferred to make her kills with the standard precision and dejection of a professional assassin without the need for any beating around the bush with her emotions.

There was the one time, however, for which Yitzy had no other alternative than to ask that Gloria indulge the favor of the one target who was a high-ranking member of a treacherous Mexican drug central, who willingly committed acts of genocide against the very people of his own country in order to further profit from the spoils of his organization's narcotics distribution and sex trafficking rackets, which all tallied to bringing in billions of dollars a year in revenue.

Chapter 22

The problem lied in where the man known as 'La Lobo' or what translates to be 'The Wolf' in English sustained a constant employ of men who were all trained in the tactics of guerilla warfare and held a penchant for killing without any forbearance to dissuade their efforts of tyranny. An army of these men were paid handsomely to provide The Wolf the protection he needed as he roamed the vast area of his estate or the territories for which his organization *'La chusmo de Bandidos,'* 'Mob of Bandits,' maintained a stronghold.

The Wolf's men also heeded his wishes to instill the wrath of fear and intimidation on those who opposed the rule of his organization's capabilities. A factor which often meant the brutal attempts of assassinations, beheadings, torture, and the vindictive death threats of family members to coincide with the acts of extortion, blackmail, and the vile measures of snatching young girls as old as the age of 12 from the comfort of their loving families to sell them off as sex slaves to the highest bidder on the black market.

To come close enough for a kill of The Wolf in his native country was virtually impossible. An opportunity arose, however, when those who had purchased the deathly pact to dispatch of him happened upon the information that The Wolf would be venturing out of his comfort zone for a chance encounter to reinsert the power of his distribution capabilities stateside with a new dealer, whom The Wolf would meet with personally, to discuss expending the business of his narcotics operation from the current states of Texas, Arizona, California, and Florida, to engage the ever-lucrative illicit trade of New York's underground market.

Somehow, Yitzy always found a way to bring to the attention of the discerning men he had an interest in the superb fact that he employed the best women of persuasion that money could buy. The happenstance was no different this time around, as Yitzy managed to work his many connections to lure the regards of his target to the services he had to offer, after The Wolf took to renting an entire floor in the famed Waldorf Astoria hotel for him and his men until he was able to conclude his business with the associate he sought out.

It had only been a few hours since The Wolf had arrived in the city, but he instantly felt the sudden need to have the pleasure of a woman to accompany him for the evening which was to be a much-welcomed change of pace from the constant sight of the stone-faced men under his employ who were currently scanning the walls of their surroundings with bug detectors to ensure the privacy of their accommodations.

After The Wolf summoned one of his men and whispered in his ear, a call was made to the downstairs concierge in order to express The Wolf's regard, to wit, a separate call was made by the very same concierge who relayed the message, "Well, you were right. It appears that our humble guest of corruption, Enrique 'La Lobo' Calderon, has developed quite the appetite for which he desires to be placated by the services you have to offer." Yitzy smiled on the receiving end of the conversation and responded, "Well done. You know what to do now," before ending the communication and interlocking his fingers to rest just below his lower lip to continue enjoying the score of an opera musical, which wafted melodically through the speakers in his office, as he waited for a return call on the update of the target.

Unlike the circumstances of the latest assignment the ladies were given, where the building attendants were not known to them beforehand, the concierge in place at the Waldorf Astoria was actually a much cherished and longtime friend of Yitzy's ever since the two were young men of the '60s and '70s. At the time, Yitzy was a wide-eyed tourist seeking his first American experience, while Arthur Shultz, on the other hand, who was affectionately named 'Artie,' was seeking to radicalize the existing views, habitual conditions, and institutions of government through the use of advocating the measures of extreme change to restore a political state of affairs to the country.

After crossing paths on a chance encounter in the midst of enjoying the spoils of a marijuana smoke fest, the two men became the best of friends and extended their association to working together as pickpockets swindlers and even stickup men, committing a slew of heists together. The proceeds of which Yitzy used to secure a bank loan and began his dream of establishing the gentlemen's club he founded to double as a safe haven for his team of female assassins. Arty couldn't see the long-term potential of Yitzy's dream at the time, so he followed his own calling and tried his hand at being a trader on the open market of the stock exchange before moving on to becoming a promoter of rock bands and nightclubs.

Arty had been doing quite well for himself until the life he sought to achieve threw him a curveball when he became financially cash strapped after the bulk of the money he invested on stocks were hopelessly lost when the market suffered a severe crash and left him bankrupt. On top of that humiliation, while not properly managing the band he was promoting, Arty had become somewhat of a 'Roadie' for the rockers who, instead of sticking to the schedule of their performance dates, would rather indulge in the acts of hard partying and the heavy use of drugs instead. A circumstance which almost cost Arty his life after he found himself overdosing on the very narcotics he began to use to cope with the many setbacks he was facing, until he finally made a way back into the care of Yitzy who provided him with every means needed for Arty to rehabilitate from his minting troubles.

Arty refused any of the financial handouts that Yitzy tried to offer him and became adamant about getting by the hard way. In gratitude for Yitzy's ongoing efforts to assist him, Arty took on odd jobs to help with the furtherance of establishing 'The Pink Lotus' by handing out flyers to advertise the services the club had to offer for the public attention of the men who would soon frequent the club.

Anything Arty may have needed was at his disposal, although he was comfortable enough to slumber on a small cot set aside for him in the basement of the Pink Lotus. All meals were provided to him free of charge from the club's restaurant grade chefs, but Arty also liked to prepare his own meals to suit to his liking. He worked as the doorman and bouncer for a time, until the day when Yitzy approached him about the to-go on a clandestine mission of his own.

As the time went on, Arty found it easier to make the sort of transition that the ladies found themselves becoming accustomed to doing, until the day he came to fall hard for a wonderful woman by the name of Roxanne, who was a resident dancer in the establishment, who began to take sensitive notice of his rough and tumble nature. The two ultimately fell deeply in love, but the day when Roxanne became pregnant with the couple's first child, Arty knew that the life Yitzy had presented for him to create a more purposeful existence for himself had to be replaced by the new means Arty had to provide for the family which meant more to him now than the feeling of his own breath.

It wasn't long before the couple welcomed their second child, both of whom were sponsored by Yitzy as the proud godfather. Through his list of contacts, Yitzy was able to procure the very position Arty worked at, now the Woldorf Astoria, by convincing the manager of the time to give his troubled but eager friend a chance at becoming a more productive member of society's working class.

The opportunity allowed Arty to perform the labor of functioning as a bellhop until he was able to rise in the ranks to finally overtake the position of management after the previous one, who happened to be a frequent patron of the Pink Lotus, went on to retire. Arty has since held the prominent title of being the chief supervisor of the fame hotel which allowed him, over the year, to create a substantial base of his own amongst the other hoteliers of different establishments, reservationists, and a host of previous, current, and future guests of all fashions. A circumstance Yitzy was able to benefit from greatly as a beneficiary of Arty's success.

*****

Although they would've been able to track him down wherever he may have landed anyway, The Wolf's arrival at the Waldorf Astoria was purely coincidental. As a result, however, Arty was able to make the best of the situation by personally delivering the yellow envelope he carried on a silver platter so that the contents could be viewed by The Wolf or a determination on what could be done to confirm to his wishes for the evening.

After a knock on the door was answered by the burly guard within, The Wolf appeared seconds after Arty made his introduction and stated the nature of his business for being there. When The Wolf removed the envelope from the platter, Arty implied the message, "I hope you find these to your liking, Senior Calderon. If not, please do not hesitate to inform me of what I can do to assist you any further."

The civility The Wolf was shown was a hidden secret which was commonplace amongst the high-class establishments such as the Waldorf Astoria who welcomed the presence of government officials, foreign dignitaries, and the likes of those who enjoyed the comity of social affluence in all walks of life, wishing to escape the glare of public scrutiny by indulging in the pleasures they discreetly sought.

The Wolf found himself to be instantly delighted as he viewed the selection of about ten women who were all of model-like quality in their own right, as the photographs depicted them while striking poses and smiling coyishly for the lens of the camera. About midway through the selections, The Wolf's heart skipped a beat when his gaze landed upon the sight of a Spanish woman who stared back at him with nonconformity to her appearance.

Sweat began to form on The Wolf's brow as the lascivious thoughts of his considerations became easily discernible on the extent of his wide-eyed expression of glee. A search for another choice was no longer needed as he replaced the rest of the photographs back into the yellow business envelope and gave it to one of his men who returned it to the manager standing in wait. The Wolf began to mumble something incoherently in a Spanish dialect as he stared into the eyes of the woman who reflected such a fierce intensity that it made his body quiver from the sheer anticipation of making her the latest conquest of his passions.

"Senior. If you can bring this…this woman to me, I will truly be grateful to you," The Wolf stated in his deeply accented English as he held high the photograph of his selection as though to highlight her mesmerizing appeal for all to behold.

"It shall be done, Senior Calderon. I will have her sent up to you immediately upon her arrival, sir," Arty responded in kind as the Wolf waved a hand in the direction of one his men who removed a thickened envelope containing what was to be the payment for the services rendered.

After his task was completed, Arty rode the elevator down in silence until the trace of a smile formed on his face. The role he played in delivering the photographs for The Wolf's consideration allowed Arty the time he needed to assess the amount of problems The Wolf and his men would be for the endgame. When he reached the privacy of his office, Arty immediately contacted Yitzy on a secure line to provide an update of his findings.

It appeared that The Wolf had only been accompanied by the five men who were all no-nonsense strongmen, willing to put their lives out on a limb to for the sake of their beloved leader. The expenditure to rent an entire floor seemed to be a bit of an overindulgence, but like many men of wealth, The Wolf didn't even bother to flinch at the price suggested which could often reach in the excess of ten-thousand dollars for a weekly endeavor.

From the looks of what he could gather, Arty didn't see much of a problem that Gloria couldn't handle. Especially after he remembered the few times when she was stacked up against odds, which were twice the amount of what The Wolf encounter could offer, before emerging unscathed and eager to complete another assignment. The problem now lay in trying to convince Gloria to actually commit to the endeavor with the extent amount of sexual tension involved.

The task of informing Gloria what she needed to do was something Arty was glad he didn't have to be a part of. That headache was left solely for Yitzy to strive against, knowing fully well the propensity of Gloria's adamance about not receiving such an assignment. Yitzy actually had to consider the option of protecting himself asking of her, but he knew then that the only way to go about it was to be straightforward with his intention.

"Is that supposed to make me feel any better?!" Gloria asked with disdain after hearing what Yitzy had to say about the circumstances at hand, concerning her needed involvement.

"Look. It's not like you have to go and actually have sex with the guy. Just go in there, make nice, then kill The Wolf and his men with the same pretty smile you used to greet him with," Yitzy replied to Gloria's concern with a statement that finally brought her to consider the possibilities of what the mission entailed.

*****

When the time came to encounter The Wolf, Gloria was ready, although it took a lot of preparation on her part to do so. What she did was try to channel the ever-bubbly personality of Dawn, who also doubled as a licensed sexual therapist on her own time, by making her kills as though she were some kind of deranged serial killer. A tactic which suited Gloria well for the moment as she practiced the intricacy of being submissive to the audience of a bathroom mirror in order to achieve the type of believability she sought for actually being a call girl to go along with her overall character.

At the mere sight of Gloria in his presence, The Wolf's palate began to salivate. He often touted himself to be quite the Casanova, but the truth happened to be that he held a propensity for committing acts of violence against the women who rejected his come-ons, by Wolf forcefully inducing his passions on them against their will. Gloria had already been informed of the form of encounter that he would soon live to regret.

"Would you care for a drink, my dear?" The Wolf inquired in his rough-hewn form of Spanish dialect as he made his way over to where an array of liquids were encased in crystal decanters. Gloria thought of playing coy to the fact that she didn't understand the language of Spanish, or maybe that she didn't consume in liquor, but decided that to take anything from The Wolf's desire would limit her ability to achieve the closeness she needed in order to complete the mission successfully, so she planned to go along with the ruse, until the perfect opportunity arose for her to implement her calculated attack.

The men under The Wolf's employ tried their best to seem impassive to the matter, but it was obvious that they were enraptured by Gloria's presence as well. An anomaly she planned to use to her full advantage as she seductively rolled her tongue around the folds of her lips and smiled flirtatiously in their direction just before the host turned to receive the answer he sought.

"I try not to drink too often, but, yes, I'll have a glass of whatever you're having," Gloria responded in English to The Wolf's offer with all the poise of a primed debutante before he became any wiser to her scheme.

With his back to her, The Wolf busied himself by preparing their drinks and turned to reveal the stemware glasses that were filled only a quarter of the way with a dark-colored wine baring the strong aroma of its fermented juices. Gloria accepted the glass from The Wolf's outstretched hand and followed his lead when The Wolf tipped the glass he held for himself and emptied the contents in one swallow.

"Mmmm," Gloria hummed in delight as she savored the rich flavor of the drink while The Wolf gaged her reactions.

The center of attention now, Gloria knew that she needed some separation to escape the ogling glances of the enforcers who stood off to the side, betraying their boss' indulgence by staring at her toned legs which were barely covered under the short dress she wore. In the attempt, Gloria began to nervously rub at her arms as though she were trying to soothe the emerging goose bumps stemming from her trepidation.

"Is everything all right?" The Wolf asked with genuine, wide-eyed concern.

In a faint whisper, Gloria responded, "Well, yes. But… I do not think I can handle all of you by myself."

"Ah!!!" The Wolf exulted as he caught onto the meaning of what Gloria was trying to convey. With a wave of his hand, the lingering men immediately began to disperse from the area in order to give their boss the privacy he commanded. The Wolf's next statement of, "Shall we begin?" was accompanied by the sinister smirk and wicked gleam in his eye which caused Gloria's previously false reaction of becoming nervous an actual one this time around as she stared into the eyes of a man who began to give her the creeps.

Gloria made the inquiry, "May I use your restroom to freshen up a bit?" To which, her host responded, "Of course you may. Come. I'll show you the way." With a total of three bathrooms to compliment the four-bedroom accommodation, Gloria was relying heavily on chance that the first restroom she was escorted to was the one where Arty planted the extra assistance she needed to successfully complete the mission with ease. When they arrived at a door, The Wolf made the statement, "You know what they say about 'Time is money'? Although I do have lots of money to spend on passion, I would much rather attend to it quickly than to waste my money foolishly."

Although it took all of her strength to do so, Gloria managed to evoke a smile on her face before responding, "I just to need two minutes to make sure that everything is how it should be for your personal enjoyment." By the time she was done with her excuse, Gloria was happy enough just to escape The Wolf's sinister smirk as she closed the door to the bathroom, with him standing there, taunting her with that smile of his.

Chapter 23

With the space she needed, Gloria immediately hurried over to where the sink was located and turned the faucet on. As the water ran, she actually used some of it to splash on her face in order to overcome some of the anxiety she felt. After gathering her thoughts, Gloria moved over to where a large flower pot was situated on the floor near the glass-enclosed shower and inhaled a deep breath. If what Arty said was true, then the plant was merely a decorative one, as was the makeshift topsoil packed tightly into the flower pot which concealed a false bottom.

The pottery itself would weigh about 25 pounds if it were to be lifted on its own, but that wasn't Gloria's concern at the moment. With her time wearing thin, she wrapped her hand around the Amin wooden stem of the plant, which resembled a 'Philodendron,' and gave it a tug while hoping for the best. To her surprise, the plant lifted with ease, to reveal a plastic to Gloria who found what she needed to complete the assignment without much difficulty.

Although it wasn't one of her own, Arty managed to leave Gloria one of her favored brand of .380-calibered pistols to go, along with a silencer to help with suppressing the sound of any ensuing gunfire. With the ability to hold a total of seven rounds, Gloria felt her chances for success strengthen exponentially with her newly acquired addition which she immediately stuffed into her purse. A soft knock on the door caused Gloria to hurry her efforts, as she took to replacing the plant back into position while sweeping whatever minimal droppings that was left behind under the large pot.

Another knock at the door was accompanied by The Wolf's soft-spoken inquiry, "Is everything all right in there?"

"Everything's fine! I'll be out in just a second!" Gloria yelled in response as she washed the remnants of dirt from her hands and shut off the water. She dug deep into her purse and removed a small aerosol can which she used to spray a floral-scented perfume around in the air that she allowed to resonate onto her clothing before going to open the door.

She didn't notice it beforehand, but Gloria's every step seemed to be an eternity in the making. She couldn't believe what was happening to her at that moment, as the purse she carried became heavy in her grip while her vision blurred uncontrollably. Before she could reach the door, it was opened by one of The Wolf's men, as he stood behind the enforcer, revealing his ever-present smirk of mischief. When the henchman walked in her direction, Gloria tried to say something in regards to the extent of her predicament, but her efforts were slurred tremendously as the enforcer hoisted her onto his massive shoulder and took her away. Gloria's vision finally came to fail her at the sight of The Wolf's sinister smirk broadening across the length of his face.

*****

Gloria awoke as though she were slapped with a ton of bricks to do so. The feeling was made even worse when she tried to sit up from her position and realized that she was constrained at the arms and legs with some sort of cloth bounding her to the bed. A fear for the worst washed over her when Gloria finally came to realize that along with her arms and legs, her mouth had been gagged tightly, and she'd been laid to rest on top of what felt like plastic covering. The thought which instantly came to her mind at that moment was that her scheme had been discovered and The Wolf was now off somewhere, preparing for his vengeance against her.

In the darkness, Gloria could hardly make out the room's décor, but she was able to locate her purse atop what appeared to be the bureau of a dresser. While fleetingly trying to shake out of her bondages, Gloria questioned whether her captors found the weapon she concealed, just before a chilling sound put a halt to her efforts. She thought that maybe it was part of her imagination, but Gloria began to discern what amounted to be the audible of a low-sounding growl.

She was certain of it now. Amongst the sound of growls, which seemed to resound more intensely now to intimidate her, Gloria saw the distinct traces of dog ears hovering round the parameters of the mattress as though in guard of a savory meal. There wasn't much of anything she could do at that point to defend herself, so she remained totally still in order to not agitate the beastly guardian any further, to put an end to the guttural sounds which began to take effect on her psyche.

Gloria let out a horrified shriek suddenly, as she felt every bone in her body quiver with repulsive dismay, when her bound and outstretched hand became sniffed by the nuzzle of a cold nose. The reaction only heightened when the animal moved to a different location and simulated the smell once more which ended off with a lick of Gloria's foot from the base of her heel to the tip of her toe.

She was left feeling utterly disgusted, but there was nothing Gloria could do about it at that point. Craning her neck, she struggled to see if she could get a glimpse of where the canine was locate and was shocked to discover the animal situated between her legs, reflecting her wide-eyed stare with a look of impassive dejection in return. No matter how much her neck strained, Gloria didn't dare to pull her view away from whatever animal this was, exchanging glances with her in the darkened room, for fear that any further movement may very well make her a tasty morsel in the palate of the guarding beast.

Not another thought could come to Gloria's mind at that moment, since she came to be predisposed with the motion of the beast rearing up on its haunches as though readying itself to devour her as a meal. Gloria realized then that she was totally naked all along in her position, as every hair on her exposed body stood with frightened terror in contemplation of what was to come next. The pall of the drapes worked well to conceal most of any light from entering the room, but as the animal came to reveal itself in the cast of the low-radiating moonlight, Gloria didn't know whether to laugh or cry at what her predicament had become.

It appeared that the beast was actually an animal of the human variety, as Enrique 'La Lobo' Calderon made use of donning a mask in resemblance of a real wolf, with only the bottom half of his face coming to be revealed as he continued to exude the low-guttural sounds of a growl while sniffing the extent of Gloria's naked flesh as though he actually were one of the large predatory 'canids' hunting in the wild.

Gloria found humor in the circumstance, but it was certainly short-lived when she felt the harsh sting of The Wolf's teeth biting into her flesh. The intensity of the bites began to vary from giving her a mild discomfort at first, to piercing Gloria's skin with wounds severe enough to cause bleeding as The

Wolf salivated the prospect of another chew over the area of her body with the glazed eyes of a madman.

Nowhere was off limits as The Wolf sank his teeth into Gloria's breast, legs, arms, and even her face while she was left powerless to stop him. She blanked out for a moment, but Gloria was instantly awakened with a hard smack to her face just before The Wolf howled a menacing outcry in triumph of his latest conquest. What came next was an absolutely horrendous and inconceivable act which Gloria would never come to forget.

Gloria tried to discern what pain The Wolf planned to inflict on her next as he reared up to her chest level and turned toward her legs to commence sniffing at her exposed flesh once more. In a dark turn, Gloria began to fear the absolute worse when The Wolf forcefully nuzzled his nose at the folds of her vagina before making a hand movement as though he were a canine clearing dirt away from the area.

Any attempt Gloria may have made to defend herself would've proven to be futile with her being tightly restrained to the bed, but after discovering the Wolf's devious intention, she vehemently thrashed about and tried to shake out of her bondages while screaming her disdain to no avail. Undoubtedly a cruel and vile act, Gloria became instantly appalled at the sight of The Wolf using her as though she were a public toilet-bowl fixture by grotesquely defecting on her bare chest.

The compact mass of feces on her body had the exact effect of acid being poured on Gloria's chest as she struggled to hold back the tears threatening to overwhelm her. In a further exertion of disgust, The Wolf climbed off of Gloria's abused body and gawked at her as though he were relishing in the delight of achievement just before taking the measure to indulge himself with the stimulation of masturbation to complete the tale of his sick effigy.

The Wolf could've easily spit in Gloria's face and attempted to commit whatever sex act imaginable to her at that point, and she wouldn't have noticed. She allowed tears to fall down the length of her face and even whimpered a bit, but it was all just another performance on her part. No longer the helpless teenager she once was, Gloria wanted nothing more now than to see The Wolf die at her hands.

It would've been much wiser for him to kill her, but after The Wolf ejaculated his semen on Gloria in a final act of callous malfeasance, he exited the room while leaving her to wallow in his wake. She didn't know for certain that The Wolf wouldn't want to risk exposing himself for the authorities to discover, when he was in town to conduct such important business to further his enterprise, without having to leave a trail of bloodshed to cover up his tracks.

Gloria received the answer she sought shortly after The Wolf's departure when three of his men entered the room she was in wearing surgical masks and latex gloves. It became obvious to her then that the encounter wasn't The Wolf's first form of sexual deviance on an unsuspecting participant. And with the surrealism with which he accomplished the task while donning the grotesque mask as though he were performing some sadistic ritual, Gloria came to surmise that it was most likely how he came to earn the namesake of 'La Lobo.'

Gloria instantly opinioned that the circumstance was a normal occurrence for the three men approaching her, as they maneuvered with impassive stares and demeanors of nonchalance to clean up after their boss' mess. One of the enforcers carried with him a container of wet wipes and used the cloths to remove the remnants of The Wolf's bowel movement while another man held open a hefty trash bag to collect the articles of soiled rubbish.

The man wiped clean any trace of The Wolf's semen as the third enforcer, who'd been standing in wait, checked the severity of Gloria's wounds before shrugging off the abnormality as though he'd seen far worse. She watched as the same man who checked her injuries removed a knife from his pocket and began cutting away at her bondages which appeared to be nothing more than silk scarves that were then discarded along with the rest of the trash.

Although severely weakened, Gloria felt her energy surging back with a vehemence to complete the mission at hand. She felt confident enough with the remaining strength she had left to possess the ability to disarm the third man of his knife and make a move to attack the other two before they could do a thing to stop her, but without a chance to put an end to The Wolf at her immediate disposal, Gloria was forced to allow the transgression of her hapless state to continue until she had the perfect opportunity to attempt her strike.

After Gloria was harshly yanked off of the mattress by the man who removed the excrement from her body, she furthered her method of playacting by continuing her whimpering and moving about as though she were still in shock by the actions that took place at her expense. The enforcer placed her skirt and undergarments in Gloria's arms and ordered, "Get dressed!" She assumed that the men in attendance were used to the many girls The Wolf came to encounter to do the same, and the fact that they didn't have the decency to allow her to cleanse herself any further only added fuel to the fire that raged within her of a volcanic magnitude.

As she dressed, Gloria looked to see the folding of the plastic covering she been laid on and disposing of it in a separate garbage bag the second enforcer held open. Her shoes and purse were shoved forcefully into her arms as the first man took ahold of Gloria and led her out of the room and into the expensive living area where The Wolf awaited their arrival dressed in an all-white robe flanked by the two remaining enforcers who were heavily armed with automatic assault rifles.

In the pit of her stomach, Gloria only felt the need to wipe the condescending smirk off of The Wolf's face as he took to commenting, "It was a pleasure to have you as my guest, my dear. I do hope that you can understand that this is a matter which needs to be kept a secret. Especially since your life may truly depend on keeping your mouth shut," The Wolf added as one of the armed men made a showing of chambering one of the rounds in his weapons as if to enforce the message that his boss was trying to convey.

"Cabrone!!!" Gloria cursed fiercely in her Spanish dialect, before continuing on with her sobs.

"That's exactly why I chose you! You have so much spirit that I needed to merge that of my own with you!!!" The Wolf responded adamantly as he gripped Gloria close with a fist full of her hair and inhaled her deeply. After previously managing to slip a hand into her purse, Gloria became elated to find that the weapon was still in her bag at the ready to do her bidding, at some point when the enforcer was leading her out of the bedroom. When The Wolf made the statement, "I hope it was as fun for you as it was for me," before salaciously licking the extent of her face with his tongue, it was all Gloria could take before she snapped altogether.

After the grotesque lick of her face, The Wolf shoved Gloria by her hair toward the direction of the exit and murmured the words, "Get rid of her." That's when he came to feel the first shot. The smirk he implanted on his face only a moment ago was now completely replaced with a look of utter shock, as he placed a hand over his ribcage area in order to try to put an end to the flow of blood which began to seep from the wound where a bullet coursed through his body in an instant.

*****

The sight of The Wolf in dismay instantly brought on a smile to Gloria's face, but there was a reason why she didn't bother to kill him immediately. Without even caring to remove her hand from the cover of her purse, Gloria moved about swiftly to dispatch of the two armed men before either of them could do anything to react. One of the men suffered from a shot to the head, while the other sustained a fatal slug to his throat. The remaining enforcer found himself in shock as he went to comfort his injured boss. By the time he could process the extent of what was happening, a rage consumed the enforcer as he took to charging at Gloria with the belief that no mere woman could have done this amount of damage on his watch. An encounter, Gloria met with a shot to the strongman's sternum while placing another right in between his eyes.

With her remaining shots, Gloria incapacitated The Wolf even further by using the silenced bullets to blow out his kneecaps before hurrying to arm herself with one of the automatic weapons from the dead enforcers as The Wolf cried out in pain. When the last two of the henchmen, who were left to clean up the rest of the mess left behind by their boss, came running out of the room with garbage bags in hand to see what was going on, they were met with intense rapid fire from the weapon Gloria held as she cut them down with stunned expressions of disbelief etched across their faces.

With the strongmen out of the way, Gloria savored every move she made as she took all the remaining time she needed to exact the vengeance she sought.

"Please don't kill me! Please!!! I'll pay you anything you want, just spare my life!!!" The Wolf pleaded as Gloria moved about with the same crazed look he had in his eyes when he accosted her in the bedroom. She watched him with sincere disdain for a moment as The Wolf begged for his life with the pleas that all fell on deaf ears.

Reminiscent of The Wolf's trademark smirk, Gloria flashed one of her own as she leveled the weapon she held in his direction and commenced firing.

"Noooo!!!" The Wolf screamed as shots tore through his body with an impact that reached his very soul with every slug that pierced him. When Gloria expended her first magazine, she frantically sought the comfort of the other weapon at her disposal and used it to her satisfaction until the metallic clanking sound of the firearm alarmed Gloria to the fact that the weapon had exceeded its capability.

Already a battered mess, Gloria wouldn't allow her vengeance on The Wolf to be deterred as she scoured through the various rooms to locate the belongings of the men in order to find what she needed to continue her onslaughter of reckoning. She happened upon a few pistols, but what Gloria found interest in were the extra clips of ammunition for the automatic weapons which she commandeered to finish what she began with an intensity that caused the bullets she fired to ricochet through the hollowed corpse of The Wolf and strike various objects which were scattered about, such as the walls and furniture fixtures of the residence.

Gloria didn't even bother to clean herself up afterward, but she did the best she could to remove any trace of herself in the abode before she placed a call to Arty and simply relayed the message, "Sorry about the mess." Her ride down in the elevator was a somber one, as her mind flashed through the insidious characteristic of The Wolf who, she surmised, has put the many women he's encountered through far worse than how she fared. As such, Gloria felt the solace in the fact that every slug she used to penetrate The Wolf's body was tantamount to her exacting revenge for the very same women who suffered at the hands of his pervasive intentions more so than she did for her own reasoning.

Her ride down in the service elevator also proved to be a form of therapy for Gloria, since she was able to avoid the detection of the surveillance cameras most commonly found to be in the main conveyors of the hotel. Something which also allowed her to escape the reflective glare of the shiny-mirrored interior. An element which would've forced Gloria to bear witness to her gruesome outlook of teeth marks, bloodstains, and death, before she was ready to fully examine the extent of her injuries on her own accord, for which she rightly took six months to recover from, although the mental damage that was inflicted upon her as a result lasted much longer.

Due to the depravity by which Gloria emptied her bullet-filled tirade into The Wolf's deserving body until he resembled the appearance of a bloodied pulp, along with the mayhem she caused to the men in his company, was the exact reason for why Arty and the establishment of the Waldorf Astoria had to work tirelessly to maintain a public relations campaign in order to ensure present and future guests that they would have nothing to fear, after the magnitude of the resulting investigation diminished their record of standing on security and their assurance of protection.

Even after renovations were made to the penthouse accommodation, the aftermath of the carnage left in Gloria's wake put a damper on anyone wanting to lease the abode for some time to come where reporters writing stories on the instance came to label the residence 'The Haunted Hideaway!' After discovering the reason why Gloria incurred the wrath of her fury on the men involved, Arty needed to apology from her, but since her demeanor to carry out missions afterward was that of a more ruthless nature, Yitzy always had to try his best to quell Gloria's tactics with the same stern warning that he gave her before she commenced with the start of the Boris and Yuri engagement. "And, Gloria—"

"I know, Yitzy. You don't want any mishaps like the last time," Gloria responded with the trace of a smirk etched across her face before Yitzy had the chance to finish his admonition, since she always found a way to stray from the effort at hand…if only a little bit.

Chapter 24

"I'm bored," Dawn implied after popping what must've been her hundredth gum bubble. "You're bored?" was the question Lauren posed in return to her passenger from the driver's seat of their stolen sports-utility vehicle before continuing on with, "I had a hot date tonight. I might've even gotten my feet massaged if I didn't have to sit here and listen to you popping your gum in my ear for over an hour." For a response, Dawn turned and looked at Lauren, stone-faced, and asked, "You mean to tell me that you had a date to get your feet massaged and you didn't bother to get someone," and rolled her eyes in jest.

The ladies in the waiting S.U.V. both heard the doors to the vehicle open suddenly as their counterparts made their way back inside with Genie commenting, "I still think we should take him in the apartment," although she had already relented to Gloria's argument that extracting their target from his place of residence had the potential of greatly exposing their scheme, with the risk of him trying to seek help from the gawking stares of neighbors and onlookers being far greater than them accosting their target on the quiet tree-lined street once he exited his car. Genie and Gloria quietly gave the other two members of their team an account of what they discovered when they entered the residence of 'The Pillager.'

With the skills of a locksmith and the heart of a burglar, Gloria was able to gain entry into the residence she sought, with the use of rudimentary lock picks, which allowed her and Genie to thoroughly scour the abode of their target in order to get a feel for what to think about what they were up against. Once inside, the two ladies didn't know what to think about what awaited them. The account they relayed to Lauren and Dawn detailed the same. After gaining the entry to the residence of their target, the two ladies were left puzzled to find… Well, nothing actually.

If not for the file that Yitzy had on hand to debrief them with, the man known to the ladies as 'The Pillager' would have certainly remained a mystery to them. The factor definitely became apparent where the elements in the abode were virtually devoid of any feeling or emotion. The only amenities to go along with the spares furnishings scattered about were a large flat-screen television set and the apparatus of a simple computer terminal harboring the traces of dust which all seemed to be quite oxymoronic computer hacker.

Photographs of family and friends, or maybe even those of female acquaintances were all nonexistent in the home as well which only helped to further thwart any attempts the ladies would make to try ascertaining the psychological makeup of their quarry. Something that was needed in order to for them to better engage their subject properly. As they moved about, the ladies came to wonder if they were on the receiving end of some ridiculous joke which neither found to be too funny at the moment.

Everything in the abode was unused and new. The linens, towels, and clothing found in the closets detailed every bit of the inertness they would have if showcased for discount on the racks of department-store displays while being passed over for more quality purchases. Even the spare toothbrush and soap dish located in the bathroom area languished in yearning for the chance at proving themselves useful for the intentions they were created for.

The more they thought about it, the more the ladies came to surmise that the circumstances of the encounter amounted to be nothing more than a setup, but after placing a call to Yitzy and receiving the assurance that they were, in fact, not being led astray, the ladies decided to stick with the plan and hoped for the success of their goal to come to fruition quickly.

"If this is a wild goose chase, I'm going to kick Yitzy's ass!" Genie lamented after the ladies found themselves waiting for about another half hour in their stolen vehicle for something to develop.

"So much for that foot massage," Lauren commented quietly to herself but caught the attention of Dawn who made the statement, "That's good for you. Maybe next time, you'll think twice about the welfare of your sidekick's feet," just before tossing out her old gum and replacing it with a new one to chew on. Gloria had to admit that it seemed like their time was being wasted, but as the thought came to her mind, the ladies all snapped to attention as the sleek red sports car their target drove pulled right ahead of them to come to a stop right in front of the building they were canvassing.

The ladies all found themselves entranced by the sudden appearance of their quarry while struggling to regain control of their thoughts for what needed to be done. "I can't feel my legs," Dawn remarked as she fawned over the sight of their target as he began to exit his vehicle. "Well, you better feel your ass moving, and quick, because we got work to do," Genie countered as she and Gloria left the automobile they were in to engage 'The Pillager' with their weapons drawn.

*****

The playful birds flying about the area were the only form of audience the ladies had to their scheme unfolding, as they chirped sounds of joy and chased each other from tree to tree to continue their enjoyment of a sun-filled day. The target didn't even seem to notice them at first, but the sight of his shocked dismay became instantly apparent as Genie cranked the shaft of her pump shotgun and held it at the level his of his chest while Gloria did the same by aiming the bulky .45-caliber pistol she carried on the mark of his head.

"Sorry, lover, but you're going to have to come with us. Somebody's paying a lot of money for the presence of your company," Genie informed the Pillager as Lauren pulled the stolen S.U.V. up to where their quarry could be extracted to the back of the vehicle without causing too much attention. To everyone's bewilderment and surprise, however, Dawn managed her way through the leveled aim of menacing weapons to place a kiss on their stunned captive's cheek before seductively whispering, "Maybe we can be together in the next lifetime. Until then, I hope you don't mind if I take that pretty car of yours for a spin?"

The Pillager didn't know whether he should reply to her or not, but as a parting measure, Dawn grabbed ahold of his butt and gave it a playful squeeze. "Just like I thought it would be," she demurred just before climbing into the brand new, candy-apple red Ferrari Berlinetta coupe. "Peter. Peter…" Dawn began while reciting the unrestricted version of her lust-filled nursery rhyme without Yitzy's nagging intervention this time around as she revved the engine to the luxury sports vehicle until it managed to peak her arousal.

He didn't feel a thing. The Pillager didn't know it, but the surprise of Dawn's kiss on his face had the added effect of providing as a distraction as she plunged the receiving end of a syringe into the back of his hip, which she later squeezed, in order to attest to the sensation of how it felt in her palm. The solution in the instrument worked instantly as The Pillager felt a wave of dizziness overwhelm his consciousness. He looked to Dawn in the driver's seat of his automobile as she dangled the syringe for him to see. "I hope you include me in your dreams, doll! See you later!" she mused as she put the sports car in gear and took off like a rocket down the street.

Genie and Gloria lowered the aim of their weapons just as The Pillager stumbled onto their shoulders. Each with an arm draped over the neck, the two ladies dragged their quarry to the back of the waiting S.U.V. and secured him inside with zipties as Genie made the statement, "Well, it looks like I won't have to kick Yitzy's ass after all." Gloria wasn't so sure about trusting the developments just yet, but with the primary objective complete, she went along with Genie's enthusiasm for the moment as the ladies drove off with their prize in tow from the success of an operation which took no longer than five minutes to accomplish.

Chapter 25

Hours later, The Pillager awoke to find himself seated in a chair, with his mouth gagged by some sort of masking tape. His arms and legs were bound tightly by the same zip ties used to transport him to his present location, which he assumed to be a seedy motel accommodation, as a large cockroach waded its way to some far-off destination by creating a path in front of his feet. As far as The Pillager could tell, he was alone for the moment, but when the door opened to flood the room with the hot and humid air of sweltering night, he took to shaking at his bondages with the wide-eyed look of a frightened hostage.

"You must be hungry," is what the voice of his captor pronounced in a melodic tone which instantly calmed the amount of anxiety he displayed. The Pillager became as mesmerized with her now as he had been when he first laid eyes on her commanding presence while she pointed a very large weapon in his direction. If there were ever a time where the circumstances could find him in a dense tropical jungle, The Pillager could easily come to assume the woman before him now to be one of the mythological Amazonian warriors of Greek folk lore, with her stout appearance of determination and features of physically fit beauty. However, instead of wielding a spear or some sort of makeshift bow, this warrior goddess carried with her a sweet-smelling bundle of fast food in her arms.

With chilled beverage in hand, Gloria used the other to peel away at the industrial-strength tape from her captive's mouth as he wasted no time in trying to plead his case.

"Pleasseee! I don't..." the rest of The Pillager's words were muffled abruptly when Gloria reapplied the tape over his mouth.

"No talking. Just eat the food you are given, because you're going to need your strength for what's to come," she cautioned before continuing on with,

"No words. Just food. If you speak again, I reapply the tape without the offer of food again. Do we have an understanding?"

The Pillager wanted to smile at how much Gloria reminded him of his mother in that moment, but he figured that it might not be a good idea to get on his captor's bad side, so he nodded his head in compliance as Gloria removed the tape once more in order to give The Pillager his first sip of the drink she held out to him before feeding him from hand to mouth.

To Gloria, the only advantage that the cheeseburgers and French fries had after her purchase were that they were still hot to the touch. Otherwise, they tasted as though they were dispensed a week old from a stubborn vending machine. To the palate of The Pillager, however, who'd been accosted and drugged unconscious for hours, he ate as though the meal were a gourmet serving of fine cuisine, deviating only a bit from Gloria's rule to make the humming sounds of his fulfilled enjoyment.

After swallowing the last bite of a burger, The Pillager strayed from his muted discourse to express the statement, "If only I could've gotten one of my ex-girlfriends to do that, I would've been married with children by now." His wide-eyed expression betrayed the knowing fact of the wrong he committed, as his stone-faced captor turned to him and admonished of the sticky tape in order to keep any more words from escaping his mouth. *Yep. Just like Mom would've done it,* The Pillager reflected while smiling inwardly to himself.

To ensure that her captive realized how grave and dire the situation was, Gloria made certain not to switch on the power to the small television the room afforded, nor make use of any reading materials as though she were not taking her responsibility seriously. Instead, Gloria bided her time by staring out of the window while cleaning the weapons she brought along with her in a scene reminiscent of how Ralph used to do it when she was still a scared, wide-eyed teenager, as her hostage looked on.

When the room to the accommodation shook violently in a tremor, as an aircraft flew low overhead in a possible position of liftoff, the realization of where he may have been brought to offered no form of solace to The Pillager as his captor stared menacingly in his direction with the muzzle of one of her weapons pointed at him intently. The innuendo replayed the very clear and blunt message of Gloria's diction, should he abstain from following her instructions to the letter.

With the elements of time proving to be a long wait, Gloria's mind became consumed with different thoughts and scenarios involved in the instance of what could she have done to alter the encounter she engaged herself in with The Wolf. A scenario which Gloria had revisited too many times to count now, but there remained the pleasurable circumstance she came to face amongst all of the rest which caused her to smile even now.

*****

After the completion of a dark task one day, Gloria was still running herself hot with the traces of gun residue on her hands when she heard the faint sound of her government name being called from an all-too-familiar voice. Intrigued, Gloria hoped that the adrenaline pumping throughout her system wasn't preying on her sensibilities as a woman made herself visible amongst the wailing sounds of sirens and the outcries echoing in the distance.

At the time, both women were at least ten years older than they were when they last saw each other. "I thought that was you," the women said in adoration as she warmed Gloria even further with her inviting smile.

"It's good to see you again, Ms. Santiago," Gloria responded flatly with her hardened demeanor coming to be overshadowed by her true feelings of joy for the instance of Gloria encountering her old foster counselor.

Now moving about with the telltale signs of graying hair while making use of prescription glasses, Ms. Santiago still maintained herself with the appearance of youthful jubilance to coincide with her passion for caring. Sensing that Gloria may have been predisposed with something other than their encounter, Ms. Santiago made the suggestion, "Can you remember how to get in touch with me? Because I'd really like to catch up with you when you…when you have the time to."

To Ms. Santiago's delight, Gloria smiled brightly in return and surprised her by dropping the heavy bag she carried to give her old counselor a big hug before replying with, "Is' it all right if we can do it now? I know of a great place for drinks not too far from here. For a nightcap perhaps?" Ms. Santiago nodded her head enthusiastically in conformity as the two set off without another care in the world while becoming caught up in the flashing light of police cruisers racing to the bloody aftermath of Gloria's latest embarkment.

Their conversation flowed effortlessly as though they were mother and daughter winding themselves down after a hearty day of shopping to engage in the latest talk of gossip. Gloria laughed emphatically after receiving an answer to why Ms. Santiago hadn't married after all these years when her counselor retorted with, "What do I need with some boring man weighing me down? I do like my male strippers though," she added with a reflective smirk that caused Gloria to laugh even harder at the implication of what Ms. Santiago meant.

Ms. Santiago had found herself enthralled by how much Gloria had blossomed into the woman she became. Gloria was forced to conjure up a lie in the regard, however, about her time of traveling to California in search of the bright lights and fame that called out to her, only to have her dreams shattered by the overbearing directors who only concerned themselves with getting into her pants rather than cast her for any roles. At that point, Gloria had been so used to lying about herself that the tale she spun was devoid of derision and didn't cause Ms. Santiago to suspect a thing, as the counselor read Gloria's emotions with genuine concern.

Gloria was surprised to find that Ms. Santiago was, in fact, still very much employed by the same foster agency as a guidance counselor. Ms. Santiago was actually on her way home from the new abode of a troubled teen when she caught sight of Gloria to help with further integrating the child into the care of the family chosen to take on the responsibility of raising her. It made Gloria smile when the counselor informed her of how much the teen reminded her of Gloria when she went through the turmoil of moving between foster homes without allowing anyone to break her spirits.

Ms. Santiago wrote down all of her contact information once more to remind Gloria of how to get in touch with her at any time should she ever need her assistance. Gloria, on the other hand, was forced to utter another falsehood in order to quell Ms. Santiago's expectancy of receiving her contact information, by telling a story of how she was currently keeping in touch. Although that too was a lie, since Gloria was actually sitting with her at a café table with a high-powered rifle disassembled in the bag at her feet.

Gloria couldn't see herself ever explaining to Ms. Santiago the ramifications of what she's been doing over the years since they last saw each other or even risk the chance of exposing her to harm's way, but she kept the possibility open for seeing the counselor again sometime in the future, which hasn't yet developed, but Ms. Santiago remained dear to her heart. After the ladies bid their farewell, since the surprise encounter with the counselor went so well, maybe she could replicate a similar feeling with the next person she sought out.

*****

It took her some time to get up the courage, but after keeping watch of her mark for over the course of a week, Gloria finally made the decision to make her move. She entered the small luncheonette when it was the least busy and took a seat at the nearest table facing the door. The move was more out of habit in regards to the way she handled most mission, but this encounter was entirely different. Gloria didn't know how the situation was going to unfold, but she felt that she was prepared enough to handle anything that came her way. *And just think... I don't even need a weapon this time around,* Gloria thought to herself while inwardly smiling.

As the waitress hustled over in contemplation of taking her order, Gloria removed the designer-aviator glasses she wore to brace herself for the worst. Upon sight of her patron, the waitress dropped the pencil and notepad she furnished for taking the order to grasp at her chest with a wide-eyed look of shock. The waitress suddenly yelped in surprise, "Oh my, God!!! Gloria???! Is that really you?!?! What are you doing here???! Where have you been?! What, wha…"

"Hello, Malala," Gloria stated to calm the emotions her old friend, Malala, was experiencing, who began convulsing with excitement. "It's good to see you too," Gloria added with a tight smile, since she wasn't too sure on how to proceed next.

The next move was entirely up to Malala to make, and she made hers by jumping at Gloria's neck in order to give the tightest hug she'd been longing to since having the disappointment of losing her best friend so long ago. "I can't believe it's really you!!!" she said to Gloria to engage her friend in conversation while, at the same time, forsaking everything going on around them.

"Hey, Mally!!! What's going on over there?!" a man donning a food-stained apron asked from behind the counter, before he continued on with, "We got customers ready to spend money over here!!!"

"Put a sock in it, Ben!!! I'm talking with a very good friend of mine!" Malala admonished him as Gloria looked to see that the only other patrons in the place besides her seemed to be four regular who all found Ben's statement to be just as alarming as they searched the area of the dinner for the same customers Ben spoke of to spend money on the type of meals he cooked, to no avail.

Snickers were consequently shared at Ben's expense as Malala started talking in rapid succession to bring Gloria up to speed on what's been going on with her life and the lives of others with whom Gloria was familiar with. In return, Gloria outlined the similar account of the fabricated tale she relayed to Ms. Santiago in order to detail her defunct stay in California, to being in between residences with no permanent places to call home.

Gloria still couldn't get over how much Malala had come into being the woman that she was today which was a far cry from the dullard of the young gothic girl Gloria knew her to be, who made use of the dark, drab clothing to go along with the equally dreary demeanor called upon for the morbid rock music that favored. The heavy makeup Malala once wore had since been replaced by a bubbly personality which Gloria found to be heartening.

From the parts of Malala's rapid conversation that she could gather, she came to find that 'Ben' was not only the proprietor and chef of the luncheonette named 'Sunrise luncheon,' but that his partner in arm, bussing the tables of the establishment was actually his precious wife of five years, Malala. The couple were now in the adorable six-year-old.

Malala tried her best to assure Gloria that the luncheonette often became far more busy at times; it was during their encounter. A fact, which Gloria knew to be true, from her time of surveilling the place for over a week after discovering Malala's whereabouts, but what really held firm in her regard was when her old friend got around to informing Gloria about the people she'd come to loathe over the years as the memories she had of them lingered in taunting fashion within the inner recesses of her mind. Information, which Gloria came to provide her undivided attention to, as Malala steadied the flow of her conversation enough for Gloria to understand the levity of it all as she spoke.

With open-mouthed fascination, Gloria listened intently as Malala detailed the misfortunates which fell upon those who came to betray her confidence, like the instance of their old acquaintance, Jeremy, who, surprisingly, still remained with the awkward girl, Mandy.

Someone he first came to meet while deep in a drunken stupor at the local prison in the area while becoming addicted to any drug he could get his hands on. The girl, Mandy, only proved to be his accomplice in the undertakings, as she managed to survive overdosing a number of times while auctioning off the fleeting virtues of her body in order to be able to provide for the couple's bare necessities.

Since Jeremy was an old friend, and Gloria didn't know Mandy well enough to judge her, she started to feel a bit dismayed by the circumstances of their turmoil, until the next instance Malala relayed to her marked the direct reason why Gloria came to feel a sense ease with the smile that emerged on her face for the reckoning that was achieved for the amount of suffering she endured at the hands of those involved.

It seems as though the very same Tommy 'The Tan' Sanderson who went on to commit the atrocity of taunting Gloria before sexually assaulting her with a band of his teammates during the time of the fabled party carried on to do quite well for himself, with the physical activity of the sport he played in at the college level. So that he caught the national attention of accomplishment, Tommy decided to celebrate his spectacular achievement before going on to chase his dream of professional stardom.

To ensure that the party he planned went off without a hitch, Tommy the Tank sought the expertise of the only person he knew who had developed a knack for accomplishing the best parties imaginable. When he approached the former head cheerleader about the endeavor, Tiffany was the only person he knew who had developed a knack for accomplishing the best parties imaginable. When he approached the former head cheerleader about the endeavor, Tiffany was only too eager to oblige the effort. "Like the last time?!" she asked with a mischievous smirk etched on her face, as Tommy responded in cahoots to her ploy, "Exactly like the last time."

Once again, Tommy's celebration was held at the vast estate of his parents, with no expenses spared on the cost of the engagement. The festivity was Roman themed in togas, with the consumption of drugs and alcohol highly favored, until the night made way for the attraction of the special kind. Like she had with Gloria, Tiffany managed to ultimately find an inebriated girl who was unaware of what was about to transpire as a swathe of gatherers began to whoop emphatically in jubilation of her appearance.

A sacrificial lamb of sorts, the girl in question was chosen for Tommy's amusement and was forced to endure the same kind of humiliation that Gloria was subjected to, only she seemed to walk away from the incident as though the encounter would hopefully bolster her 'likability.'

"Stupid huh?!" Malala remarked with a tinge of repugnance before continuing on. Like the secret ceremonial rites held in honor of a Greek or Roman deity, revelers at the party engaged in a mass sexual encounter which began at a certain hour, tantamount to the celebratory kisses, everyone in attendance arousing one another in every way possible.

In hindsight, it would be the day that Tommy would never live to forget. Feeling at the plateau of a passionate high, Tommy felt as though nothing in the world could break his spirits. He paraded around with Tiffany as though the two were destined to live happily ever after, but his plan was solely to use her as a sexual object until the time came for him to seek out a trophy wife on his path of greatness.

Tommy was entirely too intoxicated to get behind the wheel of a motor vehicle, but with his feeling of being unstoppable charging him forward, he took on the risk anyway. "Want to go for a ride?" was the question he posed to his cohort for the evening, and Tiffany, who had been equally stupefied, sat that point with her own alcohol consumption, felt giddy for the opportunity when she emphatically responded, "Yesss!!!" while clapping her hands together in excitement. The two made their way into one of the luxury vehicles his parents owned while clapping her hands together in excitement while still making use of the loose fitting Togas they wore.

The ardors of their emotion became short-lived as the two rambled on about inconsequential topics which often times took Tommy's eyes away from the road, to share in Tiffany's feeling of delight. In the haphazard course of events that ultimately followed, Tommy's source of guidance was squandered away for far too long, as the car they traveled in Veered from the direction they were heading and ended up in the wrong lane of a busy street.

What came next was a blur. As the vehicle the two were in lumbered on its own accord, a delivery truck traveling on the correct path wasn't able to move over quick enough in time to bring the large truck to a stop until it was too late.

The resulting impact caught the luxury Mercedes head on and compressed the front end of the vehicle as though it were a tin can destined for the rubbish bin.

The necessity for the 'jaws of life' mechanism had to be employed in order to erect the fallen couple from the mangled wreckage. Tiffany remained in a medically induced coma to recover from her injuries for longer than Tommy was subjected to, but when he awoke to find that both of his legs had to be severed at the knees, not even a miracle could stop the amount of tears which flowed from his eyes for days on end.

Tiffany didn't fare all that well on the other end of the equation either. The shards of glass tossed about in the accident turned her model-like features in to a hideous disaster area. She came to lose the vision on her right eye, and the reconstruction on her face afterward was forced to now walk with a considerable limp from the result of her leg being broken in three different places which required the treatment of metal rods and screws to repair.

If the effect of the injuries they sustained were tallied up, of course Tommy would feel as though he were the one to suffer the brunt of the disparity, with his dreams of becoming a professional football athlete shattered to go along with his being permanently confined to a metal chair, with the remaining stubs of his paired vertebrate proving to be a constant reminder of what could have been.

Tommy couldn't imagine life without Tiffany at this point. It took her, on the other hand, a few years of recovery and therapy to get over the anger she felt toward Tommy, but once the two came together once again, it was next to impossible to separate them. Although they were never married, Tommy and Tiffany joined with one another as though they were lifelong companions providing emotional support to each other and sharing in the addiction of painkillers.

"Serves them right!" Malala lamented in admonished fervor before instantly coming to regret the remark she made, since she didn't find it appropriate to harp on the suffering of someone else. "But damn, it's hard to do with those two!!!" she conceded with s sentiment that Gloria could agree with.

At the end of their encounter, Gloria provided Malala with the same misleading assurance that she came to give Ms. Santiago of getting together sometimes to catch up on things, but after seeing the picture of Malala's beautiful twin girls smiling blissfully with the traces of missing teeth and pimples on their faces, she couldn't help but to make good on the undertaking by attempting to visit on events such as holidays and the birthdays of her new extended family.

Malala's compassion for her family was the element which forced Gloria to think about the future of her wellbeing as well as the possibility of having children of her own. She discreetly placed a hand over her stomach at the time and beamed inwardly with joy at the enticement of the implication involved.

Chapter 26

After about another hour of becoming bored herself, Gloria encountered a scenario that nagged at her senses and posed questions, to which she desperately wanted the answer to with wide-eyed concern, with her weapon clutched in one hand and the look of viciousness attached to her gaze. The Pillager began to fear the worst, until he saw Gloria tuck the firearm into the back of the pants she wore before removing the tape from over his mouth once more

"I'm going to remove the tape from your mouth. Then I talk, and you answer. It gets no more simple than that, understood?" The Pillager knew by now that the woman before him meant business, and with no intentions of being treated once more as though he were a five-year-old child being placed on a time out, he nodded his head slowly in compliance and waited further instruction.

Gloria directed her line of inquiries as though she were conducting an actual interrogation. For an assignment which should've been cut and dried, Gloria found the instance to be either too perfectly outlaid or filled with enough holes in the story which created a substantial enigma that could only be demystified by the person in her care. Not one to beat around the bush, Gloria asked the question that she wanted answered most importantly while starting at her captive square in the eyes.

As she removed the tape from his mouth, Gloria stated, "I already know that your name is Peter Steeber, and that you are also a computer hacker making use of the monikor 'The Pillager,' but what I don't know is…why would someone go to such great lengths to have you captured? Do you know why that is?" After taking the time to stretch the muscles in his stiffened jaw, The Pillager smiled at the context of Gloria's inquiry before hurrying the sentiment when it seemed as though she was set to belt him one, to share with her the story of how the two of them came to encounter one another.

"Human test subjects?!?!" Gloria asked incredulously, with traces of skepticism etched across her face. How she came to be so engulfed in the tale conveyed was something Gloria didn't know, but she had to admit that it was a far more plausible one to hear The Pillager's chain of events than to rely solely on a file which was probably filled with falsified information.

Gloria's assumption proved to be a correct one. The file which was shared amongst her and the others to provide for a description of their target wasn't the only too convenient for belief but actually created for exactly that purpose. None of that was of an importance to Gloria at the moment, however, since the gravity of what The Pillager had to convey weighed heavily on her consciousness, with the ultimate realization that far bigger things were afoot now than she could have ever imagined.

The information of The Pillager excelling as a young computer prodigy amounted to be true. Only, his actual parents died a short time after he was born in a horrific plane crash which left him to be cared for by his elderly grandparents on a farm as they tried their best to provide for him. After the death of his remaining grandparent, The Pillager went on to find solace by immersing himself in his love for computer, until an opportunity happened to present itself for him to serve a greater purpose to his country.

While in college, The Pillager caught the attention of government recruiters who were searching desperately for the type of skills he exhibited in order to better fight the war on terror. With the skills, knowledge, and experience he soon acquired under the tutelage of the government's guiding hand was how The Pillager came to develop his talents for being the world's most sought-after computer hacker.

The government's very own National Security Agency, or N.S.A. for short, were the secretive branch of experts who put The Pillager through the rigorous training of infiltrating the world's computer systems to monitor the cash transfers of terror calls, drug smugglers, and those who were interested in bargaining to acquire weapons of mass destruction. There would be time that he would be called upon to control a satellite imaging system in order to survey the movements of terror camp or those associated with an army of guerillas seeking to overrun the regions of a particular country, but it was all just done in a day's work for The Pillager.

Entitled to a top-level security access, The Pillager had the ability to scrutinize an array of confidential data files, voice and film recordings, the financial dealings of government spending, and the schematics of advanced weaponry to go along with a host of other secretive content on a daily basis which were to remain heavily guarded form the observation of the public's opinion. On a day while making routine checks of the computerized data in storage, The Pillager came across an anomaly in the matrix of the system which prevented him from viewing the information with the level he possessed. The Pillager found it to be odd when he encountered the electronic file secured by an encryption code, but it made him smile as he viewed the irregularity as a test to sharpen his skills as hacker.

To his dismay, however, The Pillager soon became horrified by what he found. After successfully gaining access to the data hidden within, The Pillager acted quickly to commit an act of treason by downloading the information he recovered to his personal account before making the transfer to his own computer terminal at home. Becoming to be so distraught by his findings, The Pillager neglected to remove the traces of himself from the instance of his theft, which proved to be a costly mistake.

Gloria was forced to pull up a chair as The Pillager went on to explain how the encrypted files illegally downloaded was meant to conceal the atrocity of a government conspiracy which subjected the members of its own military personnel to suffer an immeasurable amount of pain in the furtherance of creating the ultimate soldier.

*****

The electronic files gathered were actually video feeds depicting the images of testimonials from government-employed neuroscientists who detailed the ongoing process of clinical trials which were conducted to study behavior and learning patterns. The participants were all of military caliber who were either ordered or consented willingly to partake in the scientific studies of combat under extreme duress.

In a moderately simple application with integrated circuitry, the scientist involved in the studies managed to make use of mini processors by implanting tiny microchips through the nasal cavity of a subject's nose and attaching it to a mass of nuclei in the brain called the 'thalamus' which serves chiefly to relay sensory impulses to and from the cerebral cortex.

The dismal maneuver, however, allowed the scientists to enhance the wave of excitation that transmits throughout the muscles, tissue, and nerve fibers which result in the physiological activity or inhibition of a subject's normal and healthy form of functioning. For a time, the results proved to be miraculous, until the side effects associated with the altering of a person's natural abilities amounted to be the consequences of a dire calamity.

In the beginning, the scientists were elated to find that the experimentation methods they created allowed their participants to become immune to the pain associated with the exertion of torture techniques such as the severing of toes and fingers, and the breaking of bones, without even a cry for agony. The ability to run faster and longer only complemented the capability to hold one's breath in excess of four minutes while possessing the power to propel for miles underwater without becoming exhausted during the rigorous physical training the subjects endured. Those in the know thought for certain that their answer to effective warfare had been successfully solved.

As the trails progressed, however, a fundamental derangement of the mind came to ensue. A factor which became evidenced by way of the delusions, hallucinations, and disorganized speech, with reckless behavior the participants experienced as characterized by a defective or a loss of contact with reality. The traces of post-traumatic stress disorder became evident when it started with a female private from the army by the name of Maggie Swanson.

As with the other participants, Private Swanson was required to undergo weekly treatment sessions. During which she was encouraged to talk freely about her personal experiences with the study, sleep patterns, and dreams, if any, in order for the information to be analyzed as a description of psychic phenomena. In the midst of her latest session, Private Swanson was alert, responsive, attentive, and even displayed a tinge of the bubbly persona she was known to have when she first volunteered to engage in the experiment's trials. Midway through the session, the private's demeanor took on a sudden change for the worst, as she began to exhibit an emotional form of disorder which proved to be life threatening.

Private Swanson began responding to an interviewer's questions about her childhood aspirations when her bright smile suddenly darkened and her outlook turned into the insipid gaze of blank dejection which became a much more common sight among the many involved with the study. Without warning, Private Swanson engaged her enemy in combat and began pummeling the unwitting interviewer without pause until he was nothing more than a bloodied mess.

Private Swanson furthered her onslaught by putting an end to the last few remaining breaths the inquisitors had left by breaking the bones in his neck with a smooth motion. If that wasn't disturbing enough, the private then proceeded to cradle the lifeless man in her arms before rearing her head back and taking a large chomp out her victim's neck and chewed on his flesh as though she were savoring the portion of a sublime meal. All captured for the standard gaze of the video cameras which were installed to record the sessions for further analysis.

Private Swanson was never heard from or seen again after the circumstances of the gory incident, but similar forms of the psychosis became apparent amongst the other subjects where patterns of disorganized behavior and suicides became the norm. Such was the case of a former Marine sergeant, who was practicing his aim with an array of weapons on the firing range, when his demeanor darkened and took on the resembling appearance of gloom which, like Private Swanson exhibited, before levelling the firearm he held and expending the remainder of the magazine in the assault rifle on those in his immediate area.

The sergeant's life came to a dramatic end when he selected a pump action shotgun to continue his attack. As the sergeant brought back to pump on the shaft and aimed in the direction of any bystanders, he took to ogling the weapon in his hands with the far-off expression he wore just before opening his mouth wide to ingest the live round which worked to remove a large portion of the sergeant's head from his shoulders.

"Further video feeds displayed the footage of our very own government's army making use of hazmat suits and using everything from blowtorches to explosives in the attempt to destroy any trace of the experiments deemed too unpredictable for scientific reason. As for the participants in the study? Well... Let's just say that the amount of body bags piled upon one another and ultimately burned to cinders was the evidence of a problem solved," The Pillager concluded to the open-mouthed shock of his bewildered audience whose words escaped her at the moment.

The Pillager went on to detail how he waited for the inevitable to happen as the government dispatched a team of special force members to seek him out. From afar, The Pillager watched as the men hunting him ransacked his former home, froze all of the assets in his accounts, and even resorted to the method of labeling him a wanted fugitive on the transitions of radio and television newscasts. The assault never wavered until The Pillager decided to gain the upper hand in the situation.

As a countermeasure, The Pillager created a firestorm of controversy by going as far as he could up the chain of command at the agency of National Security and, for a lack of better words, blackmailed his former employers into leaving him alone. As much as he could be under the circumstances. He was admonished as a traitor, a deserter, and a treacherous pig to go along with a slew of other degrading laments to warrant his condemnation, but, by then, The Pillager knew that the government's bark was worse than its bite.

The Pillager managed to keep those desperately seeking his capture at bay with the threats of uploading the files he pilfered onto the networks of the worldwide internet, with domains such as @Youtube, @Facebook, and @Instagram vying for any opportunity to appease the minds of the body of persons constituting the government's structure for the vindictive cover-up of a conspiracy.

The Pillager also tried his luck at ransoming the files in his possession for the currency of a billion dollars, but the amount of money requested proved to be a scoffed issue. The government, however, would've very much considered a more reasonable demand to keep the matter under wraps, despite its policy of not negotiating with the terrorist they labeled him to be.

The Pillager very much doubted that he would live to see a day when he would be able to spend a dime of the ill-gotten gains he received, but he did provide an assurance to his former employers that the woeful files in his possession would never see the light of day, so long as the government kept itself at a safe-enough distance from him, in return, the authoritative powers that be upheld their end of the bargain by putting a stop to the news bulletins broadcasting him as difficult for him to travel anywhere stateside or abroad.

The Pillager took the cue he was given and went underground while making use of an array of different aliases and forged documents in order to keep himself sustained as an outlaw on the run. The computer terminal became his sole means of financial support, as the old Peter Steeber then adapted to the moniker of 'The Pillager' fulltime by doing what he liked to do best as a hacker and selling the information he secreted from others to the highest bidder. The Pillager made Gloria aware that her band of femme fatales weren't the only ones that the government secretly subcontracted to seek him out, but they were, by far, the most intriguing by his estimation.

The Pillager went on to inform Gloria of how he stayed ahead of his pursuers by not being stationary and moving about from as many and updating daily. "So that explains the blank appearance of the apartment that we found, but what the hell is with that fancy car of yours? That's definitely a moving bull's eye if I've ever seen one," Gloria inquired in a condescending tone as The Pillager took the risk to smile once more before lauding, "What can I say? Other than a computer nerd, I'm one who has a love for fast cars."

The implications pouring over Gloria's mind about the circumstances transpiring around them were overwhelming. If what The Pillager was relaying amounted to be true, then it meant that her, Yitzy, and the rest of the women involved were all expendable as loose ends. It took another two hours after she removed the tape from his mouth for The Pillager to reveal the instances of his turmoil, and it only caused Gloria to feel more skeptical about the goings on around them. Routine call from Genie every few hours confirmed that Gloria was nothing more than a highly trained babysitter at the moment, since Genie and the other ladies were engaged in other assignment until their further assistance was needed.

Chapter 27

To express her concerns, Gloria placed a dire call to Yitzy in the hopes that he would see things her way. "Gloria... You always seem to find yourself astray of the rules. Why is that?" Yitzy admonished her in displeasure as Gloria made the attempt to plead her case. "You should know better than anyone, not to believe in some farfetched theory about a government-up! Especially with someone who knows that his life is on the line!!!" Yitzy persisted with his growing anger becoming more audile over the phone.

Yitzy concluded, "Just stay put and make sure you stop talking to your captive until we get further instructions on where to wash our hands of him, to complete the money transfer and our end of the agreement!" Gloria wanted to say something more on her belief but was met by an unconcerned dial tone as Yitzy ended the communication.

The Pillager became uncomfortable after Gloria's call was made, when she began to stare at him for a long moment with the same dull expression he attested to seeing on the faces of the many experimental soldiers, before she turned and began to make the movements of what appeared to be her packing up her belongings and weapons. When she turned back in his direction, The Pillager saw that Gloria now held a dagger in his hand as she walked toward him. He swallowed a big gulp of what The Pillager may have thought was the last usage of his throat as he squeezed his eyes and readied himself for an untimely demise.

Gloria made her first incision with the knife then replicated the motion a few more times to the wide-eyed shock of her captive. "Let's get out of here. We have to move quickly," Gloria commanded as The Pillager worked the kinks out of his newly freed movement with awe.

"Why are you doing this?" he asked incredulously, to which Gloria responded, "Well... Let's just say that I have a funny feeling about this entire situation."

The Pillager enthusiastically nodded his head in compliance before inquiring in a quirky manner, "Is it all right if I use the restroom first? Because sitting taped up in that chair for a number of hours had me feeling as though my insides were going to explode." Gloria nodded her head in the direction of the bathroom and watched with a cautious gaze as her captive made his way to it.

When he emerged from the bathroom, feeling a lot more refreshed and relaxed, Gloria looked The Pillager in his eyes and made the implication, "For someone who's life is in danger, you seem to be handling this situation a bit too well, especially for the gravity of what's at hand." It was then when she came to see a seriousness appear on her captive's expression as he responded, "To tell you the truth… I'm scared to death. But I've long made the decision that if I'm going to die, then I'm going to do so on my own terms and live as though every day could potentially be my last." The Pillager concluded with a sincerity that Gloria could agree with. It dawned on Gloria that Yitzy was going to be extremely pissed off by her actions, and the sentiment caused her to smile mischievously.

Riding side by side in contemplative silence in the vehicle Gloria borrowed from the motel parking lot, suspicions began to run rampant in her mind, with Yitzy rising to the top of her regards for the type of attributes she knew he possessed. Traits, which can easily develop to be a cause for concern, should Gloria finally come up with a plan to describe to herself exactly what it was that she was getting into.

*****

Yitzy's parents had long ago urged him to relocate from the sunny island of Barbados, where he was born, to seek out a better education for himself in the country of England in order for him to have a chance at the more beneficial life that his parents were never able to achieve. Yitzy maintained his reservations, but since he was young enough to have no choice in the matter, his parents borrowed whatever money they could from journey. Fresh out of high school, the goal was for Yitzy to land himself in one of London's premier learning institutions, such as the Oxford and Cambridge universities, but things didn't quite work out that way.

Financed with only the five-thousand dollars in currency that his parents managed to scrounge together, Yitzy quickly came to discover that the amount of money he possessed, which made him feel as though he were a rich man at the age of 18, was nothing to survive with for long in a bustling country where the relatives he was entrusted to stay with lived just as destitute as his parents were and whatever else was needed to keep a roof over their head. A circumstance which Yitzy just knew he couldn't settle for.

Where Yitzy thought England to be overrun by stuffy old white men, who yearned for nothing more than crumpets and Earl Grey tea, he was pleasantly surprised to find how diverse the country really was, with a tenacious devotion to its sportsmanship in the game of soccer, to go amongst the many associations involved to rival even the mount of footballers engaged in the sports in Yitzy's own country.

Although the appearance of the country seemed to be a bit dreary at times, there remained to be a rich form of quality amongst the people of the monarchial society where the currency of the English pond fared greater than the American dollar. After realizing that his life of squalor would not improve much better by working for minimum wage alone, Yitzy soon found himself to be vitality for him to attain a wealth of his own by way of implementing whatever means necessary it took to do so.

Yoking and quick on his feet, Yitzy felt confident enough with the athleticism he acquired from the field of soccer to try his hand at committing petty crimes such as burglary and the snatching of purses to coincide with other items pilfered from the ears of unsuspecting owner before making a dash to exchange the ill-gotten property for the currency he needed to provide for himself for another day. While out, attempting to snatch another purse, Yitzy's life was set for a dramatic turn when the ensuing encounter with an aged woman landed him on a path that he would have never expected.

Experienced with a number of such excursions, Yitzy thought that the attempt he planned was going to be an easy feat while finding it impossible for the woman of his regard to put up much of a resistance against his far-outmatching speed and strength. When his move was made, Yitzy grabbed firmly onto the straps of the woman's bag, which she carried in her hand, and gave it a hard tug while running at a full sprint.

Instead of the purse releasing from the grasp of its owner, however, the very same woman made a quick move of her own by forcefully bringing the bag back to her side, all while grabbing a stunned Yitzy by his throat and throwing him to ground in one smooth motion. To add further insult to Yitzy's shock and dismay, the woman removed a small caliber pistol from what appeared to be out of thin air and began taunting her captive by shouting, "Bang! Bang! Bang!!!" while she mimicked firing off the weapon by leveling the pistol at vital areas on Yitzy's body, which would have certainly killed him on impact, had the woman made good on the treat of releasing shots at him.

To coincide with her taunts, the woman laughed hysterically as she reminded Yitzy of someone practiced in the ways of witchcraft. "You like snatching purses from old women?! You like putting your life in danger for no reason?!" the women asked while continuing her laughter and prodding Yitzy with the firearm with a crazed look in her eye.

"I'm very sorry, ma'am! I'm just trying to put some food in my belly!!!" Yitzy pleaded desperately before inquiring, "Will you be calling the Bobbies on me?!" in fear of being captured by the London-based authorities and getting deported back into the care of his would-be-surely disappointed parents.

"Well, I don't care much for the authorities myself, lad. Come on and get up. Let's have a good look at ya," the woman said as she helped Yitzy to his feet.

The pistol she held vanished into thin air as quick as it has appeared, and after giving Yitzy a long look over, the woman asked, "You have no money to purchase food for yourself you say?" Yitzy shook slowly in answer as the woman's gaze narrowed. "You seem to be new around these parts. You have family here?" the woman inquired, with Yitzy providing truthful answers to the questions she raised. "Ah!!! So that explain it!" the woman lamented in glee. "You're a foreigner! No wonder why you didn't know who I am!" At the woman's sudden implication, Yitzy scanned the woman's face for any form of recognition but just couldn't place her.

The woman started intently in Yitzy's eyes and stated, "If I'd mistook you for an enemy, you could've gotten yourself killed, you know that? I could use a man like you. Would you like to come work for me?" While she waited for an answer, Yitzy didn't know whether to stay or run from the company of the crazed woman, but he ultimately nodded his agreement, and the woman responded with, "Good. You can start now by calling me Lady M," she insisted while evoking a mysterious grin on her face.

Popularly known by the moniker of Lady M, Yitzy was surprised to find that the woman, whose purse he attempted to grab, was actually a person of nefarious distinction by the name of Lady Elenor Mawer. As London's very own queen pin, Lady M befitted the role of a prominent criminal figure by maintaining an illicit organization all of her own, which had spanned over the course of decades and rivaled even those of the oldest associations run by men, engaged in the trade of underground activity.

Similar to the bloodlust of Italian and American mobsters, Lady M was able to survive numerous attempts on her life by avenging her good name and illicit status with a relentless and merciless reckoning to ensure that she was respected. Like the relationship between Ralph and Loanshark Jack, Lady M placed Yitzy under the care of her tutelage and he never bothered to look back from the opportunity she had best upon him.

*****

Very much like Gloria's mentor, Ralph, Yitzy started out with the task of collecting on the debts owed to Lady M before he yearned to prove himself more capable of carrying out the more intricate assignments given to the men whom she most trusted. Lady M first trained her star pupil on the finer points of firing a weapon along with moving in a clandestine fashion to avoid detection or to have the power of being able to maintain a surveillance without being discovered in the process.

Yitzy took well to his training and soon became a master of the crafts of blackmail, extortion, espionage, and assassination while developing a cunning only Lady M was known to possess. Yitzy performed most of the tasks he was given with little to no compensation needed in the process, since anything he ever desired was instantly provided for while he was in the caring graces of his mentor!

When an assignment became available in the states of America, Yitzy immediately volunteered to participate in the endeavor, to Lady M's hesitation at first, but after proving himself responsible enough to handle such a task, she made the proper arrangements by gathering the documents and financing needed for him to complete the mission successfully.

The undertaking was for Yitzy to do away with a man known to be a traitor to one of the many crime syndicates in England. Before providing intelligence to the British authorities as a government informant, the man in regard also managed to embezzle millions of dollars from the coffers of his former association and made a showing of it by flaunting the spoils of his plunder in the faces of those he deceived as the authorities were moving in to shake up the underworld with a mass of secret arrests, stemming from the information he supplied them with.

An example had to be made. In order to thwart the attempts of those who may have thought they could get away with such a thing as being a turncoat, an example had to be made. With the instance working to cause a ripple effect amongst the criminal entities of the United Kingdom, it didn't matter if one was an ally or enemy. Every association involved in the trade of criminality suffered a substantial loss of their supporters with many of its high-ranking members becoming targets themselves for the lure of the authoritative dragnet surrounding them.

The man, who soon became widely known as the chief Wanker, had every inclination to believe that his life was in imminent danger, as a public enemy of sorts amongst those who would most certainly resort to any means necessary to bring him to a demise. Realizing the extent of the threat, the British authorities acted quickly to call upon their American counterparts for help in providing the protection needed for their star witness to supply the testimony they would use to put a big dent in the element of the organized crime corrupting their country.

The only problem with the plan at hand was that the man entrusted into the care of the Americans wasn't the ideal person to take into the prospect of prosecutorial immunity without being able to enjoy the spoils of the loot he came to pilfer. When given the choice of participating in the witness protection program, or going at it on his own with the prize of his illicit earnings in tow, the Wanker chose the latter option and took to living on his own terms with the guise of the temporary visa he was afforded from the American government.

Of course, the British intelligence didn't take well to their coveted informant being out in the wind, but since they experienced the very same problem with him in their homeland, they couldn't make much of a stink about it as they counseled the Wanker on checking in with them regularly while desperately trying to convince him to remain out of the glare of the public eye in order to avoid getting himself killed.

Becoming a bit too comfortable in his new homeland, the Wanker took to purchasing a new sports car to go along with the lavish home he brought for himself, and the family he would soon send home for once the ordeal was concluded. The Wanker thought of himself as untouchable, with the prospect of his enemies being too far away to do a thing about his treachery and far too consumed with dodging the persistence of the authorities who sought their capture, but he would soon come to regret how wrong he was.

Lady M had long become accustomed to being a much sought-after person of criminal interest, but it upset her deeply that the Wanker would stoop so low as to disrupt the gaining of everyone's illicit endeavors to save his own skin which wasn't worth its weight in dirt anyway. As one of the elders in the underground hierarchy, Lady M provided her immediate assurance to those in the know that the matter would be handled accordingly by a man of her choosing, which is how Yitzy ultimately came into the scenario.

Yitzy soon found himself to be awed by the inner workings of American upon his arrival, but his no-nonsense approach to the matter at hand proved to be a method of efficiency on his part. The retribution intended was to convey a firm message to all parties involved that such acts of cowardice would in no way be tolerated. With the instructions he was given, Yitzy subdued the frightened subject he sought out, after quickly learning of the Wanker's whereabouts and began preparing a circumstance according to Lady M's wishes.

The measure called upon was something Yitzy would've never considered to do on his own, but the retaliation necessitated a dramatic showing of force in order to ensure that the authoritative powers involved would learn possibly one of the harshest lessons of the reality they faced. The Wanker was obviously scared out of his wits and may have thought to put up some sort of protest, but with his persecutor bearing photographs of his wife and children smiling while at play in his native England, the Wanker knew that his end was drawing near.

Careful not to leave any trace of fingerprints about, Yitzy made use of an extensive amount of duct tape to secure the malleable blocks of explosives he brought along to go around the waist and back of his captive. With the lives of his family at risk, the Wanker was given no other alternative than to comply with the demand. He was given the assurance that the members of his family would go on to lead long-lasting lives without a bother, which worked to bring him a sense of solace, as the Wanker tried his best to mentally prepare for what was about to come.

Yitzy informed the Wanker that he should die with some form of dignity instead of refraining from the demand and dying like the worthless traitor that he'd become by the concept of far more constructive means. The message to him was absolutely clear but mainly because the safety of his family was at the forefront of his concerns. When the appropriate time came, Yitzy also made sure that the Wanker carried an additional bad which held an extra amount of the explosives that Yitzy discussed to being on the timer of five minutes.

"They who plow inequity and sow mischief shall reap the same," were the last words the Wanker heard from Yitzy who watched his subject's next movements from a distance to follow the demand he was given. As soon as he felt comfortable enough to do so, the Wanker ran at a full sprint into the designated façade and began shouting, "Please help me!!! I need help!!!" he pleaded in angst as a crowd formed to find out what was happening. The police in the station house couldn't understand the Wanker's babblings as they tried to persuade him to calm down. By the time they heard him shout the words, "I'm wired with a bomb!!!" it was too late for anyone to react.

The Wanker came to believe that the minutes preprogrammed on the timer was all the time he needed to alert the authorities to the imminent threat of the matter before the bomb was set to detonate. As he would soon tragically come to find out, however, the best of his sensibilities had been hopelessly fooled by the fib Yitzy told.

With a calloused finger, Yitzy pressed a button on the device of a small detonator to activate a receiver that was carefully grafted inside a doctored block of Semtex hidden within the suicide vest the Wanker wore, which reacted quickly to an electronic pulse that was triggered. The resulting blast reverberated beneath Yitzy's feet as he kept vigil from 200 feet away, with an explosion that ultimately sent shockwaves around the world.

Lady M found herself to be satisfied beyond measure with the outcome, since the accomplishment elevated her standing all the more as a woman of high regard to those in her inner sanctum of criminality. All while the authorities of both countries were forced to remain straight-faced in order to save themselves from being smeared with humiliation due to their role of mishap in the horrendous matter.

The circumstance of the explosion was later downplayed by the government as an act of homeland terrorism while doling out the assurance that those responsible for the callous attack will be hunted down with all the time, resources, and financing it took to do so. For a number of weeks, the story became more and more of a downgrade with the media outlets, until the final result of the investigation was concluded as nothing more than a single person with access to explosive material deciding to act out on an old grudge he had with the police department while in a drunken stupor.

The mourning effects from the happenstance were still long-lasting, but it helped to obscure the true nature of the matter where any pertinent evidence that was ultimately found had magically disappeared before an official investigation could be conducted to support the validity of the findings. The British officials were still able to proceed with a slew of the indictments they commenced, although many of the cases would be dismissed, or not as strong as they would have been, had their star witness been able to provide his firsthand account of what he knew.

Yitzy, on the other hand, had changed dramatically with the course of events that followed. After completing Lady M's wishes to the letter, she encouraged him to enjoy an extended stay in the States until he would be able to travel without causing much suspicion as to the destination of his whereabouts. With time to reflect on the matter, Yitzy came to the conclusion that he could no longer be engaged to work with someone of Lady M's caliber who could so callously endanger the lives of the innocent to further her endgame of treachery. The last call Yitzy placed to Lady M was to inform her of his intentions.

For a long moment, Yitzy couldn't hear a sound coming from the other end of the line until a voice meekly responded, "That'll be a crying shame, Lad. You've become like this," Lady M insinuated as though she were pleading with Yitzy to continue his service to her.

"It's been a great apart in the way in which we choose to handle matters. And, for me… This is where it has to end between us," Yitzy responded with a finality to Lady M's dismay.

"IT's a crying shame," she implied once more as Yitzy tried to console her feelings with the statement, "Maybe, we'll cross paths again sometime in the future, but, for now, this is how it has to be."

Although he's checked up on her over the years and came to find out that Lady was still very much empowered as a prominent crime figure in England, Yitzy never bothered to make any further attempts to contact her after they parted ways with the last communication they made to each other. It was then, when after Yitzy came to encounter a young Arty at one of the many liberty fests spread about the country at the time, did he have the epiphany to establish an association of his own rearing to perform the art of assassination the right way without endangering the lives of the innocent through acts of maliciousness.

The choice to surround himself with a bevy or women was a natural one for a lady's man such as Yitzy to accomplish as he sought to bring in the females needed to run the day-to-day operations of the gentlemen's club he conjured up, to provide the perfect convert cover before going on to seek out the women whom he would later groom to complete the murderous assignments he had in store for them.

Over the course of time, Yitzy came to employ the services of a number of women to engage in the gritty endeavors he required. Some eventually departed his company for reasons similar to the likes of they didn't have the guts to continue on with such a brutal way of life, to those who became impregnated and wished to concentrate on raising a family of their own. Some were still available to answer Yitzy's beckoning call should he need them, but the four whom he came to instill his trust in the most were, by far, his favorites of them all.

Chapter 28

Although he possessed the extraordinary power of magnetism, Yitzy always seemed to attract the right kind of women to tackle on the endeavors he had in store. Chance encounters enabled him to meet females like Genie, Lauren, and Dawn, as they spiraled from the harsh circumstances they faced at the hands of men who should have sought to treat them as the goddesses they amounted to be without any side-effects to the contrary. On the verge of collapses, Yitzy made proposals to the women he engaged which were sure to bring an interesting change to the way they lived.

After ensuring that the ladies were trained in the ways of handling an assortment of weapons and the essentials for training themselves with hand-to-hand combative techniques, Yitzy integrated the women on the intricacies of planning their killings carefully, meticulously, and without any need for hurrying it in order to relatively get away with the task effortlessly, since Dawn, Lauren, and Genie took to their inceptions extremely well, but it was the interaction Yitzy had with Gloria that intrigued him the most.

Always lucky with a chance encounter, Yitzy actually happened upon Gloria after she was fresh from coming out of a grueling practice session in the Dojo where she trained. They came to cross paths on a busy street, and after exchanging glances with her, Yitzy found himself to be awed by the intensity in her stare.

Yitzy remembered the telltale signs of Gloria's cunning as she discreetly darted her eyes about in order to assess the level of danger in her immediate surroundings. It impressed him how Gloria locked her eyes with him and swiftly viewed Yitzy as a potential threat when they passed each other, and she suddenly sagged her shoulders with a slight motion as though she were readying herself to engage in combat. The threat was only averted when Yitzy broke his gaze and kept walking in the opposite direction.

After a few more paces, Yitzy turned himself around to watch the stride of confidence that Gloria exuded. With a shrug of his shoulders, Yitzy figured what harm could there be in following the object of his interest for a bit, to get a glimpse of how she interacted on the busy street they were on. As he watched, Yitzy could see Gloria making various stops to peer through the windows of stores, with her favorite being the pet shop she ventured to where Gloria spent an extra amount of time viewing.

It surprised Yitzy to see Gloria interact with a vagrant she came across, who showed an enthusiasm upon seeing her, which Yitzy took to mean a familiarity the two had with each other. When Gloria handed the man a wad of money, Yitzy couldn't remember ever seeing anyone become as happy as the vagrant had with the generous exchange, just before he started praising Gloria by the name Yitzy first mistook to be hers.

"Oh, may the Gods reach down from the heavens and bequeath you with a million blessings for your kindness, Maria! You don't know how happy you've made me! If you ever need me for anything, just say the words! Thank you! Oh, God, thank you, Maria!!!" the man rambled on in acclaim of his benefactor as Gloria wished him well before going on her way.

From the time when Yitzy encountered Gloria's menacing glare, he already had every intention of recruiting her to be a part of his association. After watching her quickly round a corner, Yitzy found himself desperately trying to catch up to Gloria while thinking of how he should broach the subject. Before he could react, however, Yitzy was surprised by a sudden karate chop that landed hard on his throat in a way that threatened to knock the wind out of him as Gloria dragged him deeper into the recesses of the alleyway and kicked at his shin to bring Yitzy to his knees.

"Who are you, and why the hell are you following me?!?!" Gloria raged in fury as she raised her hand to strike another blow. After regaining his breath, Yitzy pleaded, "Please, Maria! I mean you no harm! I would just like to know if there is some way of us working together?!" Gloria was incredulous to say the least by the revelation that Yitzy made, as she inquired, "How do you know my name, and what do you mean by 'working together'?!" Gloria figured as much when Yitzy informed her of how he came to learn of her being referred to as Maria while witnessing the interaction between Gloria and the panhandler, Eddie, but it was what he relayed to her next that came to send Gloria's thoughts on a tailspin.

Gloria managed to get past the turmoil of Ralph's demise by rampaging until her thirst for vengeance was finally quelled, but the following state of her emotional discourse proved to be the cause for Gloria wanting to vent out her frustrations on a more occasional basis. The circumstance was the exact reason why Gloria sought the comfort that firing ranges afforded her, or the harsh physical training involved in the martial arts that allowed her to cope with the severe amount of mental anguish Gloria faced.

With exertions to solidify her as being much more the angel of death than a do Gooding Saint, the proposal Yitzy made for Gloria's consideration at the time was a daring one. However, it gave her the perfect opportunity to have the type of outlet she needed to not only exhaust her digressions but would also enable her to finally put the set of skills that Ralph instilled in her to some good usage.

Gloria could come to laugh about it even now where Yitzy was lucky enough to have escaped the lethal move she had just been perfecting in the Dojo that day, moments before their chance encounter came about. The move intended wouldn't certainly render Yitzy to suffer immensely from a much more injurious effect than merely him having a sore throat and shin, had Yitzy not stated the nature of business quickly before Gloria went on to mistake him for someone aiming to achieve a reckoning against her for Gloria's killing of the Mafia boss, Vinny Ciccarelli.

For a long time, Gloria led Yitzy to actually believe that her name was indeed that of a Maria, until she was able to trust him enough to reveal her true attributes as their experiences together intensified. For Gloria, Yitzy had went on to become a sort of fresh embodiment to the image of Ralph in her mind where she came to value his insights, apprehensive ways, and even Yitzy's admonitions as though he were actually a family member with feelings that Yitzy reflected for Gloria in return.

Gloria kept the feelings she developed for the other involved close to her heart as well, but she had to remember that they were all professionals in the craft of assassination, and with the latest act of desertion to her associated duties, Gloria knew for certain that Yitzy wouldn't take too kindly to the insult she imposed upon him. Although he hadn't worked the field in a long time, Gloria knew that she had to figure Yitzy took to becoming the formidable foe he once was in order to counteract her betrayal.

Although he was mysterious, Gloria also found her captive to be quirky, intuitive, and actually quite charming, as they engaged in benign conversation to abstain if only for mere moments from the gravity of the situation at hand. Gloria kept any particulars about herself vague, with only their combined love for pianism becoming the forefront of their discussion. Perhaps she was rendered spellbound by the talk they shared. It was the only way for Gloria to explain how the drive ended within feet of her private sanctuary.

Yitzy didn't even have the information to know of where Gloria's refuge was located. For a time, she moved about the accommodations of hotel rooms in order for her to fulfill the requirements for any given endeavor, otherwise Yitzy could look to find his prized assassin curled up on one of the small beds placed in private rooms of the Pink Lotus which was usually reserved for any of the regular working women yearning for a well-deserved rest while working in between overtime shifts.

As they rode in the elevator in silence to her residence, Gloria came to wonder if her encountering The Pillager had anything to do with Ralph saving her life in the first place, from the suicidal fate she certainly would have endured years ago had she succumbed to sacrificing herself in the path of an oncoming train irrespective of the consequences that she already faced; the concept of the matter would definitely allow Gloria to have the purpose in life that she was seeking. It felt good for a change, for her to assume the role of a savior rather than her customary function as a merchant of death and destruction. Gloria just hoped that the decision she made didn't amount to be an egregious mistake on her part.

The Pillager became a bit uncomfortable with the lingering stare he was suddenly receiving from Gloria as they stood in front of the residence. The implication became quite clear as it conveyed the message of remembering Gloria's trait as a professional killer, with very little room for trust to emerge. The Pillager swallowed nervously and smiled tight-lipped to reassure the tight-lipped sentiment before inhaling a deep breath and using her keys to open the door to the personal space she cherished.

Gloria's maintenance of the residence fared no different than the one she and Genie stumbled upon together belonging to The Pillager. The furnishings of the décor were spares, aside from the object in the living-room area that The

Pillager was currently fawning over which was the only lavish expenditure that Gloria made for herself. "You own a baby grand?!" he asked incredulously while marveling over the horizontal structure displayed with its piano hinge open to reveal the beautifully tuned, steel wires hidden within.

With the insightful guidance Ralph instilled at her youthful age, Gloria was able to open her mind to the prospect of exploring the many different avenues that life had to offer. Her role playing and etiquette techniques worked well to coincide with Gloria's learning to converse in alternate languages along with her skill for performing as a pianist which were the two talents that Gloria cherished most dearly.

With the practice of her piano playing, Gloria was empowered with the ability to ease away the many tensions she encountered on any given mission, which is why she considered her personal space to be a sanctuary of sorts, where only her favored musical instrument came accompanied by an array of informative literature that was available, without any need for a television or any of the other technological advances which would dissuade set Gloria from the goals of her recuperative process.

Gloria remained stone-faced while carefully watching The Pillager as he used a sweeping hand motion to move his forefinger along the bank of keys on the piano. The result allowed the steel-wire strings to come alive with a melodic harmony of nimble tunefulness, as they were struck in sync with the felt-tipped hammers that landed with his touch. Gloria was thinking of protesting her disapproval when The Pillager took a seat on the matching white oak bench and commenced to fiddling with the ivory keys once more until her eyes automatically closed to take in The Pillager's rendition of a classical Wolfgang, Anizders Mozart arrangement.

Though he was no match for the Austrian composer's masterful stylings, the musical score was one that Gloria knew well, as she mimicked The Pillager's piano playing by simulating the notes of each chord with delicate finger touches on the side of her legs. Her next movements seemed to be those of a paranormality as Gloria opened her eyes slowly and claimed a seat next to The Pillager as he looked upon her behavior with a quizzical stare. Without being aware of the familiarity, the two began to devote themselves as a team to finish the composition of the classical arrangement, with Gloria supplying the undertone of the complex harmony and The Pillager covering the over.

The activity of their bonding caused Gloria's emotional attitude to shift dramatically in the regard of her captive. Their union only grew stronger at that instant as the rhythmic succession of the piano's organized tones drowned out any of the turmoil surrounding them. Gloria didn't know it; the gravity of the situation had become too overwhelming for her to handle or not, or maybe she just yearned to alleviate the toll of her distress with someone who could relate to her state of affairs with the amount of compassion she needed, but the next move Gloria made was one which had Gloria damning the influence that Dawn had on her decision.

As the arrangement began to fade to its conclusion, the two immersed themselves deeply within the tethers of the complex body of music as though they were classicists seeking the zenith of perfection with a dramatic finish; the pair were left panting in exhaustion, with one of The Pillager's hands coming to a rest on top of Gloria's. He smiled warmly in her direction but instantly regretted the mistake, as his sentiment was met by Gloria's menacing blank expression. When The Pillager made the attempt to express his sincerest apology, he was left utterly surprised when Gloria leaned over and…kissed him.

Gloria couldn't begin to discern what had come over her. One moment, she was a feared assassin commanding the fanatical moves of someone willing to kill on a mere whim, to someone losing the grit she once maintained on a simple moment of indiscretion to take advantage of the captive in her care, whom she was supposed to be protecting for the sake of exposing government conspiracy.

The copulation the two engaged in afterward, became as passionate as it gets, which left Gloria feeling even more guilty as though she'd stolen the last cookie from the cookie jar in greed. Once again, she took to cursing Dawn for her bad influence to the regard, but Gloria had to admit that her salacious encounter of coitus helped to immensely relieve the amount of stress she was having, as the interaction allowed her to process her thoughts more clearly again.

Although Dawn's incessant ramblings of having her own family of quirky kids with a gang of toy poodles to match only proved to be more of a worrisome burden on Gloria's psyche than it could be helpful, Gloria knew that she had to take accountability for her own lascivious actions as she looked upon the remnants of her passionate tryst which stared from their engagement at the base of the piano, to ending with The Pillager slumbering noisily in exhaustion on the bed where Gloria left him.

Chapter 29

Gloria showered, then thought to prepare them something to eat when she noticed a flash coming from her discarded pants on the floor next to the piano. She had forgotten all about disabling the ringtone on her phone by activating the vibrate feature and could now see the telltale signs of missed communications. Gloria was hesitant about it at first, but she knew that she couldn't avoid the interaction any longer as she hoisted the smartphone device to check her missed messages.

As the menu of the missed calls was displayed, Gloria immediately came to recognize one of the attempts as being Yitzy's number at the Pink Lotus, while the others were labeled under the same unlisted designation Gloria would have registered with had she made the calls which she knew to be coming from the other ladies involved in the endeavor.

The first recorded message was devoid of any pleasantries and all business, as the sound of Genie's stern voice admonished, "What the hell do you think you are doing?!!! Why aren't you where you're supposed to be at with the captive, and why aren't you answering your phone?!!! Make sure you call me back to give me an update on what the hell it is that you think you are doing, before you cast even more doubt on yourself!!!" Genie concluded with a harsh disconnect of the phone to express her anger.

The next transmission that Gloria received was one of a more cordial nature from Lauren, but Gloria could sense that the content of the intended message was far from affable as Lauren remarked, "Sweetie, is everything all right with you? I hope you realize that everybody is getting really angry with the latest stunt you pulled, especially with Yitzy rambling on about how you're attempting to ruin his reputation. You have to remember, Sky, that we're all professionals at what we do for a living, so try not to have any hard feelings about what comes next if you don't get in touch with us soon, okay?"

Gloria was well-aware of the prospect Lauren implied but hoped that she could avoid any confrontation with the other members of her team until she was able to recover the evidence The Pillager had in his possession in order to shed a better light on the subject and have them understand the extent of her concerns. Gloria couldn't stopped there after learning enough to be fully warned, but she felt a commitment to hear what the other messages entailed as she actually found humor in the correspondence that Dawn left for her.

"You better not be trying to steal my man from me, Sky, I saw him first!!!" Dawn lamented with a sentiment which instantly erected a mischievous smirk on the corners of Gloria's lips as Dawn continued with, "You better warn him that if he does anything with you, that he should be doing with me over and over again, I'll burn his expensive car down to ashes and you know I will!!!" She stated in jest before warning, "But, seriously though… I hope you know what you're doing, Sky, because I've never seen Yitzy this angry before. I think he wants your head on a platter."

When Dawn's message was concluded, Gloria found herself breathing in deeply as she took in Yitzy's message of, "A killer with a conscience? My dear Gloria, I'm hoping you realize that the mere concept is an extreme breach of the ethical standards by which you've chosen to live by." Yitzy's communication was short concise and eerily serene, Gloria thought, as she raised the level of the threat to coincide with the fact that Yitzy's final message was the last one of its kind from anyone involved in the matter for a period of over two hours since the last message was received.

*****

Gloria began to feel as though the world was collapsing on top of her. With the gravity of the messages weighing heavily on her consciousness, Gloria dressed and retrieved one of her weapons just before going to rouse The Pillager out of his slumber. When she entered the bedroom, loading the clip into the chamber of the weapon she carried, Gloria watched with amazed disbelief as the man in the bed she'd slept countless nights alone in began to stir out of his sleep. The smile which blossomed on her face when Gloria reflected on the intimate time the pair spent together quickly dissipated as she focused on the possibility of what they may encounter shortly.

The Pillager couldn't remember a time when he had such a fitful sleep. He certainly didn't want to open his eyes, but he smiled nonetheless as the thought of getting another glimpse at his Amazonian temptress came to mind. When The Pillager slowly parted his eyes open to what sounded like a pistol being loaded, he immediately became alert when he was met by Gloria's menacing gaze as she held a large-caliber weapon at her side. If Gloria had wanted him dead at that point, there was nothing that The Pillager could do about it, but after a long moment of encountering her intense stare, Gloria made the command, "Get up and get dressed. We have to move."

The Pillager dressed himself quickly and ate a few of the sandwiches that Gloria prepared for them before they headed out to face whatever the world had in store for them once more. As the two made their way past the piano to the exit, the pair shared knowing glances, with The Pillager begging the question with his eyes and Gloria mischievously smirking in response before she stated, "Who knows? Maybe we can do another duet together sometime in the near future. We just have to make it out of this mess alive, then maybe… Just maybe." The Pillager felt thoroughly appeased by the response she gave, and Gloria thought for a split second that she could see an extra pep in The Pillager's step as the two made their way to expose a conspiracy.

The plan was for the two of them to stay mobile until Gloria felt it was safe enough for them to recover the data files which The Pillager claimed to have stashed in a bank safety-deposit box under an assumed name. The merchant mind in Gloria immediately considered the intention of managing the damning evidence for a profit to the highest bidding news outlets, but even the most experienced of assassins lived by a strict code of honor and, as such, Gloria's moral aptitude would not allow her to seek a financial gain while on her quest for the principals of justice.

The day was seasonably warm, but Gloria made use of a bulky sweat suit in order to remain in comfortable attire which also worked well to conceal the weapons she intended to carry. At her side, Gloria also held a small duffel bag concealing an extra assortment of weapons and a change of clothing if needed to go along with the spare identification now naming her as Jasmine Baez. A lawyer, Gloria thought with a smile.

The intention was for the two to find accommodations at a nearby motel which allow them the easiest access to the bank of their regard after Gloria made the proper provisions to ensure that no threat of a surveillance was imminent. As they exited the building and were heading to a vehicle that Gloria had reserved for situations such as this, a thought suddenly occurred to her.

The streets where Gloria's refuge was located could only be described as an assassin's paradise where the roads and walkways were hardly ever cluttered with busy pedestrians and the neighbors were often engulfed in their own self-righteous worlds of high-tech security systems and personal servants, with very little room for children in their ever-demanding lives of business and leisure travels. On this day, however, Gloria found her surroundings to be bizarrely tranquil with not even the birds making much of a fuss for being active. Suddenly, she saw a gleam in the corner of her eye which accompanied the sound of vehicle doors closing before the first shot was fired in the direction of her and The Pillager.

The Pillager was taken by surprise when the reflexes of Gloria tugged at his shirt and brought him down to a crouching position just as a bullet was whizzing past his head. As she guided him to the cover of a parked car, Gloria heard Dawn lament, "Hi, Honey, I'm here for you!!! You miss me, Baby?!?!" she screamed in feigned adoration for The Pillager before making use of her suppressed weapon to send a hail of automatic gunfire at the two as they ran for the cover they sought.

"Shit," Gloria grumbled with disdain to herself as she took the opportunity to sneak in a quick peek at the oncoming incursion. What dismayed her the most was to find that her plans to avoid a confrontation until she controlled the evidence needed to prove her digression was now hopelessly lost. Gloria knew she had to engage in a defensive manner in order to get out of the mess alive, as she cocked back the slide on the chamber of her weapon to prepare for the worst while still hoping for the best.

Genie happened to be one of the first women Yitzy recruited to embark on the journey he proposed, which was why she was often called upon to be in charge of supervising the group missions as well as the many goings on with the regular women working the rooms full of gnawing admirers at the Pink Lotus. It was designation she was assigned to now as Gloria watched her whisper in the ear of Lauren to direct her into enveloping Gloria and The Pillager while Dawn and Genie converged from opposite directions with their weapons blazing.

Their specialties differed when it came to the requirements for contract killing, but the women were also available for other incidental work such as abduction, with Yitzy training them well to make wounds that no doctor would be able to undo. The factor was one Gloria knew well, as she began to feel as though the odds were now stacked heavily against her with only one viable option left for survival. "Do you know how to handle a weapon?" was the question Gloria posed to her cohort who slowly nodded his assent after overcoming his initial state of wide-eyed awe. Gloria moved quickly to remove another pistol out of the bag she carried and handed it to The Pillager as she gave him instructions on what needed to be done.

A coin flipped is like the barbed spector of war on one side while the other is the white dove of peace. With an instance such as this, Gloria could see no possibility for the latter alternative at the moment as Dawn wailed, "Sorry about this, Sky, but you know the rules! Oh! And as for you, sweet Peter! Since you chose her over me… I burned your pretty car down to the ground!!!" she exclaimed in jest before unloading another round of fire at the vehicle the pair hid behind as the other attackers released shots of their own.

When there was finally a break in the gunfire, with Gloria hearing the telltale sounds of expended magazines being changed, she yelled, "Now!!!" as she and The Pillager returned fire at their designated targets. When The Pillager fired off his weapon, Gloria could hear exasperated yelps as Lauren exclaimed that she'd been hit with Genie concurring that she had been too. Dawn's eyes opened wide with the horror of being the focus of Gloria's steadied aim. Dawn thought her death was imminent as she started down the barrel of the pistol from her distance while Gloria squeezed on the trigger under her finger in rapid succession.

Dawn could instantly feel the buzz of the bullets breeze by her ears with the resemblance of dragonflies which were intended for the direction of an alternate target. The result caused her to be propelled forward as the vehicle behind her erupted in an explosion when the shots that Gloria fired off ripped through the gas tank of the sports utility vehicle the women arrived in which sparked the destructive chain reaction that followed.

With the attack on them thwarted for the moment, Gloria took the opportunity to grab ahold of The Pillager and her belongings to make their way out of the area as the sounds of approaching sirens began to ruminate loudly in the distance. In a time of reproof, Gloria admonished, "Why did you have to shoot them?!?! I told you to just scare them off!!!" To which The Pillager vehemently responded, "Are you serious?!?! They were trying to kill us!!! Would you rather have them shoot us first?!?!"

Gloria fully understood The Pillager's reasoning, but she was so mad about the happening that she could've broken every bone in his body in retaliation, but Gloria knew that she shared in the fault of the culpability as well. As they located the car that Gloria managed to have in secret, she was left with only the solace of seeing all three of these injured women scurrying to get away, with Dawn using her elbow to smash the window of a random vehicle which she would rapidly hotwire to enable their escape as the other two women climbed into the vehicle's rear, groaning in agony.

When the only tool you have is a hammer, then everything looks like a nail, Gloria thought with regards to her need for the use of excessive force, but, for now, she and The Pillager were safe enough to continue on with their clandestine mission to save the world. Gloria just hoped that the women of the team could find it in their hearts to forgive the mishaps of her judgment while also desiring to never have to encounter something like the vehemence of their unfriendly assail ever again.

Chapter 30

The pair managed to find themselves at a far off motel which was perfectly desolate for them to relax and recuperate from the intensity of their adrenaline-fueled encounter. The Pillager seemed remarkably tranquil, Gloria thought, but after the energy of her vigorousness subsided, all she wanted to devote her attention to, at that moment, was to find out how her whereabouts came to be discovered so quickly.

The vibration originating from the base of her pocket came to demand attention from Gloria with an urgency that couldn't be ignored. When she retrieved the electronic device from her pocket, Gloria looked to find a threatening message was left on her phone by Dawn who transcribed the text, 'I hope that you don't think that this is over. Because this is far from over. We won't be so nice with you the next time around. D.' Gloria released an exasperated breath in frustration as she flopped to take a seat on the bed upon discovering an intriguing development.

The content of Dawn's message isn't what concerned Gloria. However, it had everything to do with the fact that she neglected to remember the phone's capability to easily track her whereabouts should she ever find herself in a dangerous situation. Which was the very reason Yitzy issued the similar device to all the women under his employ as a safety precaution should any of the ladies ever fall victim to being abducted or any of the other hazard to their lives. Although the measure was only limited to tracking an individual to a generalized area, the method helped to dramatically narrow down any viable options until a more specific designation could be ascertained.

In Gloria's case, she remembered the instance of leaving Yitzy a final message before exiting her residence, which read something like, 'I'm so sorry about how this turned out, Yitzy, but once I bring you the evidence of a conspiracy, you'll understand my point of view.' The apologetic text was what Gloria surmised was the instrumental factor in allowing her fellow assassins to narrow down her positioning, as their only requirements afterward was to wait for a sighting of the pair in order to follow the instructions they were given. The mere concept caused Gloria to meticulously scrub all the data applications from her phone while also removing the global positioning antenna.

When Gloria finally looked up from her task of disabling any links to surveillance her whereabouts, her vision landed on the sight of The Pillager smiling mischievously in her direction. Now the object of her attention, he took to expressing himself in a way that Gloria found to be odd. "You intrigue me, Sky," The Pillager began. His smile widened as he examined the worried expression etching across Gloria's features. "I never really did catch your name, but I assume that it's what your friends refer to you as from what I heard that crazy one shouting. Anyway, I like your style a whole lot which is why I thought to be honest with you and inform you that I'm not really who you think I am," The Pillager revealed with his smirk becoming even more menacing.

Gloria's senses placed were on high alert by the statement The Pillager made, but any sudden moves she may have wanted to make to defend herself were stunted when The Pillager brought the weapon he had concealed behind his leg to the forefront of Gloria's heightened awareness in order to have her understand the level of the threat she was up against. Before any further words could be exchanged, The Pillager squeezed off two quick shots in Gloria's direction. One of which landed in a random area on her right side, while the other found its mark on the opposite side where her shoulder was located.

****

"Well, now I guess I can feel comfortable enough without need for these, now won't I?" The Pillager stated as he removed the glasses from his face. Gloria tried her best to control her injured wheezing after sustaining the impact of bullets originating from the suppressed barrel of one of her very own weapons... Her favored .380-caliber pistol.

"Sky. Sky. Sky. My, how naïve you are," The Pillager bemused as he took to speaking in a condescending manner to patronize Gloria's faults. "I must admit. You took to the theory of a possible government conspiracy quite well. Especially if it meant the potential for cleaning your name and conscience with an act of being the savior, huh? I'm sorry, my bear, but that isn't how it works for people like us."

"I take it that your look of surprise isn't solely due to my wounding you, is it? Yes, I, like you, am a contracted killer. Hired to dispatch of you and your band of colleagues by someone whom all of you should know quite well by now. Ever heard of your precious Yitzy referring to a woman by the name of 'Lady M'? It's okay if you haven't. I'm sure your boss has, since she's always kept him in her regards," The Pillager rambled on in revelation as though he were conducting a tutorial on being a scoundrel.

By this point, The Pillager seemed to be nothing more than a braggadocio as he inspected the severity of Gloria's wound with his gaze while outlining a tale of compelling events to account for the pair's current state of transgressive affairs. What Gloria found to be most insulting was the fact that the entire circumstance of The Pillager's deception was predicated on nothing more than the basis of pure greed.

It became apparent that Lady M never really did get over the fact of losing Yitzy so many years ago to the treachery of his willful negligence toward her. After soon coming to learn of Yitzy trying his hand at establishing his own association in the trade of contract killing, Lady M felt elated to have been the one who reared him, with the hopes that her power would be strengthened immensely by Yitzy's extension in the States coinciding with the stature of Lady M's commanding presence in the United Kingdom. However, her plan didn't quite go according to plan.

Yitzy didn't know it, but it was Lady M who often subcontracted him and his ladies to take care of the odds and ends she had in store as a sort of congratulatory present for the good fortune of him starting his own business, but she came to feel spurned when her continuous attempts to reconnect with Yitzy were disregarded as an undesirable happenstance. His insolent behavior proved to be a constant slap in the face of Lady M, which caused her to grow bitter in Yitzy's regard, as she took to resenting even the mentioning of his name and accomplishments.

Though a woman in her late 70s, Lady M's mind was still quick as a whip, with her desire to convey a tyranny only ripening with her age. "So, you see?! This is how I came to be!" The Pillager proclaimed while extending his arms open to substantiate the point he his, but, for now, she found herself to be at a severe disadvantage while being forced to endure more of The Pillager's mockery as he ranted on.

"You see, my dear Sky… You are merely a pawn in a grueling game of survival," The Pillager commented as he continued on with, "Although I happened upon Lady M shortly after the tenure of your boss had ended, the betrayal of his ultimately departure worked to cast a dark cloud over all of us who came to be under her employ. Where no matter what we did, we were never good enough to measure up to her precious Yitzy Hammond," The Pillager bemoaned with a tinge of jealousy becoming evident in his tone of voice.

"Just think about being ridiculed every day over a bunch of meager women being able to do a better job than me and my mates did in the task of contract killing? Purely preposterous, you understand?!" The Pillager admonished her, with Gloria's eyes widening at the implication of a surprising element. "You guessed right, my dear. I am a true nobleman of England. Unlike your deserter of a boss, I know where my loyalties lie," The Pillager implored with every ounce of his natural tongue becoming audible over his anger.

"You like my accent? Ever see a show on your American television titled 'House'? Well, the star, Hugh Laurie, is actually a Londoner you know. He was a great influence on my wanting to capture the true essence of the American language. Listen to an example, 'Hello. Hello. Hello, I like your coat, may I borrow it?'" The Pillager rambled on as he mocked the intricacy of translation with a characteristic that Gloria came to view as being borderline psychotic.

"Anyway, my intention was to eventually kill you and the rest of your mates without any help from my chums across the pond, but the magical moment we shared in your place of residence earned you a special place in my regards. It's the reason why I'm abstaining from my goal a bit, to give you a one-time chance at being your own woman, free to seek out a life of your choosing, but your mates will not fare so lucky." Gloria saw her opportunity then to exact her revenge, but she had to have patience. She wanted to ask how much of what she'd been told about him was a lie but didn't have to as The Pillager ranted on and enlightened her on his own.

"Well, as you may have gathered… Everything you've come to learn about me has been fabricated by none other than Lady M herself. Although, I must say, she did use pieces of my actual life to construct what she referred to as an 'elaborate guise' to woo the type of attention her prized Yitzy would be vying for, to earn a healthy payday," The Pillager informed Gloria with a detail she knew to be true, since Yitzy only sought the best assignments for his girls to encounter as long as the financial gain was worth their while.

*****

As the Pillager gave his dubious account, Gloria came to learn that the illusory file Yitzy received was in stark contrast to The Pillager's actual livelihood which left him emotionally disturbed to say the least. She had wondered why the specifics on The Pillager's parents were so vague, but Gloria found that there was no special form of prestigious homeschooling for the man before her.

The Pillager's parents were both abusive alcoholics who often carried out their aggressions in all-out brawls while their son bared witness and often became the object of backlash from their turmoil. The Pillager even found it hysterical to reveal to Gloria that had any of her team members even bothered to check if he had any inclination of how to work a computer system, they would've instantly came to discover that he didn't know anything about operating one of the terminals after pressing on the power button.

The Pillager also informed Gloria that his ability to perform on the piano stemmed from his parents' feeble attempt to keep him out of trouble and on the straight and narrow by seeking out the strict aid of nuns who were instrumental in initiating his reform with the harsh use of wooden rulers on his bare knuckles, should he ever not take to the guidance they were instilling in him seriously. "What can I say? The piano lessons stuck. The rules… Not so much," The Pillager concluded as his mischievous grin emerged in reflection of the thought.

The severity of Gloria's wounds weren't as grave as she may have made them out to be. She just hoped that The Pillager saw it that way. Fortunately, he seemed it be satisfied with her current state of distress as he began packing her belongings into the bags she brought along with the impression that she was unarmed and powerless to stop him.

"You've been a jolly-good sport about this, Sky. I'm sorry for wounding you the way I did, but your legend precedes you. After learning of what you did to that dreadful chap 'La Lobo' and his men, I knew you were a force to be reckoned with. So, your injury is what the gravity of the situation called for, you understand," The Pillager informed her in order to give Gloria an explanation for his need to cause her harm.

"Well, I guess this is it, Sky. If you ever find yourself across the pond in London, make sure to look me up under the name of Michael Bormann. Maybe we can conduct another blissful harmony of music together again," The Pillager boasted while gesturing his departure as though he were a family member saying his final goodbye until the mark of the next holiday season arose.

Although the instance could in no way be a match for the level of treachery she endured at the hands of The Wolf, the betrayal would still be one that Gloria came to learn from for years to come. Where she had fallen victim to the ingenious acts intended to deceive or cheat her over the years, Gloria now refused to allow any of the experiences she had to overwhelm her current emotions the way it would have when she was younger with an impulse to commit suicide. Nowadays, she just chalked up her turmoils to being the nature of the beast she found herself to be in, for the way in which she chose to live.

Gloria was barely able to discern The Pillager's word when he lauded himself to being more of a philanderer than the name she'd come to refer to him by, when a smile suddenly blossomed on her face. Although in a great deal of pain, the sudden glee Gloria felt was the result of something originating from when a vision of her mentor sprang to life in her mind.

The mental toughness Ralph instilled in her proved to be an invaluable lesson on life, Gloria thought, where she came to accept the concept of being a survivalist whenever the threat of anarchy remains to be persistent. It was the very thought Gloria carried with her now as her smile broadened with the teachings of Ralph's constant insistence that she be prepared for the worst coming to mind while The Pillager began to head for his exit.

"It would sadden me greatly if you were to experience any ill will toward me for our meeting of wits, but this is the true nature of what your business entails, you understand. No hard feelings on my part, Luv. I just hope we can meet together again one day under much more palpable circumstances. Until then… Cheerio, darling!" The Pillager proclaimed as he reached for the door knob after making his final statement. Unfortunately, for him, it would be the last movement he would ever came to make again.

The first shot to enter him did so with an impact at the back of his skull with a burst of speed that quickly ended The Pillager's life. For good measure,

Gloria fired off the remaining bullet from the barrel of the tow shot derringer she easily kept hidden in an ankle holster to land at the base of his neck just before The Pillager slumped to the floor. Gloria was just glad to have finally shut up his excessive blabbering as she kicked his body over in order to confirm his demise.

Gloria came to determine that The Pillager's corpse may likely decompose before anyone was the wiser as to what occurred between them. After tending to her wounds, which were nonlife-threatening, Gloria changed into her spare clothing and tried to remove any traces of herself from the motel room, starting with the bloodied sheet set. With lots of explaining and apologizing to do, Gloria hoped that the discourtesy she showed toward her fellow team could be forgiven as she sought to make her fellow team.

The philosophies of human beings aren't necessarily flawed, but rather the humans who try to interpret them. In Gloria's case, however, she didn't feel the need to discern which system of philosophical concepts were out there for her to discover. She just wanted to right the wrongs that'd been done to her and her team of femme fatales while learning to cope with the behavioral tendencies she'd come to possess.

If it's a war that Lady M is seeking, then it was Gloria's top priority to exact her vengeance with a fervor to settle the controversy at hand, in a way which would allow any and all possible adversaries wishing to injure, overthrow, or confound the efforts of her and her associates to be aware that they would ultimately suffer the fate of harsh consequences, should Gloria yearn to accomplish her revengeful desires.

The End